William Carew Hazlitt

A select collection of old English plays

William Carew Hazlitt

A select collection of old English plays

ISBN/EAN: 9783742858603

Manufactured in Europe, USA, Canada, Australia, Japa

Cover: Foto ©Andreas Hilbeck / pixelio.de

Manufactured and distributed by brebook publishing software
(www.brebook.com)

William Carew Hazlitt

A select collection of old English plays

OLD ENGLISH PLAYS.

VOL. II.

INTERLUDE OF YOUTH.

LUSTY JUVENTUS.   JACK JUGGLER.

NICE WANTON.

HISTORY OF JACOB AND ESAU.

DISOBEDIENT CHILD.

MARRIAGE OF WIT AND SCIENCE.

A SELECT COLLECTION

OF

OLD ENGLISH PLAYS.

ORIGINALLY PUBLISHED BY ROBERT DODSLEY
IN THE YEAR 1744.

FOURTH EDITION,

NOW FIRST CHRONOLOGICALLY ARRANGED, REVISED AND ENLARGED,
WITH THE NOTES OF ALL THE COMMENTATORS
AND NEW NOTES

BY

W. CAREW HAZLITT.

VOLUME THE SECOND.

LONDON:

REEVES AND TURNER, 196 STRAND
AND 185 FLEET STREET.
1874

THE INTERLUDE OF YOUTH.

A

MR HALLIWELL'S PREFACE[1] TO THE FORMER EDITION.

The "Interlude of Youth" is probably the most interesting early-printed moral play that has descended to our times, and it may therefore be considered somewhat singular that it has hitherto escaped the notice of the publication societies. Its great rarity may, however, account for this circumstance, only two or three copies of any edition being known to exist. Waley's edition appeared probably about the year 1554, and has a woodcut on the title-page of two figures, representing Charity and Youth, two of the characters in the interlude. Another edition was printed by Copland, and has also a woodcut on the title-page, representing Youth between Charity, and another figure which has no name

---

[1] The "Interlude of Youth." From the rare black-letter edition, printed by Waley about the year 1554. Edited by James Orchard Halliwell, Esq. . . . . . Brixton Hill, 1849, 4to. 75 copies privately printed.

over its head. The colophon is : "Imprented at London, in Lothbury, over against Sainct Margarytes church, by me, Wyllyam Copland." See Collier's "History of Dramatic Poetry," vol. ii., p. 313. "The 'Interlude of Youth,'" observes Mr Collier, "is decidedly a Roman Catholic production, and I have therefore little doubt that it made its appearance during the reign of Mary ;" and he adds, p. 315, "on the whole, this piece is one of the most amusing and most humorous of the class to which it belongs." A fragment of a black-letter copy of the interlude is preserved at Lambeth Palace,[1] and is described by Mr Maitland in his "List of Early Printed Books," p. 311.

[1 Apparently of an otherwise undescribed edition. See Hazlitt's "Handbook," p. 464.]

INTERLUDE OF YOUTH.

———◆———

CHARITY.

Jesu that his arms did spread,
And on a tree was done to dead,
From all perils he you defend !
I desire audience till I have made an end,
For I am come from God above
To occupy his laws to your behove,
And am named Charity ;
There may no man saved be
Without the help of me,
For he that Charity doth refuse,
Other virtues though he do use,
Without Charity it will not be,
For it is written in the faith :
Qui manet in charitate in Deo manet.
I am the gate, I tell thee,
Of heaven, that joyful city ;
There may no man thither come,
But of charity he must have some,
Or ye may not come, i-wis,
Unto heaven, the city of bliss ;
Therefore Charity, who will him take,
A pure soul it will him make
Before the face of God :
In the A B C, of books the least,

It is written *Deus charitas est.*
Lo ! charity is a great thing,
Of all virtues it is the king :
When God in earth was here living,
Of charity he found none ending.
I was planted in his heart ;
We two might not depart.[1]
Out of his heart I did spring,
Through the might of the heaven-king :
And all priests that be,
May sing no mass without charity :
And charity to them they do not take,
They may not receive him, that did them make
And all this world of nought.

YOUTH.

Aback, fellows, and give me room,
Or I shall make you to avoid soon !
I am goodly of person ;
I am peerless, wherever I come.
My name is Youth, I tell thee,
I flourish as the vine-tree :
Who may be likened unto me,
In my youth and jollity ?
My hair[2] is royal and bushed thick ;
My body pliant as a hazel-stick ;
Mine arms be both big[3] and strong,
My fingers be both fair and long ;
My chest big as a tun,
My legs be full light for to run,
To hop and dance, and make merry.
By the mass, I reck not a cherry,
Whatsoever I do !
I am the heir of all my father's land,

---

[1] Part asunder.   [2] [*hearte*, Waley's ed.]
[3] [Waley's and Copland's eds., *fair*.]

And it is come into my hand :
I care for no more.

CHARITY.

Are you so disposed to do,
To follow vice, and let virtue go ?

YOUTH.

Yea, sir, even so :
For now-a-days he is not set by,
Without he be unthrifty.

CHARITY.

You had need to ask God mercy ;
Why did you so praise your body ?

YOUTH.

Why, knave, what is that to thee ?
Wilt thou let [1] me to praise my body ?
Why should I not praise it, and it be goodly ?
I will not let for thee.

CHARITY.

What shall it be, when thou shalt flit
Fro thy wealth into the pit ?
Therefore of it be not too bold,
Lest thou forethink [2] it, when thou art old :
Ye may be likened to a tree,
In youth flourishing with royalty,
And in age it is cut down,

---

[1] Hinder.   [2] Regret.

And to the fire is thrown :
So shalt thou, but thou amend,
Be burned in hell without end !

YOUTH.

Ye whoreson, trowest thou so ?
Beware, lest thou thither go !
Hence, caitiff, go thy way,
Or with my dagger I shall thee slay !
Hence, knave, out of this place,
Or I shall lay thee on the face !
Sayest thou that I shall go to hell,
For evermore there to dwell ?
I had liever thou had evil fare.[1]

CHARITY.

Ah, yet, sir, do by my reed,
And ask mercy for thy misdeed,
And thou shalt be an heritor of bliss,
Where all joy and mirth is ;
Where thou shalt see a glorious sight
Of angels singing, with saints bright,
Before the face of God.

YOUTH.

What, sirs, above the sky ?
I had need of a ladder to climb so high !
But what, and the ladder slip ?
Then I am deceived yet,
And if I fall, I catch a queck ;
I may fortune to break my neck,

---

[1] A line, rhyming with this, seems to have dropped out.

And that joint is ill to set :
Nay, nay, not so.

CHARITY.

Oh, yet remember, and call to thy mind,
The mercy of God passeth all thing.
For it is written by noble clerks,
The mercy of God passeth all works ;
That witnesseth Holy Scripture, saying thus :
Miseratio domini super omnia opera ejus :
Therefore doubt not God's grace ;
Thereof is plenty in every place.

YOUTH.

What, methink ye be clerkish,
For ye speak good gibb'rish !
Sir, I pray you, and you have any store,
Soil[1] me a question, ere ye cast any more,
Lest when your cunning is all done,
My question have no solution.
Sir, and it please you this,
Why do men eat mustard with salt fish ?
Sir, I pray you soil me this question
That I have put to your discretion.

CHARITY.

This question is but a vanity ;
It longeth not to me
Such questions to assoil.

YOUTH.

Sir, by God, that me dear bought,
I see your cunning is little or nought ;

---

[1] Solve.

And I should follow your school,
Soon ye would make me a fool !
Therefore crake no longer here,
Lest I take you on the ear,
And make your head to ache :

CHARITY.

Sir, it falleth not for me to fight,
Neither by day, ne by night ;
Therefore do by my counsel, I say,
Then to heaven thou shalt have thy way.

YOUTH.

No, sir, I think ye will not fight ;
But to take a man's purse in the night
Ye will not say nay ;
For such holy caitiffs
Were wont to be thieves,
And such would be hanged as high
As a man may see with his eye :
In faith, this same is true.

CHARITY.

God save every Christian body
From such evil destiny,
And send us of his grace
In heaven to have a place !

YOUTH.

Nay, nay, I warrant thee,
He hath no place for thee ;
Weenest thou he will have such fools
To sit on his gay stools ?
Nay, I warrant thee, nay !

HUMILITY.

Well, sir, I put me in God's will,
Whether he will me save or spill ;
And, sir, I pray you do so,
And trust in God, whatsoever ye do.

YOUTH.

Sir, I pray thee hold thy peace,
And talk to me of no goodness ;
And soon look thou go thy way,
Lest with my dagger I thee slay !
In faith, if thou move my heart,
Thou shalt be weary of thy part,
Ere thou and I have done.

CHARITY.

Think what God suffered for thee,
His arms to be spread upon a tree ;
A knight with a spear opened his side,
In his heart appeared a wound wide,
That bought both you and me !

YOUTH.

God's fast ! what is that to me ?
Thou daw, wilt thou reed me
In my youth to lose my jollity ?
Hence, knave, and go thy way,
Or with my dagger I shall thee slay !

CHARITY.

O sir, hear what I you tell,
And be ruled after my counsel,

That ye might sit in heaven high
With God and his company.

YOUTH.

Ah, yet of God thou wilt not cease
Till I fight in good earnest ;
On my faith I tell thee true,
If I fight, it will thee rue
All the days of thy life.

CHARITY.

Since[1] I see it will none otherwise be ;
I will go to my brother Humility,
And take good counsel of him,
How it is best to be do therein.

YOUTH.

Yea, marry, sir, I pray you of that ;
Methink it were a good sight of your back ;
I would see your heels hither,
And your brother and you together
Fettered fine fast !
I-wis, and I had the key,
Ye should sing well-away,
Ere I let you loose !

CHARITY.

Farewell, my masters everychone !
I will come again anon,
And tell you how I have done.

YOUTH.

And thou come hither again,
I shall send thee hence in the devil's name.

---

[1] [Old copies, *Sir.*]

What ! now I may have my space
To jet here in this place;
Before I might not stir,
When that churl Charity was here ;
But now, among all this cheer,
I would I had some company here ;
I wish[1] my brother Riot would help me,
For to beat Charity
And his brother too.

RIOT.

Huffa ! huffa ![2] who calleth after me ?
I am Riot, full of jollity.
My heart as light as the wind,
And all on riot is my mind,
Wheresoever I go.
But wot ye what I do here ?
To seek Youth my compeer :
Fain of him I would have a sight,
But my lips hang in my light.
God speed, master Youth, by my fay.

YOUTH.

Welcome, Riot, in the devil's way !
Who brought thee hitherto ?

RIOT.

That did my legs, I tell thee :
Methought thou did me call,
And I am come now here
To make royal cheer,
And tell thee how I have done.

---

[1] [Old copies, *i-wis.*]
[2] See Hazlitt's "Popular Poetry," iv., 239.

YOUTH.

What! I weened thou hadst been hanged,
But I see thou art escaped,
For it was told me here
You took a man on the ear,
That his purse in your bosom did fly,
And so in Newgate you did lie.

RIOT.

So it was, I beshrew your heart :
I come lately from Newgate,
But I am as ready to make good cheer,
As he that never came there ;
For, and I have spending,
I will make as merry as a king,
And care not what I do ;
For I will not lie long in prison,
But will get forth soon,
For I have learned a policy
That will loose me lightly,
And soon let me go.

YOUTH.

I love well thy discretion,
For thou art all of one condition ;
Thou art stable and steadfast of mind,
And not changeable as the wind.
But, sir, I pray you at the least,
Tell me more of that jest,
That thou told me right now.

RIOT.

Moreover, I shall tell thee,
The Mayor of London sent for me

Forth of Newgate for to come,
For to preach at Tyburn.

YOUTH.

By our Lady ! he did promote thee,
To make thee preach at the gallow-tree !
But, sir, how didst thou 'scape ?

RIOT.

Verily, sir, the rope brake,
And so I fell to the ground,
And ran away, safe and sound :
By the way I met with a courtier's lad,
And twenty nobles of gold in his purse he had :
I took the lad on the ear,
Beside his horse I felled him there :
I took his purse in my hand,
And twenty nobles therein I fand.[1]
Lord, how I was merry !

YOUTH.

God's fate ! thou didst enough there
For to be made knight of the collar.

RIOT.

Yea, sir, I trust to God Allmight
At the next sessions to be dubbed a knight.

YOUTH.

Now, sir, by this light !
That would I fain see,

---

[1] Found.

And I plight thee, so God me save,
That a sure collar thou shalt have ;
And because gold collars be so good cheap,
Unto the roper I shall speak
To make thee one of a good price,
And that shall be of warrantise.

RIOT.

Youth, I pray thee have ado,
And to the tavern let us go,
And we will drink divers wine,
And the cost shall be mine ;
Thou shalt not pay one penny, i-wis,
Yet thou shalt have a wench to kiss,
Whensoever thou wilt.

YOUTH.

Marry, Riot, I thank thee,
That thou wilt bestow it on me,
And for thy pleasure so be it ;
I would not Charity should us meet,
And turn us again,
For right now he was with me,
And said he would go to Humility,
And come to me again.

RIOT.

Let him come, if he will ;
He were better to bide still ;
And he give thee crooked language,
I will lay him on the visage,
And that thou shalt see soon,
How lightly it shall be done ;
And he will not be ruled with knocks,

We shall set him in the stocks,
To heal his sore shins !

YOUTH.

I shall help thee, if I can,
To drive away that hangman ;
Hark, Riot, thou shalt understand
I am heir of my father's land,
And now they be come to my hand,
Methink it were best therefore,
That I had one man more
To wait me upon.

RIOT.

I can speed thee of a servant of price,
That will do thee good service ;
I see him go here beside ;
Some men call him Master Pride ;
I swear by God in Trinity
I will go fetch him unto thee,
And that even anon.

YOUTH.

Hie thee apace and come again,
And bring with thee that noble swain.

RIOT.

Lo, Master Youth, here he is,
A pretty man and a wise ;
He will be glad to do you good service
In all that ever he may

YOUTH.

Welcome to me, good fellow,
I pray thee, whence comest thou ?
And thou wilt my servant be,
I shall give thee gold and fee.

PRIDE.

Sir, I am content, i-wis,
To do you any service
That ever I can do.

YOUTH.

By likelihood thou should do well enou' ;
Thou art a likely fellow.

PRIDE.

Yes, sir, I warrant you,
If ye will be ruled by me,
I shall you bring to high degree.

YOUTH.

What shall I do, tell me,
And I will be ruled by thee.

PRIDE.

Marry, I shall tell you :
Consider ye have good enou'
And think ye come of noble kind ;
Above all men exalt thy mind ;
Put down the poor, and set nought by them ;
Be in company with gentlemen ;
Get up and down in the way,

And your clothes look they be gay ;
The pretty wenches will say then,
Yonder goeth a gentleman ;
And every poor fellow that goeth you by,
Will do off his cap, and make you courtesy :
In faith, this is true.

YOUTH.

Sir, I thank thee, by the rood,
For thy counsel that is so good ;
And I commit me even now
Under the teaching of Riot and you.

RIOT.

Lo, Youth, I told you
That he was a lusty fellow.

YOUTH.

Marry, sir, I thank thee
That you would bring him unto me.

PRIDE.

Sir, it were expedient that ye had a wife,
To live with her all your life.

RIOT.

A wife ? nay, nay, for God avow,
He shall have flesh enou',
For, by God that me dear bought,
Over-much of one thing is nought ;
The devil said he had liever burn all his life
Than once for to take a wife ;
Therefore I say, so God me save,

He shall no wife have :
Thou hast a sister fair and free,
I know well his leman she will be ;
Therefore I would she were here,
That we might go and make good cheer
At the wine somewhere.

YOUTH.

I pray you hither thou her do bring,
For she is to my liking.

PRIDE.

Sir, I shall do my diligence
To bring her to your presence.

YOUTH.

Hie thee apace, and come again ;
To have a sight I would be fain
Of that lady free.

RIOT.

Sir, in faith I shall tell you true,
She is fresh and fair of hue,
And very proper of body ;
Men call her Lady Lechery.

YOUTH.

My heart burneth, by God of might,
Till of that lady I have a sight.

(Intret Superbia cum Luxuria et dicat Superbia.)

PRIDE.

Sir, I have fulfilled your intent,
And have brought you in this present,
That you have sent me for.

YOUTH.

Thou art a ready messenger ;
Come hither to me, my heart so dear,
Ye be welcome to me as the heart in my body.

LECHERY.

Sir, I thank you, and at your pleasure I am ;
Ye be the same unto me.

YOUTH.

Masters, will ye to tavern walk ?
A word with you here will I talk,
And give you the wine.

LECHERY.

Gentleman, I thank you verily,
And I am all ready
To wait you upon.

RIOT.

What, sister Lechery ?
Ye be welcome to our company.

LECHERY.

Well, wanton, well, fie for shame '
So soon ye do express my name :

What! if no man should have known,
I-wis I shall you beat! well, wanton, well!

RIOT.

A little pretty niset,[1]
Ye be well nice, God wot!
Ye be a little pretty pye! i-wis, ye go full gingerly.

LECHERY.

Well, I see your false eye
Winketh on me full wantonly;
Ye be full wanton, i-wis.

YOUTH.

Pride, I thank you of your labour
That you had to fetch this fair flow'r.

PRIDE.

Lo, youth, I told thee
That I would bring her with me.
Sir, I pray you tell me now,
How she doth like you?

YOUTH.

Verily, well she pleaseth me,
For she is courteous, gentle, and free.
How do you, fair lady?
How fare you, tell me.

LECHERY.

Sir, if it please you, I do well enou',
And the better that you will wit.

[1] [Vele's ed. nilet.]

YOUTH.

Riot, I would be at the tavern fain,
Lest Charity us meet and turn us again :
Then would I be sorry, because of this fair lady.

RIOT.

Let us go again betime,
That we may be at the wine,
Ere ever that he come.

PRIDE.

Hie thee apace, and go we hence ;
We will let for none expense.

YOUTH.

Now we will fill the cup and make good cheer ;
I trust I have a noble here.
Hark, sirs, for God Almighty,
Hearest thou not how they fight ?
In faith we shall them part.
If there be any wine to sell,
They shall no longer together dwell ;
No, then I beshrew my heart.

RIOT.

No, sir, so mot I the,
Let not thy servants fight within thee ;
For it is a careful life
Evermore to live in strife ;
Therefore, if ye will be ruled by my tale,
We will go to the ale,
And see how we can do ;
I trust to God that sitteth on high,

Think not too long, I pray ye ;
If misfortune come soon enou',
Ye shall think it a little [too] soon.

YOUTH.

Yet, sirs, let this cease,
And let us talk of goodness.

RIOT.

He turneth his tail, he is afeard ;
But, faith, he shall be scared ;
He weeneth by flattering to please us again,
But he laboureth all in vain.

CHARITY.

Sir, I pray you me not spare,
For nothing I do care
That ye can do to me.

RIOT.

No, whoreson ? sayest thou so?
Hold him, Pride, and let me go ;
I shall set a pair of rings,
That shall set to his shins,
And that even anon.

PRIDE.

Hie thee apace and come again,
And bring with thee a good chain,
And hold him here still.

CHARITY.

Jesus, that was born of Mary mild,
From all evil he us shield,
And send you grace to amend,
Ere our life be at an end ;
For I tell you truly,
That ye live full wickedly ;
I pray God it amend !

RIOT.

Lo, sirs, look what I bring.
Is not this a jolly ringing ?
By my troth, I trow it be :
I will go with Charity.
How say'st thou, Master Charity ?
Doth this gear please thee ?

CHARITY.

They please me well indeed !
The more sorrow, the more meed !
For God said, while he was a man,
Beati qui persecutionem patiuntur propter justitiam ;
Unto his apostles he said so,
To teach them how they should do.

PRIDE.

We shall see how they can please ;
Sit down, sir, and take your ease ;
Methink these same were full meet
To go about your fair feet.

YOUTH.

By my truth, I you tell
They would become him very well ;

Therefore hie that they were on,
Unto the tavern that we were gone.

RIOT.

That shall ye see anon,
How soon they shall be on ;
And after we will not tarry long,
But go hence with a merry song.

PRIDE.

Let us begin all at once.

YOUTH.

Now have at thee, by Cock's bones,
And soon let us go !
          [*Exeunt Pride, Youth, Riot, and Lechery.*

CHARITY.

Lo, masters, here you may see beforne,
That the weed overgroweth the corn :
Now may ye see all in this tide,
How vice is taken, and virtue set aside.
Yonder ye may see youth is unstable,
But evermore changeable ;
And the nature of men is frail,
That he wotteth not what may avail
Virtue for to make.
O good Lord, it is a pitiful case,
Sith God hath lent man wit and grace
To choose of good and evil,
That man should voluntarily
To such things himself apply,
That his soul should spill.

HUMILITY.

Christ that was crucified, and crowned with thorn,
And of a virgin for man was born,
Some knowledge send to me
Of my brother Charity.

CHARITY.

Dear brother Humility,
Ye be welcome unto me ;
Where have ye be so long ?

HUMILITY.

I shall do you to understand,
That I have said mine evensong ;
But, sir, I pray you tell me now,
How this case happened to you ?

CHARITY.

I shall tell you anon ;
The fellows that I told you on,
Have me thus arrayed.

HUMILITY.

Sir, I shall undo the bands
From your feet and your hands.
Sir, I pray you tell me anon
Whither they be gone,
And when they come again.

CHARITY.

Sir, to the tavern they be gone,
And they will come again anon,
And that shall you see.

HUMILITY.

Then will we them exhort
Unto virtue to resort,
And to forsake sin.

CHARITY.

I will help you that I can
To convert that wicked man.

YOUTH.

Aback ! gallants, and look unto me,
And take me for your special,
For I am promoted to high degree,
By right I am king eternal ;
Neither duke ne lord, baron ne knight,
That may be likened unto me,
They be subdued to me by right,
As servants to their masters should be.

HUMILITY.

Ye be welcome to this place here ;
We think ye labour all in vain ;
Wherefore your brains we will stir,
And keel[1] you a little again.

YOUTH.

Sayest thou my brains thou wilt stir,
I shall lay thee on the ear,
Were thou born in Trumpington,[2]

---

[1] Cool.

[2] [Trumpington is in Essex, a county proverbial, rightly
or wrongly, for the stupidity of its inhabitants]

And brought up at Hogsnorton ? [1]
By my faith it seemeth so ;
Well, go, knave, go !

CHARITY.

Do by our counsel and our reed,
And ask mercy for thy misdeed ;
And endeavour thee, for God's sake,
For thy sins amends to make
Ere ever that thou die.

RIOT.

Hark, Youth, for God avow,
He would have thee a saint now ;
But, Youth, I shall you tell
A young saint an old devil ;
Therefore I hold thee a fool,
And thou follow his school.

YOUTH.

I warrant thee I will not do so ;
I will be ruled by you two.

PRIDE.

Then shall ye do well,
If ye be ruled by our counsel ;
We will bring you to high degree,
And promote you to dignity.

---

[1] [Equivalent to calling him a churl. See Hazlitt's
"Proverbs," 1869, pp. 315-316 and 489 ; and Halliwell's
"Dictionary," v. Hogsnorton. But in none of the instances
cited there do we find Trumpington mentioned.]

HUMILITY.

Sir, it is a pitiful case,
That ye would forsake grace,
And to vice apply.

YOUTH.

Why, knave, doth it grieve thee !
Thou shalt not answer for me.
When my soul hangeth on the hedge once,
Then take thou, and cast stones,
As fast as thou wilt !

CHARITY.

Sir, if it please you to do thus,
Forsake them and do after us,
The better shall you do.

RIOT.

Sir, he shall do well enou',
Though he be ruled by neither of you ;
Therefore crake no longer here,
Lest you have on the ear,
And that a good knock.

PRIDE.

Lightly see thou avoid the place,
Or I shall give thee on the face.
Youth, I trow that he would
Make you holy, ere ye be old ;
And, I swear by the rood,
It is time enough to be good,
When that ye be old.

YOUTH.

Sir, by my truth, I thee say
I will make merry, whiles I may,
I cannot tell you how long.

PRIDE.

Yea, sir, so mot I thrive,
Thou art not certain of thy life ;
Therefore thou wert a stark fool
To leave mirth and follow their school.

HUMILITY.

Sir, I shall him exhort
Unto us to resort,
And you to forsake.

PRIDE.

Ask him if he will do so,
To forsake us and follow you two ;
Nay, I warrant you, nay !

HUMILITY.

That shall you see even anon ;
I will unto him gone,
And see what he will say.

RIOT.

Hardily go on thy way ;
I know well he will say nay.

YOUTH.

Yea, sir, by God that me dear bought,
Methink ye labour all for nought ;
Weenest thou that I will for thee
Or thy brother Charity
Forsake this good company ?
Nay, I warrant you.

PRIDE.

No, master, I pray you of that,
For anything forsake us not,
And all our counsel rule you by ;
Ye may be emperor, ere ye die.

YOUTH.

While I have life in my body,
Shall I be ruled by Riot and thee.

RIOT.

Sir, then, shall ye do well,
For we be true as steel ;
Sir, I can teach you to play at the dice,
At the queen's game [1] and at the Irish ; [2]
The treygobet [3] and the hazard [4] also,
And many other games mo ;
Also at the cards I can teach you to play,
At the triump and one-and-thirty,

---

[1] See "Popular Antiquities of Great Britain," ii. 286.
[2] "Popular Antiquities of Great Britain," ii. 315.
[3] Should we not read *Hey-go-bet !*
[4] See Hazlitt's "Popular Poetry," iii. 73–4.

Post,[1] pinion,[2] and also aums-ace,
And at another they call dewce-ace ;
Yet I can tell you more, and ye will con me thank,
Pink [3] and drink, and also at the blank,[4]
And many sports mo.

YOUTH.

I thank thee, Riot, so mot I the,
For the counsel thou hast given me ;
I will follow thy mind in every thing,
And guide me after thy learning.

CHARITY.

Youth, leave that counsel, for it is nought,
And amend that thou hast miswrought,
That thou may'st save that God hath bought.

YOUTH.

What say ye, Master Charity ?
What hath God bought ?
By my troth, I know not
Whether he goeth in white or black ;
He came never at the stews,
Nor in no place, where I do use ;
I-wis he bought not my cap,

---

[1] *Post and pair.*
[2] [We do not find this mentioned elsewhere. The same remark applies to *aums-ace.*]
[3] [Halliwell, in his " Dict." *v.* Pink, says :—" A game, the same as post and pair." Surely this is not so. It seems rather to be used, here at least, in the sense of *gamble.* But *pink*, after all, may signify something very different, viz., *lechery.*]
[4] The target or butts.

Nor yet my jolly hat;
I wot not what he hath bought for me;
And he bought anything of mine,
I will give him a quart of wine,
The next time I him meet.

CHARITY.

Sir, this he did for thee;
When thou wast bond, he made thee free,
And bought thee with his blood.

YOUTH.

Sir, I pray you tell me,
How may this be :
That I know, I was never bond
Unto none in England.

CHARITY.

Sir, I shall tell you—
When Adam had done great trespass,
And out of Paradise exiled was;
Then all the souls, as I can you tell,
Were in the bondage of the devil of hell,
Till the Father of heaven, of his great mercy,
Sent the Second Person in Trinity
Us for to redeem,
And so with his precious blood
He bought us on the rood,
And our souls did save.

YOUTH.

How should I save it, tell me now,
And I will be ruled after you
My soul to save.

RIOT.

What, youth ; will ye forsake me ?
I will not forsake thee.

HUMILITY.

I shall tell you shortly ;
Kneel down and ask God mercy,
For that you have offended.

PRIDE.

Youth, wilt thou do so ?
Follow them, and let us go ?
Marry, I trow, nay.

YOUTH.

Here all sin I forsake,
And to God I me betake ;
Good Lord, I pray thee have no indignation,
That I, a sinner, should ask salvation.

CHARITY.

Now thou must forsake Pride,
And all Riot set aside.

PRIDE.

I will not him forsake,
Neither early ne late ;
I ween'd he would not forsake me ;
But if it will none otherwise be,
I will go my way.

YOUTH.

Sir, I pray God be your speed,
And help you at your need.

RIOT.

I am sure thou wilt not forsake me,
Nor I will not forsake thee.

YOUTH.

I forsake you also,
And will not have with you to do.

RIOT.

And I forsake thee utterly :
Fie on thee, caitiff, fie !
Once a promise thou did me make,
That thou would me never forsake,
But now I see it is hard
For to trust the wretched world ;
Farewell, masters, everychone.

HUMILITY.

For your sin look ye mourn,
And evil creatures look ye turn ;
For your name, who maketh inquisition,
Say it is Good Contrition
That for sin doth mourn.

CHARITY.

Here is a new array,
For to walk by the way,
Your prayer for to say.

HUMILITY.

Here be beads[1] for your devotion,
And keep you from all temptation ;
Let not vice devour.
When you see misdoing men,
Good counsel give them,
And teach them to amend.

YOUTH.

For my sin I will mourn,
All creatures I will turn ;
And when I see misdoing men,
Good counsel I shall give them,
And exhort them to amend.

CHARITY.

Then shall ye be an heritor of bliss,
Where all joy and mirth is.

YOUTH.

To the which eternal
God bring the persons all
Here being, amen !

HUMILITY.

Thus have we brought our matter to an end
Before the persons here present ;
Would every man be content,
Lest another day we be shent.

CHARITY.

We thank all this presence
Of their meek audience.

---

[1] [Copland's ed. *books.*]

HUMILITY.

Jesu that sitteth in heaven so high,
Save all this fair company : [1]
Men and women that here be,
Amen, amen, for Charity. [2]

---

[1] [This line is omitted in Waley's ed.]
[2] [The colophon of Waley's ed. is : Imprinted at London by John waley, dwellyng in foster lane.]

LUSTY JUVENTUS.

A MORALITY.

An Enterlude called Lusty Juuentus, lyuely describing the frailtie of youth: of natur prone to vyce: by grace and good counsayll traynable to vertue.

The parsonages that speake.

Messenger,	*Hypocrisie,*
Lusty Juuentus,	*Felowship,*
Good Counsaill,	*Abhominable Lyuyng,*
Knowledge,	*Gods mercifull promises.*
Sathan the deuyll,	

Foure maye playe it easely, takyng such partes as they thinke best: so that any one take of those partes that be not in place at once.

[Col.] Imprynted at London, in Lothbury, ouer agaynst Sainct Margarits Church, by Wyllyam Copland. 4°, black-letter.[1]

---

[1] [The colophon of Vele's ed. is at the end *infrâ*.]

HAWKINS'S PREFACE.

THE editor has been favoured with two copies of this moral interlude ; one of which is preserved in the library belonging to Lincoln Cathedral,[1] the other is in the possession of Mr Garrick. It was written in the reign of Edward the Sixth by one R. Wever, of whom the editor can give the reader no further information. The former was printed at London by Abraham Vele. The latter is a very different copy from the other. A more obsolete spelling runs through the whole, and it contains great variations besides, which the reader will find at the bottom of each page. The conclusion being imperfect, the printer's colophon is wanting, so that it cannot be known where this edition was printed. According to Dr Percy's tables, it was printed by Richard Pinson.[2]

The design of this interlude was to expose the super-

---

[1] [Afterwards parted with to Dr Dibdin. A second copy is in the Bodleian.]

[2] [An error. No edition by Pinson is known, or is likely to have ever existed. The impression referred to is Copland's. *See* Hazlitt's "Handbook," p. 649–50.]

stitions of the Romish Church, and to promote the
Reformation. The stage (as the learned Dr Percy observes) in those days literally was what wise men have
always wished it—a supplement to the pulpit : chapter
and verse are as formally quoted as in a sermon. See
" Prologue of the Messenger," &c. From this play we
learn that most of the young people were new gospellers,
or friends to the Reformation ; and that the old were
tenacious of the doctrines imbibed in their youth, for
thus the Devil is introduced lamenting the downfall of
superstition—

> The old people would believe still in my laws,
> But the younger sort lead them a contrary way ;
> They will not believe, they plainly say,
> In old traditions and made by men,
> But they will live as the scripture teacheth them, &c.

And in another place Hypocrisy urges—

> The world was never merry,
> Since children were so bold ;
> Now every boy will be a teacher,
> The father a fool, and the child a preacher.

[This is certainly a piece of rather heavy and tedious
morality, replete with good instruction, but didactic to
a fault. It is deficient in the curious allusions, which
abound in other productions of the same kind; and
even that mysterious character, *Abominable Living*,
whose introduction promises some amusement and
illustration, moves off the scene almost immediately
after her first appearance, while *Little Bess*, whose
entrance might have been a vehicle for some diverting
or sentimental situation, does not " come on " at all.]

LUSTY JUVENTUS.

THE PROLOGUE OF THE MESSENGER.

FOR as much as man is naturally prone
To evil from his youth, as Scripture doth recite,[1]
It is necessary that he be speedily withdrawn
From concupiscence of sin, his natural appetite :
An [2] order to bring up youth Ecclesiasticus doth
      write,—
An untamed horse will be hard, saith he,
And a wanton child wilful will be.
   Give him no liberty in youth, nor his folly
      excuse,
Bow down his neck, and keep him in good awe,
Lest he be stubborn : no labour refuse
To train him to wisdom and teach him God's law,
For youth is frail and easy to draw
By grace to goodness, by nature to ill :
That nature hath ingrafted, is hard to kill.
   Nevertheless, in youth men may be best
Trained to virtue by godly mean ;
Vice may be so mortified and so supprest,

---

[1] Gen. viii. ; Jer. xvii. ; Eccles. xxx.
[2] *And*, Copland's edition.

That it shall not break furth, yet the root will
  remain ;
As in this interlude by youth you shall see plain,
From his lust by Good Counsel brought to godly
  conversation,
And shortly after to frail nature's inclination.
  The enemy of mankind, Satan, through Hypo-
  crisy
Feigned or chosen holiness of man's blind intent,
Forsaking [1] God's word, that leadeth right way,
Is brought to Fellowship and ungracious company,
To Abhominable Living till he be wholly bent,
And so to desperation, if good counsel were not
  sent
From God, that in trouble doth no man forsake
That doth call, and trust in him for Christ's sake.
  Finally, youth by God's special grace
Doth earnestly repent his abhominable living
By the doctrine of good counsel, and to his solace
God's mercy entereth to him reciting
God's merciful promises, as they be in writing :
He believeth and followeth, to his great consola-
  tion. [2]
And these parts ye shall see briefly played in their
  fashion.

Here entereth LUSTY JUVENTUS, *or* YOUTH, *singing
as followeth :*

In a herber [3] green, asleep [4] where as I lay,
The birds sang sweet in the middes of the day ;
I dreamed fast of mirth and play :
  In youth is pleasure, in youth is pleasure.

---

[1] *Forsakyn,* Copland's edition.
[2] *Consolaion,* Vele's edition.
[3] *Arbour,* Copland's edition.
[4] *Aslope,* Copland's edition.

Methought I walked still to and fro,
And from her company I could not go ;
But when I waked, it was not so :
     In youth is pleasure, in youth is pleasure.

Therefore my heart is surely pight [1]
Of her alone to have a sight,
Which is my joy and heart's delight :
     In youth is pleasure, in youth is pleasure.

Finis.

LUSTY JUVENTUS, *or* YOUTH, *speaketh.*

What, ho ?   Are they not here ?
I am disappointed, by the blessed mass !
I had thought to have found them making good
    cheer ;
But now they are gone to some secret place.
Well, seeing they are gone, I do not greatly pass ; [2]
Another time I will hold them as much,
Seeing they break [3] promise, and keep not the
    tweche. [4]
    What shall I do now to pass away the day ?
Is there any man here that will go to game ?
At whatsoever he [5] will play,
To make one I am ready to the same :
Youth full of pleasure is my proper name.
To be alone is not my appetite, [6]
For of all things in the world I love merry com-
    pany.
    Who knoweth where is e'er a minstrel ?

---

[1] *Surel i-pight,* Copland's edition.   [2] Care.
[3] *Brake,* Copland's edition.   [4] Touch.
[5] *Ye,* Copland's edition.
[6] *Appetyte,* Vele's edition.

By the mass, I would fain go dance a fit.[1]
My companions[2] are at it, I know right well ;
They do not all this while in a corner sit :
Against another time they have taught me[3] wit :
I beshrew their hearts for serving me this,[4]
I will go seek them, whether I hit or miss.

Here entereth GOOD COUNSEL, *to whom* YOUTH
yet speaketh.

Well i-met, father, well i-met :
Did you hear any minstrels play,
As you came hitherward upon your way ?
And if you did, I pray you wish[5] me thither,
For I am going to seek them, and, in faith, I know
      not whither.

GOOD COUNSEL.

Sir, I will ask you a question by your favour :
What would you with the minstrel do ?

JUVENTUS.

Nothing but have a dance or two,
To pass the time away in pleasure.

---

[1] The word *fitte* sometimes signified a part or division of
a song ; but in its original acceptation a poetic strain, verse,
or poem : from being applied to music, the word was easily
transferred to dancing, as in the above passages. See Dr
Percy's "Relics of Anc. Eng. Poetry," vol. ii., p. 297 [edit.
1765].—*Hawkins.*
[2] *Compacions,* Copland's edition.
[3] *My,* Copland's edition.   [4] Thus.
[5] *Wyse,* Vele's edition.

GOOD COUNSEL.

If that be the matter, I promise you sure,
I am the more sorrier that it should so be ;
For there is no such passing the time appointed in
    the Scripture,
Nor yet thereunto it doth not agree !
I wish that ye would so use your liberty,
To walk as you are bound to do,
According to the vocation which God hath called
    you to.

JUVENTUS.

Why, sir, are you angry, because I have spoken so ?
By the mass, it is alone for my appetite.

GOOD COUNSEL.

Show me your name, I pray you heartily,
And then I will my mind express.

JUVENTUS.

My name is called Juventus, doubtless :
Say what you will, I will give you the hearing.

GOOD COUNSEL.

For as much as God hath created you of nothing,
Unto his own likeness by spiritual illumination,
It is unmeet that ye should lead your living
Contrary to his godly determination.
Saint Paul unto the Ephesians giveth good exhorta-
    tion,

Saying, walk circumspectly, redeeming the time;
That is, to spend it well, and not to wickedness
    incline.

JUVENTUS.

No, no, hardily none of mine;
If I would live so strait, you might count me a
    fool;
Let them keep those rules, which are doctors
    divine,
And have be brought up all their days in school.

GOOD COUNSEL.

Moses in the law exhorteth his people,
As in the book of Deuteronomy he doth plainly
    write,
That they should live obedient and thankful;
For in effect [1] these words he doth recite:
All ye this day stand before the Lord's sight,
Both princes, rulers, elders, and parents,
Children, wives, young, and old; therefore obey his
    commandments.

JUVENTUS.

I am too young to understand his documents; [2]
Wherefore did all they stand before his presence?

GOOD COUNSEL.

To enter with God peace and alliance,
Promising that they would him honour, fear, and
    serve:

---

[1] *For infecte,* Copland's edition.
[2] Teachings.

All kind of people were bound in those covenants,
That from his law they should never swerve ;
For God useth no partiality.

JUVENTUS.

What, am I bound, as well as the clergy,
To learn and follow his precepts and law ?

GOOD COUNSEL.

Yea, surely, or else God will withdraw
His mercy from you, promised in his covenant ;
For, except you live under his obedience and awe,
How can you receive the benefits of his Testament ?
For he that [1] submitteth himself to be a servant,
And his master's commandment will not fulfil nor
    regard,
According as he hath done, is worthy his reward.

JUVENTUS.

It is as true a saying as ever I heard ;
Therefore your name, I pray you [2] now tell,
For, by my truth, your communication I like won-
    ders well.

GOOD COUNSEL.

My name is called Good Counsel.

JUVENTUS.

Good Counsel ?
Now, in faith, I cry you mercy :

---

[1] *That*, omitted in Copland's edition.
[2] *You*, omitted in Copland's edition.

I am sorry that I have you thus offended ;
But, I pray you, bear with me patiently,
And my misbehaviour shall be amended :
I know my time I have rudely spended,
Following my own lust, being led by ignorance ;
But now I hope of better knowledge through your
        acquaintance.

GOOD COUNSEL.

I pray God guide you with his gracious assistance
Unto the knowledge of his truth, your ignorance
        to undo,
That you may be one of those numbered Christians,
Which followeth the lamb whither he doth go :
The lamb Jesus Christ my meaning is so,
By sure faith and confidence in his bitter death
        and passion,
The only price of our health and salvation.

JUVENTUS.

Sir, I thank you for your hearty oration :
And now, I pray you, show me your advisement,
How I may live in this my vocation,
According to God's will and commandment.

GOOD COUNSEL.

First of all, it is most expedient,
That you exercise yourself in continual prayer,
That it might please the Lord omnipotent
To send unto you his holy spirit and comforter,
Which will lead you every day and hour
Unto the knowledge of his word and verity,
Wherein you may learn to live most christianly.

JUVENTUS.

O Lord, grant me of thy infinite [1] mercy
                                    [*He kneeleth.*
The true knowledge of thy [2] law and will,
And illumine my heart with spirit continually,
That I may [3] be apt thy holy precepts to fulfil;
Strengthen me, that I may persever still
Thy commandments to obey :
And then shall I never slip nor fall away.
                                    [*He riseth.*

GOOD COUNSEL.

Full true be these words, which Christ himself did
        say,
He that seeketh shall surely find.

KNOWLEDGE *entereth.*

Behold, Youth, now rejoice we may,
For I see Knowledge of God['s] [4] Verity stand here
        behind :
He is come now to satisfy your mind
In those things which you will desire ;
Therefore together let us approach him near.

JUVENTUS.

Ah, Good Counsel, now [5] it doth appear,
That God never rejecteth the humbles[t] petition.

---

1 *Infinitie,* Vele's edition.
2 *The,* Copland's edition.
3 *Way,* Copland's edition.
4 Both the copies read *God.*
5 *New,* Copland's edition.

KNOWLEDGE.

Now the Lord bless you all with his heavenly
    benediction,
And with his fiery love your hearts inflame,
That of his merciful promises you may have the
    fruition,
The subtlety of the devil utterly to defame.
Now, good Christian audience, I will express my
    name,
The True Knowledge of God's Verity, this[1] my
    name doth hight,
Whom God hath appointed to give the blind their
    sight.

GOOD COUNSEL.

All praise be given to that Lord of might,
Which hath appointed you hither at this present
    hour;
For I trust you will so instruct youth aright,
That he shall live according to God's pleasure.

JUVENTUS.

And I thank Jesus Christ my Saviour,
That he is come to my company.

KNOWLEDGE.

I thank you, my friends, most heartily
For your gentle salutation.

JUVENTUS.

Sir, I will be so bold, by your deliberation,
To open my mind unto you now,

---

[1] *Thus*, Copland's edition; but the sense is the same.

Trusting that, by your good exhortation,
I shall learn those things which I never knew :
This one thing chiefly I would learn of you,
How I may my life in this my vocation lead,
According as God hath ordained and decreed.

KNOWLEDGE.

The prophet David saith, that the man is blessed,
Which doth exercise himself in the law of the
    Lord,
And doth not follow the way of the wicked ;
As the first psalm doth plainly record :[1]
The fourscore and thirteenth psalm thereunto doth
    accord ;
Blessed is the man whom thou teachest, O Lord,
    saith he,
To learn thy[2] law, precepts, word, or verity.
And Christ in the gospel saith manifestly :
Blessed is he which heareth the Word of God and
    keepeth it ;
That is, to believe his word and live accordingly,
Declaring the faith by the fruits of the spirit,
Whose fruits are these, as St. Paul to the Galathi
    doth write,
Love, joy, peace, long suffering, and faithfulness,
Meekness, goodness, temperance, and gentleness.

GOOD COUNSEL.

By[3] these words, which unto you he doth express,
He teacheth that you ought to have a steadfast
    faith ;

---

[1] *Accorde,* Copland's edition.
[2] *The,* Copland's edition.
[3] *Be,* Copland's edition.

Without the which [1] it is impossible doubtless
To please God, as Saint Paul saith :
Where faith is not, godly living decayeth ;
For whatsoever is not of faith, saith St. Paul, is
    sin,
But where a perfect faith is, there is good working.

JUVENTUS.

It seemeth to me, that this is [2] your meaning,
That, when I observe God's commandments and
    the works of charity,
They shall prevail unto me nothing,
Except I believe to be saved thereby.

KNOWLEDGE.

No, no, you are deceived very blindly ;
For faith in Christ's merits doth only justify,
And make us righteous in God's sight.

JUVENTUS.

Why should I then in good [3] works delight,
Seeing I shall not be saved by them ?

GOOD COUNSEL.

Because they are required of all Christian men,
As the necessary fruits of true repentance.

KNOWLEDGE.

But the reward of the heavenly inheritance
Is given us through faith, for Christ's deservings :

---

[1] *The which*, omitted in Copland's edition.
[2] *Is*, omitted, Copland's edition.
[3] *God*, Vele's edition.

As St. Paul declareth in the fourth chapter to the
    Romans,
Therefore we ought not to work as hirelings :
Seeing Christ hath purged us once from all our
    wicked living,
Let us no more wallow therein,
But persever, like good branches, bearing fruit in
    him.

JUVENTUS.

Now I know where about you have been :
My elders never taught me so before.

GOOD COUNSEL.

Though your elders were blind, doubt not you
    therefore ;
For Saint Peter saith, vain is the conversations
Which ye receive by your elders' traditions,

JUVENTUS.

I will gladly receive your godly admonitions :
But yet, I pray you, show me the cause
That they, being men of great discretions,
Did not instruct me in God's laws,
According to his will and ordinance.

KNOWLEDGE.

Because they themselves were wrapped in ignorance,
Being deceived by false preachers.

JUVENTUS.

O Lord, deliver me from wicked teachers,
That I be not deceived with their false doctrine.

GOOD COUNSEL.

To God's word you must only incline;
All other doctrine clean set apart.

JUVENTUS.

Surely that I will from the bottom of my heart ;
And I thank the living God which hath given me
    the knowledge
To know his doctrine from the false and pervart,[1]
I being yet young and full tender of age ;
And that he hath made me partaker of the heavenly
    inheritage,
Of his own[2] mercy, and not of my deserving,
For hell I have deserved by my sinful working.
I know right well, my elders and parents
Have of a long time deceived be
With blind hypocrisy and superstitious intents,
Trusting in their own works, which is nothing but
    vanity ;
Their steps shall not be followed for me :
Therefore, I pray you, show me a brief conclusion,
How I ought to live in Christian religion.

KNOWLEDGE.

The first beginning of wisdom, as saith the wise
    Solomon,
Is to fear God with all thy[3] heart and power ;
And then thou must believe all his promises with-
    out any exception,
And that he will perform them both constant and
    sure :

---

[1] *Pervarce*, Copland's edition.
[2] *One*, Copland's edition.
[3] *They*, Copland's edition.

And then, because he is thy only Saviour,
Thou must love him with all thy soul and mind,
And thy neighbour as thyself, because he hath so
    assigned.

JUVENTUS.

To love my neighbour as myself? I cannot be so [1]
    kind :
I pray you tell me, what mean you?

KNOWLEDGE.

My meaning is, as Christ saith in the sixth chapter
    of Matthew, [2]
To do to him as you would be done to.

JUVENTUS.

I pray God give me grace so for to do,
That unto his will I may be obedient.

GOOD COUNSEL.

Here you shall receive Christ's testament
To comfort your conscience, when need shall re-
    quire,
To learn the contents thereof, see that you be
    diligent ;
The which all Christian men ought to desire,
For it is the well or fountain most clear,
Out of the which doth spring sweet consolation
To all those that [3] thirst after eternal salvation.

---

[1] *To,* Copland's edition.
[2] *Chap. Math.,* Copland's edition.
[3] *Which,* Vele's edition.

KNOWLEDGE.

Therein shall you find most wholesome preserva-
    tion
Both in troubles, persecutions, sickness, and ad-
    versity,
And a sure defence in the time of temptation,
Against whom the devil cannot prevail with all
    his army :
And, if you persever therein unfeignedly,
It will set your heart at such quietness and rest,
Which cannot [1] never be turned with storms nor
    tempest.

GOOD COUNSEL.

With this thing you must neither flatter nor jest,
But stedfastly believe it every day and hour,
And let your conversation openly protest,
That of your heart it is the most precious treasure :
And then your godly example shall other men pro-
    cure
To learn and exercise the same also :
I pray God strengthen you so for to do.

JUVENTUS.

Now for this godly knowledge which you have
    brought me to,
I beseech the living God reward [2] you again :
From your company I will never depart nor go,
So long as in this life I do remain ;
For in this book I see manifest and plain,
That he that followeth his own lusts and imagina-
    tion,

---

[1] *Not*, omitted in Vele's edition.
[2] *To reward*, Vele's edition.

Keepeth the ready path to everlasting damnation :
And he that leadeth[1] a godly conversation
Shall be brought[2] to such quietness, joy, and peace,
Which in comparison passeth all worldly gloriation,
Which cannot endure, but shortly cease.
Both the time and hour I may now bless,
That I met with you, father Good Counsel,
To bring me to the knowledge of this[3] heavenly
    gospel.

KNOWLEDGE.

This your profession I like very well,
So that you intend to live according ;
I pray God, your living do not rebel,
But ever agree unto your saying,
That, when ye shall make accounts or reckoning,
Of this talent which you have received,
You may be one of those, with whom the Lord
    shall be pleased.

GOOD COUNSEL.

For this conversation of Youth the Lord's name be
    praised :
Let us now depart for a season.   [*Exit.*

KNOWLEDGE.

To give God the glory it is convenient and reason :
If you will depart, I will not tarry.   [*Exit.*

---

[1] *Leadete*, Copland's edition.
[2] *Borught*, Copland's edition.
[3] *His*, Copland's edition.

JUVENTUS.

And I will never forsake your company,
While I live in this world.   *[Exit.*[1]

Here entereth the DEVIL.

O, O, all too late !
I trow this gear will come to naught ;
For I perceive my power doth abate,
For all the policy that ever I have wrought :
Many and sundry ways I have fought,
To have the Word of God deluded utterly ;
O for sorrow ! yet it will not be.
I have done the best that I can,
And my mistress also in every place,
To root it clean from the heart of man ;
And yet for all that it flourisheth apace ;
I am sore in dread to show my face,
My auctority and works are so greatly despised,
My inventions, and all that ever I have devised.
O, O, full well I know the cause,
That my estimation doth thus decay ;
The old people would believe still in my laws,
But the younger sort lead them a contrary way ;
They will not believe, they plainly say,
In old traditions and made by men,
But they will live, as the Scripture teacheth them.
Out, I cry, upon them, they do me open wrong,
To bring up their children thus in knowledge ;
For, if they will not follow my ways, when they
   are young,
It is hard turning them when they come to age :
I must needs find some means this matter to 'suage ;

---

[1] *Exit,* omitted in Copland's edition.

I mean, to turn their hearts from the Scripture
    quite,
That in carnal pleasures they may have more
    delight.
Well, I will go haste[1] to infect this youth
Through the enticement of my son Hypocrisy,
And work some proper feat to stop his mouth,
That he may lead his life carnally :
I had never more need my matters to apply.
O my child Hypocrisy, where art thou ?
I charge thee of my blessing appear before me now.
                    [*Here entereth* HYPOCRISY.

HYPOCRISY.

O, O, quoth he, keep again the sow ;
I come as fast as I can, I warrant you :
Where is he that hath the sow to sell ?
I will give him money, if I like her well ;
Whether it be sow or hog, I do not greatly care,
For by my occupation I am a butcher.

DEVIL.

O my child, how dost thou fare ?

HYPOCRISY.

Sancti amen, who have we there ?
By the mass, I will buy none of thy ware ;
Thou art a chapman for the devil.

DEVIL.

What, my son, canst thou not tell,
Who is here, and what I am ?
I am thine own father Satan.

---

[1] Copland's edit. *taste.*

HYPOCRISY.

Be you so, sir ? I cry you mercy then ;
You may say I am homely, and lack learning,
To liken my father's voice unto a sow's groaning :
But, I pray you, show me the cause and why,
That you called me hither so hastily ?

DEVIL.

Ah, Hypocrisy, I am undone utterly.

HYPOCRISY.

Utterly undone ! nay, stop there hardily ;
For I myself do know the contrary
By daily experience :
Do not I yet reign abroad ?
And as long as I am in the world,
You have some treasure and substance.
I suppose I have been the flower
In setting forth thy laws and power
Without any delay :
By the mass, if I had not been,
Thou haddest not been worth a Flander's pin
At this present day.
The time were too long now to declare,
How many and great the number are,
Which have deceived be ;
And brought clean from God's law
Unto thy yoke and awe,
Through the enticement of me.
I have been busied since the world began,
To graff thy laws in the heart of man,
Where they ought to be refused :
And I have so mingled God's commandments
With vain zeals and blind intents,

That they be greatly abused.
I set up great idolatry
With all[1] kind of filthy sodometry,
To give mankind a fall :
And I [have] brought up such superstition,
Under the name of holiness and religion,
That deceived almost all.
As holy cardinals, holy popes,
Holy vestments, holy copes,
Holy hermits and friars,
Holy priests, holy bishops,
Holy monks, holy abbots,
Yea, and all obstinate[2] liars :
Holy pardons, holy beads,
Holy saints, holy images,
With holy, holy blood,
Holy stocks, holy stones,
Holy clouts, holy[3] bones ;
Yea, and holy holy wood.
Holy skins, holy bulls,
Holy rochets and cowls,
Holy crouches and staves,
Holy hoods, holy caps,
Holy mitres, holy hats ;
Ah good holy holy knaves.
Holy days, holy fastings,
Holy twitching, holy tastings,
Holy visions and sights,
Holy wax, holy lead,
Holy water, holy bread,
To drive away spirits.
Holy fire, holy palm,
Holy oil, holy cream,

---

[1] *A*, Copland's edition.
[2] *Abstinate*, Copland's edition.
[3] *Hole*, Copland's edition.

And holy ashes also ;
Holy brooches, holy rings,
Holy kneeling, holy censings,
And a hundred trim-trams mo.
Holy crosses, holy bells,
Holy relics, holy jewels,
Of mine own invention ;
Holy candles, holy tapers,
Holy parchments, holy papers :
Had not you a holy son ?

DEVIL.

All these things, which thou hast done,
My honour and laws hath maintained ;
But now, O alas ! one thing is begun,[1]
By the which my kingdom is greatly decayed ;
I shall lese all, I am sore afraid :
Except thy help, I know right plain,
I shall never be able to recover it again.
God's Word is so greatly sprung up in youth,
That he little regardeth my laws or me ;
He telleth his parents that is very truth,
That they of long time have deceived be :
He saith according to Christ's verity
All his doings he will order and frame,
Mortifying the flesh with the lusts of the same.

HYPOCRISY.

Ah, sirrah, there beginneth the game :
What, is Juventus become so tame,
To be a New Gospeller ?

---

[1] *Begone*, Copland's edition.

DEVII.

As fast as I do make, he doth mar ;
He hath[1] followed so long the steps of Good
    Counsel,
That Knowledge and he together doth dwell ;
For who is so busy in every place as youth,
To read and declare the manifest truth ?
But, O Hypocrisy, if thou could stop his mouth,
Thou shouldst win my heart for ever.

HYPOCRISY.

What would you have me to do in the matter ?
Show me therein your advisement.

DEVIL.

I would have thee go incontinent,
And work some crafty[2] feat or policy,
To set Knowledge and him at controversy ;
And his company thyself greatly use,
That God's Word he may clean abuse.

HYPOCRISY.

At your request I will not refuse
To do that thing, which in me doth lie :
Doubt ye not, but I will excuse
Those things, which he doth plainly deny ;
And I will handle my matters so craftily,
That, ere he cometh to man's state,
God's Word and his living shall be clean at the
    bate.

---

[1] *That,* Copland's edition.
[2] *Craft,* Vele's edition.

DEVIL.

Thou shalt have my blessing both early and late ;
And, because thou shalt all my counsel keep,
Thou shalt call thy [1] name Friendship.

HYPOCRISY.

By the mass, it is a name full meet
For my proper and amiable person.

DEVIL.

O, farewell, farewell, my son ;
Speed thy business, for I must be gone.　　　　[*Exit.*[2]

HYPOCRISY.

I warrant you, let me alone.
I will be with Juventus anon,
And that, ere he be ware ;
And, i-wis, if he walk not straight,
I will use such a sleight,
That shall trap him in a snare.
How shall I bring this gear to pass ?
I can tell now, by the mass,
Without any more advisement :
I will infect him with wicked company,
Whose conversation shall be so fleshly,
Yea, able to overcome an innocent.
This wicked Fellowship
Shall him company keep
For a while :
And then I will bring in

---

[1] *My*, Copland's edition.
[2] *Exit* omitted in Copland's edition.

Abhominable [1] Living,
Him to beguile.
With words fair I will him 'tice,
Telling him of a girl nice,
Which shall him somewhat move ;
Abhominable Living though she be,
Yet he shall no other ways see,
But she is for to love.
She shall him procure
To live in pleasure,
After his own phantasy ;
And my matter to frame,
I will call her name
Unknowen Honesty.
This [2] will I convey
My matter, I say,
Somewhat handsomely ;
That, through wicked Fellowship
And false pretended Friendship,
Youth shall live carnally.
Trudge, Hypocrisy, trudge !
Thou art a good drudge,
To serve the devil :
If thou shouldest lie and lurk,
And not intend thy work,
Thy master should do full evil.

---

[1] Abhominable. So the word is constantly spelt. It is
worth remarking, in order to fix the adjustment of a passage
in Shakespeare's "Love's Labour's Lost," A. 4, S. 1: This
is abhominable which he would call abominable. Capell's
edition, nearly agreeable to the quartos, or, this is abominable which we would call abhominable. So Theobald and
Hanmer, according to the folios. The two great and
learned editors, Warburton and Johnson, read *vice versa :*
This is abominable which he would call abhominable, which
destroys the poet's humour, such as it is, who is laughing at
such fanatical phantasms and rackers of orthography as
affect to speak fine.—*Hawkins.*   [2] Thus.

Here entereth YOUTH, *to whom* HYPOCRISY
yet speaketh.

What, Master Youth?
Well i-met, by my truth;
And whither away?
You are the last man,
Which I talked [1] on,
I swear, by this day.
Methought by your face,
Ere you came in place,
It should be you:
Therefore I did abide
Here in this tide [2]
For your coming, this is true.

JUVENTUS.

For your gentleness, sir, most heartily I thank you,
But yet you must hold me somewhat excused;
For to my simple knowledge I never knew,
That you and I together were acquainted:
But nevertheless, if you do it renew,
Old acquaintance will soon [3] be remembered.

HYPOCRISY.

Ah, now I see well, Youth is feathered,
And his crumbs he hath well gathered,
Since I spake with him last;
A poor man's tale cannot now be heard,
As in times past.
I cry you mercy, I was somewhat bold,
Thinking that you mastership would

---

[1] *Called*, Copland's edition.
[2] *Here in this tide* omitted, Copland's edition.
[3] *Some*, Copland's edition.

Not have been so strange ;
But now I perceive, that promotion
Causeth [1] both man, manners, and fashion
Greatly for to change.

JUVENTUS.

You are to blame this [2] me to challenge ;
For I think I am not he, which you take me for.

HYPOCRISY.

Yes, I have known you ever since you were bore ;
Your age is yet under a score,
Which I can well remember :
I-wis, i-wis, you and I
Many a time have been full merry,
When you were young and tender.

JUVENTUS.

Then, I pray you, [3] let us reason no lenger ;
But first show your nomination.

HYPOCRISY.

Of my name to make declaration
Without any dissimulation,
I am called Friendship :
Although I be simple and rude of fashion,
Yet by lineage and generation
I am nigh kin to your mastership.

---

[1] *Canseth,* Copland's edition.
[2] Thus.
[3] *You,* omitted in Copland's edition.

JUVENTUS.

What, Friendship?
I am glad to see that you be merry ;
By my truth, I had almost you forgot,
By long absence brought out of memory.

HYPOCRISY.

By the mass, I love you so heartily,
That there is none so welcome to my company :
I pray you, tell me whither are you going?

JUVENTUS.

My intention is, to go hear a preaching.

HYPOCRISY.

A preaching, quod-a? ah, good little one :
By Christ, she will make you cry out of the
      winning,
If you follow her instruction so early in the morning.

JUVENTUS.

Full great [1] I do abhor this your wicked saying ;
For, no doubt, they increase much sin and vice :
Therefore I pray you, show not your meaning,
For I delight not in such foolish fantasies.

HYPOCRISY.

Surely, then you are the more unwise :
You may have a spurt amongst them now and
      then ;
Why should not you, as well as other men ?

---

[1] Greatly.

JUVENTUS.

As for those filthy doings [1] I utterly detest them ;
I will hear no more of your wicked communication.

HYPOCRISY.

If I may be so bold by your deliberation,
What will you do at a preaching ?

JUVENTUS.

Learn some wholesome and godly teaching
Of the true minister of Christ's gospel.

HYPOCRISY.

Tush, what he will say, I know right well ;
He will say that God is a good man, [2]
He can make him no better, and say the best he
    can.

JUVENTUS.

I know that, but what then ?
The more that God's Word is preached and taught,

---

[1] *As for al those fylthe doinges*, Copland's edition.

[2] Shakespeare puts these words, with great humour, into
the mouth of Dogberry, in "Much ado about Nothing," A.
3, S. 8.   Though the quartos and folios concur in this reading, the moderns uniformly read, *He's a good man.   N.B.—*
The old reading is restored by Mr Capell.

The author seems here to ridicule the blasphemous questions discussed by the schoolmen among the Papists in his
time, as, Whether the Pope be God or man, or a mean
betwixt both? &c.   See Archbishop Whitgift's "Sermon
before Queen Elizabeth." 1574.   Sig. B 2.—*Hawkins.* [In
Germany they have a similar saying at present, and it seems
to be used in this sense : God is a good person, he lets
things take their course.]

The greater the occasion is to all Christian men
To forsake their sinful livings, both wicked, vile
　　　and naught :
And to repent their former evils, which they have
　　　wrought,
Trusting by Christ's death to be redeemed :
And he that this doth shall never be deceived.

HYPOCRISY.

Well said, master doctor, well said !
By the mass, we must have you into the pulpit :
I pray you be remembered, and cover your head :
For indeed you have need to keep in your wit :
Ah, sirrah, who would have thought it,
That youth had been such a well-learned man !
Let me see your portous,[1] gentle Sir John !

JUVENTUS.

No, it is not a book for you [2] to look on,
You ought not to jest with God's Testament.

HYPOCRISY.

What, man ? I pray you be content :
For I do nothing else, but say my phantasy :
But yet, if you would do after my advisement,
In that matter you should not be so busy ;
Was not your father as well-learned as ye ?
And if he had said then as you have now done,
I-wis he had been like to make a burn.

---

[1] Portous, the ancient name for a Breviary. *Blount.*
Here it signifies the Bible.—*Hawkins.*
[2] *You* omitted, Copland's edition.

JUVENTUS.

It were much better for me than to return
From my faith in Christ and the profession of his
    word.

HYPOCRISY.

Whether is better a halter or a cord,
I cannot tell, I swear by God's mother:
But I think [1] you will have the one or the other:
Will you lose all your friends' good will,
To continue in that opinion still?
Was there not as well-learned men before as
    now?
Yea, and better too, I may say to you?
And they taught [2] the younger sort of people
By the elders to take an example:
And if I did not love you, as nature doth me
    bind,
You should not know so much of my mind.

JUVENTUS.

Whether were [3] I better to be ignorant and blind,
And to be damned in hell for infidelity;
Or to learn godly knowledge, wherein I shall find
The right path-way to eternal felicity?

HYPOCRISY.

Can you deny, but it is your duty
Unto your elders to be obedient?

---

[1] *Thynge*, Copland's edition.
[2] *Thought*, Copland's edition.
[3] *Where*, Vele's edition.

JUVENTUS.

I grant I am bound to obey my parents
In all things honest and lawful.

HYPOCRISY.

Lawful, quod-a? ah, fool, fool!
Wilt [1] thou set men to school,
When they be old?
I may say to you secretly,
The world was never merry,
Since children were so bold :
Now every boy will be a teacher,
The father a fool, and the child a preacher ;
This is pretty gear :
The foul presumption [2] of youth
Will turn shortly to great ruth,
I fear, I fear, I fear.

JUVENTUS.

The sermon will be done, ere I can come there :
I care not greatly whether I go or no ;
And yet for my promise, by God I swear,
There is no remedy but I must needs go :
Of my companions there will be mo,
And I promised them, by God's grace,
To meet them there as the sermon was.

HYPOCRISY.

For once breaking promise do not you pass ;
Make some excuse the matter to cease,

---

[1] *Wil*, Copland's edition.
[2] *The foole presumptious*, Copland's edition.

What have they to do ?
And you and I were, I wot[1] where,
We would be as merry as there,
Yea, and merrier too.

JUVENTUS.

I would gladly in your company go ;
But, if my companions should chance to see,
They would report full evil by me :
And peradventure, if I should[2] it use,
My company they would clean refuse.

HYPOCRISY.

What, are those fellows so curious,
That yourself you cannot excuse ?
I will teach you the matter to convey ;
Do what your own lust, and say as they say ;
And if you be reproved with your own affinity,
Bid them pluck the beam out of their own eye :
The old popish priests mock and despise,
And the ignorant people, that believe their lies,
Call them papists, hypocrites, and joining of the
    plough ;
Face[3] out the matter, and then good enough !
Let your book at your girdle be tied,
Or else in your bosom that he may be spied ;
And then it will be said both with youth and age,
Yonder fellow hath an excellent knowledge.
Tush, tush !
I could so beat[4] the bush,

---

[1] *I wote wote where,* Copland's edition.
[2] *Would,* Copland's edition.
[3] *Fare,* Copland's edition.
[4] *Beare,* Copland's edition.

That all should be flush,
That ever I did.

JUVENTUS.

Now, by my truth, you are merrily disposed ;
Let us go thither as you think best.

HYPOCRISY.

How say you ? shall we go to breakfast ?
Will you go to the pie-feast ?
Or, by the mass, if thou wilt be my guest,
It shall cost thee nothing ;
I have a furny card in a place,
That will bear a turn besides the ace,
She purveys now apace
For my coming :
And if thou wilt sibber [1] as well as I,
We shall have merry company :
And I warrant thee, if we have not a pie,
We shall have a pudding.

JUVENTUS.

By the mass, that meat I love above all thing ;
You may draw me about the town with a pudding. [2]

---

[1] *Jybben,* Vele's edition.

[2] This passage will receive illustration from the following
quotation out of Bishop Latimer's Sermon, preached before
King Edward the Sixth, about the year 1550 : "A good
fellow on a tyme bad another of hys frendes to a breakefast,
and sayed, Yf you wyl come, you shal be welcome ; but I
tell you afore hande, you shal haue but sclender fare, one
dysh and that is al. What is that, said he? A puddynge
and nothynge els. Mary, sayed he, you cannot please me
better; of all meates that is for myne owne toth : you may
draw me round about the town with a pudding." Sig. G vii.
—*Hawkins.*

HYPOCRISY.

Then you shall see my cunning :
A poor shift for a living
Amongest poor men used is ;
The kind heart of hers
Hath eased my purse,
Many a time ere this.   [*Here entereth* FELLOWSHIP.

FELLOWSHIP.

I marvel greatly where Friendship is ;
He promised to meet me here ere this time :
I beshrew his heart, that his [1] promise doth miss ;
And then be ye sure, it shall not be mine.

HYPOCRISY.

Yes, Fellowship, that it shall be thine,
For I have tarried here this hour or twain ;
And this honest gentleman in my company hath
    been,
To abide your coming, this thing is plain.

FELLOWSHIP.

By the mass, if you chide, I will [2] be gone again ;
For in faith, Friendship, I may say to thee,
I love not to be there, where chiders be.

HYPOCRISY.

No, God it knoweth, you are so full of honesty,
As a mary-bone is full of honey :

---

[1] *Thys*, Copland's edition.
[2] *Wylt*, Vele's edition.

But, sirrah, I pray you, bid this gentleman wel-
  come,
For he is desirous in your company to come :
I tell you he is a man of the right making ;
And one that hath excellent learning ;
At his girdle he hath such a book,
That the Popish priests dare not in him look :
This is a fellow for the nonce.

FELLOWSHIP.

I love him the better, by God's[1] precious bones :
You are heartily welcome, as I may say,
I shall desire you of better acquaintance ;[2]
That of your company be bold I may,
You may be sure, if in me it lie
To do you pleasure, you should it find :
For, by the mass, I love you both with heart and
  mind.

JUVENTUS.

To say the same to you your gentleness doth me
  bind ;
And I thank you heartily for your kindness.

HYPOCRISY.

Well[3] you see this gentleman fines[4]
Your gentleness and your kindness,
I thank him, and I thank you ;

---

[1] *Dogs*, Copland's edition.
[2] This mode of expression occurs in Shakespeare's "Midsummer Night's Dream," A. 3, S. 3, needlessly altered by
some to, I shall desire of you more acquaintance.—*Hawkins.*
[3] Original, *wyl.*　　　　　　　　　　[4] Query, *defines.*

And I think, if the truth were sought,[1]
The one bad and the other naught,
Never a good, I make God a vow!
But yet, Fellowship, tell me one thing,
Did you see little Bess this morning?
We should have our breakfast yesternight, she said,
But she hath forgotten it now, I am afraid.

FELLOWSHIP.

Her promise shall be performed and paid;
For I spake with her, since the time I rose,
And then she told me how the matter goeth:
We must be with her between eight and nine,
And then her master and mistress will be at the
    preaching.

JUVENTUS.

I purposed myself there to have been;
But this man provoked me to the contrary,
And told me that we should have merry company.

FELLOWSHIP.

Merry, quod-a? we cannot choose but be merry;
For there is such a girl where as we go,
Which will make us to[2] be merry, whether we
    will or no.

HYPOCRISY.

The ground is the better on the which she doth go;
For she will make better cheer with that[3] little,
    which she can get,

---

1 *Wer ysought*, Copland's edition.
2 *To* omitted, Copland's edition.
3 *A*, Copland's edition.

Than many a[1] one can with a great banket of
    meat.

JUVENTUS.

To be in her company my heart is set ;
Therefore, I pray you, let us be gone.

FELLOWSHIP.

She will come for us [2] herself anon ;
For I told her before, where we would stand,
And then, she said, she would beck us with her
    hand.

JUVENTUS.

Now, by the mass, I perceive that she is a gallant :
What, will she take pains to come for us hither ?

HYPOCRISY.

Yea, I warrant you ; therefore you must be familiar
    with her :
When she cometh in place,
You must her embrace
Somewhat handsomely ;
Lest she think it [3] danger,
Because you are a stranger,
To come in your company.

JUVENTUS.

Yea,[4] by God's foot, that I will be busy,

---

[1] *A* omitted, Copland's edition.
[2] *For us* omitted, Copland's edition.
[3] *She thinketh danger*, Copland's edition.
[4] These two lines I have given to Juventus against the
authority of the copies.—*Hawkins.*

And I may say to you, I can play the knave
    secretly. [*Here entereth* ABHOMINABLE LIVING.[1]

ABHOMINABLE LIVING.

Hem! come away quickly,
The back door is open;[2] I dare not tarry:
Come, Fellowship, come on away!

HYPOCRISY.

What, Unknown Honesty? a word!
                        [*Draws* A. L. *aside.*[3]
You shall not go yet, by God I swear;
Here is none but your friends, you need not to
        fray,
Although this strange young gentleman be here.

JUVENTUS.

I trust, in me she will think no danger;
For I love well the company of fair women.

ABHOMINABLE LIVING.

Who, you? nay, ye are such a holy man,
That to touch one ye dare not be bold;
I think,[4] you would not kiss a young woman,
If one would give you twenty pound in gold.

---

[1] The entrance of Abhominable Living is not marked in
the copies.—*Hawkins.*
[2] *Opned,* Copland's edition.
[3] [This is not marked in the copies.]
[4] *Thyng,* Copland's edition.

JUVENTUS.

Yes, by the mass, that I would ;
I could find in my heart to kiss you in your smock.

ABHOMINABLE. LIVING.

My back is broad enough to bear away that mock ;
For one hath told me many a time,
That you[1] have said you would use no such wanton's
  company as mine.

JUVENTUS.

By dog's[2] precious wounds, that was some whore-
  son[3] villain ;
I will never eat meat that shall do me good,
Till I have cut his flesh, by God's precious blood :
Tell me, I pray you, who it was,
And I will trim the knave, by the blessed mass.

ABHOMINABLE LIVING.

Tush ! as for that, do not you pass ;
That which I told you was but for love.

HYPOCRISY.

She did nothing else but prove,
Whether a little[4] thing would you move
To be angry and fret ;
What, and if one had said so ?

---

[1] *Iou*, Copland's edition.
[2] Both the copies concur in this reading.—*Hawkins.* [A
common corruption of the Divine name.]
[3] *Horson*, Copland's edition.
[4] *Lile*, Vele's edition.

Let such trifling matters go,
And be good to men's flesh for all that.

JUVENTUS [*He kisseth* ABHOMINABLE LIVING.]

To kiss her since she came, I had clean forgot :
You are welcome to my company.

ABHOMINABLE LIVING.

Sir, I thank you most heartily ;
By your kindness it doth appear.

HYPOCRISY.

What a hurly-burly is here !
Smick smack, and all this gear !
You will to tick-tack,[1] I fear,
If you[2] had time :
Well, wanton, well ;
I-wis, I can tell,
That such smock-smell
Will set your nose out of tune.

ABHOMINABLE LIVING.

What, man ? you need not to fume,
Seeing he is come into my company now ;
He is as well welcome as the best of you :
And if it lie in me to do him pleasure,
He shall have it, you may ye sure.

FELLOWSHIP.

Then old acquaintance is clean out of favour :

---

[1] *Take*, Copland's edition.
[2] *Thou*, Copland's edition.

Lo, Friendship, this gear goeth with a sleight ;[1]
He hath driven us twain out of conceit.

HYPOCRISY.

Out of conceit, quod-a? no, no ;
I dare well say, she thinketh not so :
How say you, Unknown Honesty?
Do not you love Fellowship and me?

ABHOMINABLE LIVING.

Yea, by the mass, I love you all three ;
But yet indeed, if I should say the truth,
Amongst all other, welcome Master Youth.

JUVENTUS.

Full greatly I do delight to kiss your pleasant
　　　mouth :　　[*He kisseth* ABHOMINABLE LIVING.
I am not able your kindness to recompence ;
I long to talk with you secretly, therefore let us
　　go hence.

ABHOMINABLE LIVING.

I agree to that ; for I would not for twenty pence,[2]
That it were known where I have been.

HYPOCRISY.

What, and it were known? it is no deadly[3] sin :
As for my part, I do not greatly care,
So that they find not your proper buttocks bare.

---

[1] *Afsleight*, Copland's edition.
[2] This and the following line is given to Juventus in
Copland's edition.—*Hawkins*.
[3] *It were no daly*, Copland's edition.

ABHOMINABLE LIVING.

Now much fie upon you! how bawdy[1] you are!
I-wis, Friendship, it mought[2] have been spoken at
    twice:
What think you, for your saying that the people
    will surmise?

JUVENTUS.

Who dare be so bold us to despise?
And if I may hear a knave speak one word,
I will run thorough his cheeks with my sword.

FELLOWSHIP.

This is an earnest fellow, of God's Word!
See, I pray you, how he is disposed to fight!

JUVENTUS.

Why should I not, and if my cause be right?
What, and if a knave do me beguile,
Shall I stand crouching like an owl?
No, no; then you might count me a very cow;
I know what belongeth to God's law as well as you.

ABHOMINABLE LIVING.

Your wit therein greatly I do allow;
For, and if I were a man, as you are,
I would not stick to give a blow,
To teach other knaves to beware,
I beshrew you twice, and if you do spare,
But lay load on the flesh, whatsoever befall,
You have strength enough to do it with all.

---

[1] *Badi*, Copland's edition.
[2] *Mouth*, Copland's edition.

FELLOWSHIP.

Let us depart, and if that we shall;
Come on, masters, we twain will go before.

JUVENTUS.

Nay, nay, my friend, stop there;
It is not you, that shall have her away,
She shall go with me, and if she go to-day—

HYPOCRISY.

She shall go with none of you, I dare well say :

ABHOMINABLE LIVING.

To forsake any of your company I would be very
      loth;
Therefore I will follow you all three.

HYPOCRISY.

Now I beshrew his heart, that to that will not
      agree ;
But yet because the time shall not seem very
      long,
Ere we depart, let us have a merry song.

They sing as followeth :

Why should not youth fulfil his own mind,
As the course of nature doth him bind?
Is not everything ordained to do his kind?
      Report me to you, report me to you.

Do not the flowers spring fresh and gay,
Pleasant and sweet in the month of[1] May?
And when their time cometh, they fade away.
  Report me to you, report me to you.

Be not the trees in winter bare?
Like unto their kind, such they are;
And when they spring, their fruits declare.
  Report me to you, report me to you.

What should youth do with the fruits of age,
But live in pleasure in his[2] passage?
For when age cometh, his lusts will suage.
  Report me to you, report me to you.

Why should not youth fulfil his own mind,
As the course of nature doth him bind? &c.
     [They go forth.

  Here entereth GOOD COUNSEL.

O merciful Lord, who can cease to lament,
Or keep his heart from continual mourning,
To see how Youth is fallen from thy word and
  testament,[3]
And wholly inclined to Abhominable Living?
He liveth nothing according to his professing;[4]
But, alas! his life is to thy word['s] abusion,
Except thy great mercy, to his utter confusion.
O, where is now[5] the godly conversation,

---

 [1] *Of* omitted, Copland's edition.
 [2] *Thys,* Copland's edition.
 [3] *And testament* omitted, Copland's edition.
 [4] *Profession,* Copland's edition.
 [5] *Now* omitted, Copland's edition.

Which should be among the professors[1] of thy
    word !
O, where may a man find now one faithful con-
    gregation,[2]
That is not infected with dissension or discord ?
Or amongst whom are all vices utterly abhorred ![3]
O, where is the brotherly love between man and
    man !
We may lament the time our vice began.
O, where is the peace and meekness, long suffering
    and temperance,
Which are the fruits of God's holy spirit ?
With whom is the flesh brought under obedience,
Or who readeth the scripture with intent to follow
    it ?
Who useth not now covetousness and deceit ?
Who giveth unto the poor that which is due ?
I think, in this world few that live now.
O, where is the godly example, that parents should
    give
Unto their young family by godly and virtuous
    living ?
Alas ! how wickedly[4] do they themselves live,
Without any fear of God or his righteous threaten-
    ing !
They have no respect unto the dreadful reckoning,
Which shall be required of us, when the Lord shall
    come,
As a rightful judge at the day of doom.
O, what a joyful sight was it for to see,
When Youth began God's word to embrace ?
Then he promised Godly Knowledge and me,

---

[1] Both the copies read *professour.—Hawkins.*
[2] *Congregation* omitted, Copland's edition.
[3] *Abhord utterly,* Copland's edition.
[4] *Wicked,* Copland's edition.

That from our instruction he would never turn his
    face;
But now he walketh, alas! in the ungodly's chase!
Heaping sin upon sin, vice upon vice:
                [*Here entereth* JUVENTUS.
He that liveth most ungodly is counted most wise—

JUVENTUS.

Who is here playing at the dice?
I heard one speak of cinque [1] and sice; [2]
His words did me entice
Hither to come.

GOOD COUNSEL.

Ah, Youth, Youth, whither dost thou run?
Greatly I do bewail thy miserable estate;
The terrible plagues, which in God's law are written,
Hang over thy head both early and late:
O fleshly Capernite, stubborn and obstinate,
Thou hadst liever forsake Christ, thy Saviour and
    King,
Than thy fleshly swinish lusts and abhominable
    living.

JUVENTUS.

What, old whoreson, art thou a-chiding?
I will play a spurt, why should I not?
I set not [3] a mite by thy checking:

---

[1] Juventus, coming in and hearing imperfectly the words
sin and *vice*, very naturally mistakes them for terms used
at dice: we may presume, therefore, that the genuine
reading should be *cinque and sice.—Hawkins.*

[2] *Cyce,* Copland's edition.

[3] *Not* omitted, Copland's edition.

What hast thou to do, and if I lose my coat ?
I will trill the bones, while I have one groat ;
And, when there is no more ink in the pen,[1]
I will make a shift,[2] as well as other men.

GOOD COUNSEL.

Then I perceive you have forgotten clean
The promise, that you made unto Knowledge and
    me :
You said such fleshly fruits should not be seen :
But to God's word your life should agree.
Full true be the words of the prophet Hosè,
No verity nor knowledge of God is now in the
    land,
But abhominable vices hath gotten the upper
    hand.

JUVENTUS.

Your mind therein I do well understand :
You go about my living to despise,
But you will not see the beams in your own eyes.

GOOD COUNSEL.

The devil hath you deceived, which is the author
    of lies,
And trapped[3] you in his snare of wicked Hypo-
    crisy ;
Therefore all that ever you do devise,
Is to maintain your fleshly liberty.

---

[1] [An indelicate figure, which occurs in jest-books and
other early literature.]
[2] *Shyfe*, Copland's edition.
[3] *Trape*, Copland's edition.

JUVENTUS.

I marvel, why you do this[1] reprove me;
Wherein do I my life abuse?

GOOD COUNSEL.

Your whole conversation I may well accuse,
As in my conscience just occasion I find;
Therefore be not offended, although I express my
    mind.

JUVENTUS.

By the mass, if thou tell not truth, I will not be
    behind
To touch you as well again.

GOOD COUNSEL.

For this thing most chiefly I do complain:[2]
Have you not professed the knowledge of Christ's
    gospel?
And yet, I think, no more ungodliness doth reign
In any wicked heathen, Turk, or infidel;
Who can devise that sin or evil,
That you practise not from day to day?
Yea, and count it nothing but a jest or a play.
Alas! what wantonness remaineth in your flesh!
How desirous are you to accomplish your own will!
What pleasure and delight have you in wickedness!
How diligent are you your lusts to fulfil!
St Paul saith, that you ought your fleshly lusts to
    kill:
But unto his teaching your life ye will not frame;
Therefore in vain you bear a Christian name.

---

[1] Thus.   [2] *Complaye*, Copland's edition.

Read the Five to the Galatians, and there you
    shall see,
That the flesh rebelleth against the spirit,
And that your own flesh is your[1] most utter[2]
    enemy,
If in your soul's health you do delight :
The time were too long now to recite,
What whoredom, uncleanness, and filthy com-
    munication
Is dispersed with youth in every congregation.
To speak of pride, envy, and abhominable oaths,
They are the common practices of youth,
To avance your flesh, you cut and jag your clothes,
And yet ye are a great gospeller in the mouth :
What shall I say for this blaspheming[3] the truth ?
I will show you what St Paul doth declare
In his Epistle to the Hebrews and the tenth
    chapter.
For him, saith he, which doth willingly sin or
    consent,
After he hath received the knowledge of the
    verity,
Remaineth no more sacrifice, but a fearful looking
    for judgment,
And a terrible[4] fire, which shall consume the adver-
    sary ;
And Christ saith that this blasphemy
Shall never be pardoned nor forgiven
In this world, nor in the world to come.

JUVENTUS [He lieth down].

Alas, alas ! what have I wrought and done !

---

[1] *Our*, Copland's edition.
[2] *Veter*, Copland's edition.
[3] *Blasphemyng*, Copland's edition.
[4] *Terible*, Copland's edition.

Here in this place I will fall down desperate ;
To ask for mercy now, I know, it is too late.
Alas, alas ! that ever I was begat !
I would to God I had never been born !
All faithful men, that behold this [1] wretched state,
May very justly laugh me to scorn ;
They may say, my time I have evil-spent and
    worn,
Thus in my first age to work my own destruction :
In the eternal pains is my part and portion.

GOOD COUNSEL.

Why, Youth, art thou fallen into desperation ?
What, man, pluck up thine heart, and rise,
Although thou see nothing now but thy condemna-
    tion,
Yet it may please God again to open thy eyes :
Ah, wretched creature, what doest thou surmise ?
Thinkest not that God's mercy doth exceed thy sin ?
Remember his Merciful Promises, and comfort thy-
    self in him.

JUVENTUS.

O sir, this state is so miserable, the which I lie in,
That my comfort and hope from me is separated :
I would to God I had never been !
Woe worth the time, that ever I was created !

GOOD COUNSEL.

Ah, frail [2] vessel, unfaithful and faint-hearted,
Doest thou think that God is so merciless,
That when the sinner doth repent, and is converted,
That he will not fulfil his merciful promises ?

---

[1] *His*, Vele's edition.
[2] *Fair*, Copland's ed.

JUVENTUS.

Alas, sir ! I am in such heaviness,
That his promises I cannot remember.

GOOD COUNSEL.

In thy wickedness continue no lenger ;
But trust in the Lord without any fear,
And his Merciful Promises shall shortly appear.

JUVENTUS.

I would believe, if I might them hear,
With all my heart, power and mind.

GOOD COUNSEL.

The living God hath him hither assigned :
Lo, where he cometh even here by,
Therefore mark his sayings diligently.
        [*Here entereth* GOD'S MERCIFUL PROMISES.
The Lord, by his prophet Ezekiel, saith in this
    wise plainly,
As in the thirty-third chapter it doth appear :
Be converted, O ye children, and turn unto me,
And I shall remedy the cause of your departure ;
And also he saith in the eighteenth chapter,
I do not delight in a sinner's death,
But that he should convert and live : thus the Lord
    saith.

JUVENTUS.

Then must I give neither credit nor faith
Unto St Paul's saying, which this man did allege.

GOD'S MERCIFUL PROMISES.

Yes, you must credit them, according unto know-
    ledge;
For St Paul speaketh of those which resist the
    truth by violence,
And so end their lives without repentance.
Thus [1] Saint Augustine [2] doth them define,
If unto the Lord's word you do your ears incline,
And observe these things which he hath com-
    manded,
This sinful state, in the which you have lain,
Shall be forgotten and never more remembered:
And Christ himself in the gospel hath promised,
That he, which in him unfeignedly doth believe,
Although he were dead, yet shall he live.

JUVENTUS [*He riseth*].

These comfortable sayings doth me greatly move
To arise from this wretched place.

GOD'S MERCIFUL PROMISES.

For me his mercy sake thou shalt obtain his grace,
And not for thine own desertes, this must thou know;
For my sake alone, ye shall receive solace;
For my sake alone, he will thee mercy show:
Therefore to him, as it is most due,
Give most hearty thanks with heart unfeigned,
Whose name for evermore be praised.

GOOD COUNSEL.

The prodigal son, as in Luke we read,
Which in vicious living his good doth waste,

---

[1] *This*, Vele's edition.   [2] *Austine*, Copland's edition.

As soon as his living he had remembered,
To confess his wretchedness he was not aghast;
Wherefore his father lovingly him embrac'd,
And was [1] right joyful, the text saith plain,
Because his son was returnen [2] again.

JUVENTUS.

O sinful flesh, thy pleasures are but vain:
Now I find it true, as the scripture doth say,
Broad [3] and pleasant is the path which leadeth
    unto pain,
But unto eternal life full narrow is the way. [4]
He that is not led by God's spirit surely goeth
    astray;
And all that ever he doth shall be clean abhorred;
Although he brag and boast never so much of
    God's word.
O subtle Satan, full deceitful is thy snare;
Who is able thy falsehood to disclose?
What is the man, that thou doest favour or spare,
And doest not [5] tempt him eternal joys to lose?
Not one in the world, surely I suppose.
Therefore happy is the man, which doth truly
    wait,
Always to refuse thy deceitful and crafty bait.
When I had thought to live most christianly,
And followed the steps of Knowledge and Good
    Counsel,
Ere I was aware, thou haddest deceived me,

---

[1] *Is*, Copland's edition.
[2] *Returned*, Vele's edition.
[3] *Borde*, Vele's edition.
[4] Mr Garrick's copy is imperfect, and ends at this mark.
—*Hawkins.*
[5] *Not*, Vele's edition.

And brought me into the path, which leadeth unto
    hell :
And of an earnest professor of Christ's gospel
Thou madest me an hypocrite, blind and pervert,
And from virtue unto vice thou hadst clean turned
    my heart.
First, by hypocrisy thou didest me move,
The mortification of the flesh clean to forsake,
And wanton desires to embrace and love ;
Alas ! to think on it my heart doth yet quake :
Under the title of Friendship to me ye spake,
And so to wicked Fellowship did me bring,
Which brought me clean to Abhominable Living.
Thus, I say, Satan did me deceive,
And wrapped me in sin many a fold ;
The steps of Good Counsel I did forsake and
    leave,
And forgot the words which before to me he
    told :
The fruits of a true christian in me waxed cold ;
I followed mine own lusts, the flesh I did not
    tame,
And had them in derision which would not do the
    same.
Yet it hath pleased God of his endless mercy
To give me respite my life to amend ;
From the bottom of my heart I repent my ini-
    quity,
I will walk in his laws unto my life's end :
From his holy ordinance I will never descend,
But my whole delight shall be to live therein,
Utterly abhorring all filthiness and sin.
[1] *All Christian* people which be here present,
May learn by me hypocrisy to know,

---

[1] The following lines being torn are filled up by con-
jecture with the words printed in *italics.—Hawkins.*

With which the devil, as with a poison most
    pestilent,
Daily seeketh all men to overthrow :
Credit not all things unto the outward show,
But try them with God's word, that squire [1] and
    rule most just,
Which never deceiveth them, that in him put
    their trust.
Let no flattering friendship, nor yet wicked com-
    pany,
Persuade you in no wise God's word to abuse ;
But see that you stand steadfastly unto the verity,
And according to the rule thereof your doings
    frame and use,
Neither kindred nor fellowship shall you excuse,
When you shall appear before the judgment seat,
But your own secret conscience shall then give an
    audit.
All you that be young, whom I do now represent,
Set your delight both day and night on Christ's
    Testament :
If pleasure you tickle, be not fickle, and suddenly
    slide,
But in God's fear everywhere see that you abide :
In your tender age seek for knowledge, and after
    wisdom run,
And in your old age teach your family to do as
    you have done :
Your bodies subdue unto virtue, delight not in
    vanity ;
Say not, I am young, I shall live long, lest your
    days shortened be :
Do not incline to spend your time in wanton toys
    and nice,

---

[1] Square.

For idleness doth increase much wickedness and
    vice :
Do not delay the time, and say, my end is not
    near ;
For with short warning the Lord coming shall
    suddenly appear.
God give us grace, his word to embrace, and to
    live thereafter,
That by the same his holy name may be praised
    ever.

GOOD COUNSEL.

Now let us make our supplications together
For the prosperous estate of our noble and virtuous
    king,[1]
That in his godly proceedings he may still persevere,
Which seeketh the glory of God above all other
    thing :
O Lord, endue his heart with true understanding,
And give him a prosperous life long over us to
    reign,
To govern and rule his people as a worthy captain.

JUVENTUS.

Also let us pray for all the nobility of this realm ;
And, namely, for those whom his[2] grace hath
    authorised
To maintain the public wealth over us and them,
That they may see his gracious acts published ;
And that they, being truly admonished
By the complaint of them which are wrongfully
    oppressed,
May seek reformation, and see it redressed.

---

[1] Edward VI.   [2] *Is*, Vele's edition.

GOOD COUNSEL.

Then shall this land enjoy great quietness and rest :
And give unto God most hearty thanks therefore,
To whom be honour, praise, and glory for ever-
      more.[1]

---

[1] [The colophon of Vele's edition is : "Finis. quod R.
Wever. Imprinted at London in Paules churche yeard, by
Abraham Vele, at the sygne of the Lambe." Of Copland's
edition, besides the Garrick copy, there is a second, formerly
Heber's, in the Devonshire collection.]

JACK JUGGLER.

*A new Enterlued for Chyldren to playe named Iacke
Iuggler both wytte and very playsent. Newly Imprented.*

The Players' Names.

Mayster Boungrace,	*A Galant.*
Dame Coye, .	*A Gentlewoman.*
Iacke Iugeler,	*The vyce.*
Ienkin Careway,	*A Lackey.*
Ales trype and go, .	*A Mayd.*

*[Colophon.] Imprinted at London in Lothbury by
me Wyllyam Copland. 4to, black letter.*

Beneath the players' names occurs a woodcut, of
which we annex a facsimile.

INTRODUCTION.

[Some account of this piece may be found in Haslewood's Preface, which precedes our text of " Thersites."
It may be added, that whatever shortcomings may be apparent in these productions from a literary and dramatic point of view, they are by no means devoid of a fair share of shrewd humour and pointed vivacity, and are, moreover, not unimportant contributions, especially when their early date is considered, to the illustration of manners. The low-comic view predominates in most of them, and we meet with occasional grossnesses which, so far as " Jack Juggler " itself is concerned, are the more remarkable when it is recollected that the performance was presented by youths. In none of these ruder specimens of the drama is any distribution to be found into acts and scenes; nor is it invariably clear how the entrances and exits were introduced.

As to the groundwork of this interlude, Mr Child observes :—[1]]

---

[1] [" Four Old Plays," 1848, 9–12.]

"Plautus's tragi-comedy of 'Amphitryon' has been perhaps more popular on the modern stage than any other ancient play. It is the groundwork of one of the best comedies of the great Molière, and of a once favourite English drama, which Sir Walter Scott, in an introduction not everywhere distinguished by his usual judgment, styles 'one of the happiest effusions of Dryden's comic muse.' It has been several times translated into our tongue, and by Bonnell Thornton, with an elegance, spirit, and correctness that leave nothing to be desired.

"This is not the place to expatiate on the merits of the Latin play; but the assertion may be hazarded without much risk, that both the original and Thornton's version are, taken as wholes, considerably superior to any of the imitations. Indeed, the character of Alcmena, as drawn by Plautus, so truly innocent, simple, and loving, her distress on being suspected by her husband, and his agony at finding her, as he believes, dishonest, immediately suggest, as the accomplished translator has observed, a not discreditable comparison with our 'Othello.' We may add, too, that the conclusion of the fourth act, where Amphitryon, 'perplexed in the extreme,' and defying the gods in the intensity of his despair, rushes to the house to wreak his vengeance on his family, and is struck down by lightning, rises to grandeur, almost to sublimity, and must produce immense dramatic effect in the representation. Very little of this sort of thing appears in the modern play. What Dryden has made of Alcmena will be understood, when we observe that he adapted her to the standard of contemporary taste. Yet Scott has strangely said, that, 'in the scenes of a higher cast, Dryden far outstrips both the French and Roman poet!'

"The reader will not find any such important characters as gods and generals in the drama before him. 'Jack Juggler' can hardly be called an imitation of the comedy of Plautus. It is the play of 'Amphitryon' without the part of Amphitryon, and resembles more than anything else one of those pieces made up of the comic portions of plays, which used to be called 'drolls.' In fact, 'Jack Juggler' is a caricature even of the comic parts. All dignity is stripped from the characters, every ridiculous feature is much exaggerated, and the language and incidents are ingeniously vulgarized to reduce everything to the grotesque, the quaintness of the expressions greatly heightening the effect to a modern reader. The amiable Alcmena becomes a 'verie cursed shrew.' General Amphitryon sinks into Master Boungrace, a commonplace 'gentilman,' somewhat subject, we suspect, to being imposed upon by his wife and servants. Bromia, the insignificant and well-conducted attendant, is changed into the smart and malicious Aulsoon tripe and goo.

"There is no proper plot to the piece, the whole action consisting in getting Jenkin Careawaie into as much trouble as possible, when he is left to go to bed with aching bones, and wishing bad luck to his second self. He does not get off with a beating from Jack and his master. The servant-maid lends her tongue, and her mistress both tongue and hand, for the amusement

of the spectators and the revenge of Jack Juggler.
Those who are acquainted with the tedious perform-
ances of those times will recognise with pleasure an
uncommon raciness and spirit in this little interlude.
The lines are rude, but sharp and bold, and Dame Coye
may even be called a well-drawn and original character.

"In Mr Wright's 'Early Mysteries, and other Latin
Poems of the Twelfth and Thirteenth Centuries,' will
be found a rather clever and once very popular poem,
founded on 'Amphitryon,' the 'Geta' of Vital of Blois.
Amphitryon in this is a student of Greek learning, and
the awkwardness of Alcmena's situation, after Jupiter's
visit is got over, by her assuring her confiding husband
that she thinks the whole affair must have been a
dream."

JACK JUGGLER.

THE PROLOGUE.

Interpone tuis interdum gaudia curis,
Vt possis animo quemvis sufferre laborem.
Do any of you know what Latin is this?
Or else would you have an Expositorem
To declare it in English *per sensum planiorem?*
It is best I speak English, or else within a while
I may percase mine own self with my Latin be-
    guile.

The two verses, which I rehearsed before,
I find written in the Book of Cato the wise
Among good precepts of living a thousand more,
Which to follow there he doth all men avise
And they may be Englished briefly in this wise :
Among thy careful business use sometime mirth
    and joy,
That no bodily work thy wits break or 'noy.

For the mind (saith he), in serious matters occupied,
If it have not some quiet mirth and recreation
Interchangeable admixed, must needs be soon
    wearied,

And (as who should say) tried through continual
    operation
Of labour and business without relaxation.
Therefore intermix honest mirth in such wise
That your strength may be refreshed, and to
    labours suffice.

For as meat and drink, natural rest and sleep,
For the conservation and health of the body,
Must needs be had, so the mind and wits to keep
Pregnant, fresh, industrious, quick and lusty,
Honest mirth and pastime is requisite and necessary:
For, *Quod caret alterna requie durabile non est:*
Nothing may endure (saith Ouid) without some
    rest.

Example proof hereof in earth is well found,
Manifest, open, and very evident;
For except the husbandman suffer his ground
Sometimes to rest, it woll bear no fruit vera-
    ment;
Therefore they let the field lie every second year
To the end that, after rest, it may the better corn
    bear.

Thus then (as I have said) it is a thing natural,
And naturally belonging to all living creatures,
And unto man especially above others all,
To have at times convenient pastance, mirth and
    pleasures,
So they be joined with honesty, and kept within
    due measures;
And the same well allowed not only the said Cato,
But also the Philosophers, Plutarch, Socrates, and
    Plato.

And Cicero Tullius, a man sapient and wise,
Willeth the same, in that his first book,
Which he wrote and entituled of an honest man's
    office :
Who so is disposed thereupon to look,
Where to define and affirm he boldly on him
    took,
That to hear interludes is pastime convenient
For all manner men, and a thing congruent.

He reckoneth that namely as a very honest dis-
    port,
And above all other things commendeth the old
    comedy,
The hearing of which may do the mind comfort;
For they be replenished with precepts of philo-
    sophy :
They contain much wisdom, and teach prudent
    policy ;
And though they be all writers of matters of none
    importance,
Yet they show great wit, and much pretty con-
    veyance.

And in this manner of making Plautus did excel,
As recordeth the same Tullius, commending him
    by name :
Wherefore this maker delighteth passingly well
To follow his arguments, and draw out the same,
For to make at seasons convenient pastimes, mirth
    and game :
As now he hath done this matter, not worth an
    oyster shell,
Except percase it shall fortune to make you laugh
    well.

And for that purpose only this maker did it write,
Taking the ground thereof out of Plautus first
    comedy
And the first sentence of the same; for higher
    things indite
In no wise he would, for yet the time is so queasy,
That he that speaketh best, is least thank-worthy.
Therefore, sith nothing but trifles may be had,
You shall hear a thing that only shall make you
    merry and glad.

And such a trifling matter, as when it shall be done,
Ye may report and say ye have heard nothing
    at all.
Therefore I tell you all, before it be begun,
That no man look to hear of matters substantial,
Nor matters of any gravity either great or small
For this maker showed us that such manner things
Do never well beseem little boys' handlings.

Wherefore, if ye will not sourly your brows bend
At such a fantastical conceit as this,
But can be content to hear and see the end,
I woll go show the Players what your pleasure is ;
Which to wait upon you I know be ready ere this.
I woll go send them hither into your presence,
Desiring that they may have quiet audience.

JACK JUGGLER.

Our Lord of heaven and sweet Saint John
Rest you merry, my masters everychone ;
And I pray to Christ and sweet Saint Stephen
Send you all many a good even !

And you too, sir, and you, and you also,
Good even to you an hundred times and a thousand
    mo.
Now by all these crosses of flesh, bone, and blood,
I reckon my chance right marvellous good,
Here now to find all this company,
Which in my mind I wished for heartily ;
For I have laboured all day, till I am weary,
And now am disposed to pass the time, and be
    merry.
And I think none of you, but he would do the
    same,
For who woll be sad, and needeth not, is foul to
    blame ;
And as for me, of my mother I have been taught
To be merry when I may, and take no thought.
Which lesson I bare so well away,
That I use to make merry once a day.
And now, if all things happen right,
You shall see as mad a pastime this night,
As you saw this seven years, and as proper a toy
As ever you saw played of a boy.
I am called Jack Juggler of many an one,
And in faith I woll play a juggling cast anon.
I woll conjure the nowl,[1] and God before !
Or else let me lese my name for evermore.
I have it devised, and compassed how,
And what ways I woll tell and show to you.
You all know well Master Bongrace,[2]
The gentleman that dwelleth here in this place?
And Jenkin Careaway his page, as cursed a lad,
And as ungracious as ever man had,
An unhappy wage, and as foolish a knave withal,
As any is now within London wall.

---

[1] [Mr Child printed *moull.*]
[2] A fanciful name. See Halliwell's *Dict., v. Bonegrace.*

This Jenkin and I been fallen at great debate
For a matter, that fell between us a-late ;
And hitherto of him I could never revenged be,
For his master maintaineth him, and loveth not
  me ;
Albeit, the very truth to tell,
Nother of them both knoweth me not very well.
But against all other boys the said gentleman
Maintaineth him all that he can.
But I shall set little by my wit,
If I do not Jenkin this night requite.
Ere I sleep, Jenkin shall be met,
And I trust to come partly out of his debt ;
And when we meet again, if this do not suffice,
I shall pay Jenkin the residue in my best wise.
It chanced me right now in the other end of the
  next street
With Jenkin and his master in the face to meet.
I abode there a while, playing for to see
At the bucklers, as well became me.
It was not long time ; but at the last
Back cometh my cousin Careaway homeward full
  fast :
Pricking, prancing, and springing in his short coat,
And pleasantly singing with a merry note.
Whither away so fast ? tarry a while, said one.
I cannot now, said Jenkin, I must needs be gone.
My master suppeth hereby at a gentleman's place,
And I must thither fetch my dame, Mistress Bon-
  grace.
But yet, ere I go, I care not much
At the bucklers to play with thee one fair touch.
To it they went, and played so long,
Till Jenkin thought he had wrong.
By Cock's precious podstick, I will not home this
  night,
Quod he, but as good a stripe on thy head light !

Within half an hour, or somewhat less,
Jenkin left playing, and went to fetch his mistress ;
But by the way he met with a fruiterer's wife :
There Jenkin and she fell at such strife
For snatching of an apple, that down he cast
Her basket, and gathered up the apples fast,
And put them in his sleeve, then came he his way
By another lane, as fast as he may ;
Till he came at a corner by a shop's stall,
Where boys were at dice, faring at all ;
When Careaway with that good company met,
He fell to faring withouten let,
Forgetting his message, and so did he fare,
That when I came by, he gan swear and stare,
And full bitterly began to curse,
As one that had lost almost all in his purse.
For I know his old guise and condition,
Never to leave, till all his money be gone.
For he hath no money but what he doth steal,
And that woll he play away every deal.
I passed by, and then called unto my mind
Certain old reckonings, that were behind
Between Jenkin and me, whom partly to recom-
    pense
I trust by God's grace, ere I go hence.
This garments, cape, and all other gear,
That now you see upon me here,
I have done on all like unto his
For the nonce ; and my purpose is
To make Jenkin believe, if I can,
That he is not himself, but another man.
For except he hath better luck than he had,
He woll come hither stark staring mad.
When he shall come, I woll handle my captive so,
That he shall not well wot whither to go.
His mistress, I know, she woll him blame,
And his master also will do the same ;

Because that she of her supper deceived is,
For I am sure they have all supped by this.
But, and if Jenkin would hither resort,
I trust he and I should make some sport,
If I had sooner spoken, he would have sooner been
  here,
For me seemeth I do his voice hear.

CAREAWAY.

Ah, sir, I may say I have been at a feast :
I have lost two shillings and sixpence at the least.
Marry, sir, of this gains I need make no boast ;
But, the devil go with all, more have I lost !
My name is Careaway, let all sorrow pass !
I woll ere to-morrow night be as rich as ever I was ;
Or at the furthest within a day or twain :
My master's purse shall pay me again.
Therefore ho ! Careaway, now woll I sing *hei, hei!*
But, by the Lord, now I remember another thing :
By my faith, Jenkin, my mistress and thou
Are like to agree—God knoweth how—
That thou comest not for her incontinent,
To bring her to supper, when thou were sent ?
And now they have all supped, thou wolt surely
  abi',
Except thou imagine some pretty and crafty lie.
For she is, as all other women be,
A very cursed shrew, by the blessed Trinity,
And a very devil, for if she once begin
To fight or chide, in a week she woll not lin ;
And a great pleasure she hath specially now of
  late
To get poor me now and then by the pate ;
For she is an angry piece of flesh, and soon dis-
  pleased,
Quickly moved, but not lightly appeased.

We use to call her at home Dame Coy,
A pretty gingerly piece, God save her and St Loy !
As dainty and nice as an halfpenny-worth of silver
    spoons,
But vengeable melancholy in the afternoons.
She useth for her bodily health and safeguard
To chide daily one fit to supperward ;
And my master himself is worse than she,
If he once thoroughly angered be.
And a maid we have at home, Alison Trip-and-go :
Not all London can show such other two :
She simpereth, she pranketh, and jetteth without fail,
As a peacock that hath spread and showeth her
    gay tail :
She minceth, she bridleth, she swimmeth to and fro :
She treadeth not one hair awry, she trippeth like
    a doe
Abroad in the street, going or coming homeward :
She quavereth and warbleth, like one in a galliard,
Every joint in her body and every part :
O, it is a jolly wench to mince and divide a fart.
She talketh, she chatteth like a pie all day,
And speaketh like a parrot popinjay,
And that as fine as a small silken thread,
Yea, and as high as an eagle can fly for a need.
But it is a spiteful lying girl, and never well,
But when she may some ill tale by me tell ;
She woll, I warrant you, anon at the first
Of me imagine and say the worst,
And whatsoever she to my mistress doth say,
It is written in the gospel of the same day.
Therefore I woll here with myself devise
What I may best say, and in what wise
I may excuse this my long tarrying,
That she of my negligence may suspect nothing.
For if the fault of this be found in me,
I may give my life for halfpennies three.

[*Hic cogitabundo similis sedeat.*]

Let me study this month, and I shall not find
A better device than now is come to my mind.
Mistress, woll I say, I am bound by my duty
To see that your womanhood have no injury;
For I hear and see more than you now and then,
And yourself partly know the wanton wiles of
　　men.
When we came yonder, there did I see
My master kiss gentlewomen two or three,
And to come among others me-thought I see,[1]
He had a marvellous great phantasy:
Anon he commanded me to run thence for you,
To come sup there, if you would; but (I wot not
　　how)
My heart grudged, mistrusting lest that I, being
　　away,
My master would some light cast play;
Whereupon, mistress, to see the end,
I tarried half supper-time, so God me mend!
And, besides that there was such other company
As I know your mistress-ship setteth nothing by;
Gorgeous dames of the court and gallants also,
With doctors and other rufflers mo:
At last when I thought it time and season,
I came to certify you, as it was reason;
And by the way whom should I meet
But that most honest gentleman in the street,
Which the last week was with you here,
And made you a banket and bouncing cheer?
Ah, Jenkin, quod he, good speed! how farest thou?
Marry, well, God yield it you, master, quod I:
　　how do you?
How doth thy mistress? is she at home?
Yea, sir, quod I, and suppeth all alone;

---

1 Old copy, *byrye.*

And but she hath no manner good cheer,
I am sure she would gladly have you there.
I cannot come now, said he, I have business ;
But thou shalt carry a token from me to thy
    mistress.
Go with me to my chamber at yon lane-end,
And I woll a dish of costards unto her send.
I followed him, and was bold, by your leave,
To receive and bring them here in my sleeve.
But I would not for all England, by Jesus Christ,
That my master Bongrace hereof wist,
Or knew that I should any such gear to you bring,
Lest he misdeem us both in some worse thing ;
Nor show him nothing of that I before said,
For then indeed, sir, I am arrayed : [1]
If you do, I may nothing hereafter unto you tell,
Whether I see my master do ill or well.
But [2] if you now this counsel keep,
I woll ease you perchance twice in a week ;
You may say you were sick, and your head did ache :
That you lusted not this night any supper make,
Specially without the doors ; but thought it best
To abide at home and take your rest ;
And I will to my master to bring him home,
For you know he woll be angry, if he come alone.
This woll I say and face it so well,
That she shall believe it every deal.
How say you, friends, by the arms of Robin Hood,
Woll not this excuse be reasonable good ?
To muse for any better great folly it is ;
For I may make sure reckoning of this
That, and if I would sit stewing this seven year,
I shall not else find how to save me all clear.

---

[1] Disconcerted, put out in my plans. See Halliwell, *v.*
aray.
  [2] Original reads *that.*

And I durst jeopard an hundred pound,
That some bawdry might now within be found;
But except some of them come the sooner,
I shall knock such a peal, that all England shall
     wonder.

JACK JUGGLER.

Knock at the gate hardily again, if thou dare :
And seeing thou wolt not by fair words beware,
Now, fists, me-thinketh, yesterday seven past,
That four men asleep at my feet you cast,
And this same day you did no manner good,
Nor were not washen in warm blood.

JENKIN CAREAWAY.

What whoreson is this that washeth in warm blood !
Some devil broken loose out of hell for wood !
Four hath he slain, and now well I see,
That it must be my chance the fifth to be !
But rather than thus shamefully to be slain,
Would Christ my friends had hanged me, being
     but years twain !
And yet, if I take good heart and be bold,
Percase he woll be more sober and cold.

JACK JUGGLER.

Now, hands, bestir you about his lips and face,
And strike out all his teeth without any grace !
Gentleman, are you disposed to eat any fist-meat !—

JENKIN CAREAWAY.

I have supped, I thank you, sir, and list not to
     eat :
Give it to them that are hungry, if you be wise.

JACK JUGGLER.

It [1] shall do a man of your diet no harm to sup
    twice :
This shall be your cheese to make your meat
    digest,
For I tell you these hands weigheth of the best.

JENKIN CAREAWAY.

I shall never escape : see, how he waggeth his hands !

JACK JUGGLER.

With a stroke they will lay a knave in our Lady-
    bonds, [2]
And this day yet they have done no good at all.

JENKIN CAREAWAY.

Ere thou essay them on me, I pray thee lame them
    on the wall—
But speak you all this in earnest or in game ?—
If you be angry with me, truly you are to blame ;
For have you any just quarrel to me ?

JACK JUGGLER.

Ere thou and I part, that woll I show thee—

JENKIN CAREAWAY.

Or have I done you any manner displeasure ?—

---

[1] Original reads *yet*.

[2] Original has *boons*. The sense appears to be that " Jack
Juggler" will, by killing Careaway, leave him to the mercy
of the Virgin.

JACK JUGGLER.

Ere thou and I part, thou shalt know, thou mayest
    be sure—

JENKIN CAREAWAY.

By my faith, if you be angry without a cause,
You shall have amends made with a couple of
    straws ;
By thee I set whatsoever thou art ;
But for thy displeasure I care not a fart.
May a man demand whose servant you be ?

JACK JUGGLER.

My master's servant I am, for verity !

JENKIN CAREAWAY.

What business have you at this place now !

JACK JUGGLER.

Nay, marry, tell me what business hast thou ?.
For I am commanded for to watch and give
    diligence
That, in my good Master Bongrace's absence,
No misfortune may happen to his house, certain.

JENKIN CAREAWAY.

Well now I am come, you may go hence again,
And thank them that so much for my master hath
    done :
Showing them that the servants of the house be
    come home,
For I am of the house, and now in woll I go.

JACK JUGGLER.

I cannot tell whether thou be of the house or no ;
But go no near,[1] lest I handle thee like a stranger ;
Thank no man but thyself, if thou be in any danger.

JENKIN CAREAWAY.

Marry, I defy thee, and plainly unto thee tell,
That I am a servant of this house, and here I dwell.

JACK JUGGLER.

Now, so God me snatch, but thou go thy ways,
While thou mayest, for this forty days
I shall make thee not able to go nor ride
But in a dung-cart or wheelbarrow lying on one
    side.

JENKIN CAREAWAY.

I am a servant of this house, by these ten bones—[2]

JACK JUGGLER.

No more prating, but get thee hence at once !

JENKIN CAREAWAY.

Why, my master hath sent me home in[3] his mes-
    sage—

JACK JUGGLER.

Pick and walk, a knave, here away is no passage—

---

[1] *i.e.*, Nearer.   [2] ? Finger-bones.   [3] *i.e.*, On.

JENKIN CAREAWAY.

What, wilt thou let me from mine own master's
　　house ?

JACK JUGGLER.

Be tredging, or in faith you bear me a souse.[1]
Here my master and I have our habitation,
And hath continually dwelled in this mansion,
At the least this dozen years and odd ;
And here woll we end our lives, by the grace of
　　God.

JENKIN CAREAWAY.

Why, then, where shall my master and I dwell ?

JACK JUGGLER.

At the devil, if you lust : I cannot tell.

JENKIN CAREAWAY.

In nomine patris, now this gear doth pass :
For a little before supper here our house was ;
And this day in the morning I woll on a book
　　swear,
That my master and I both dwelled here.

JACK JUGGLER.

Who is thy master ? tell me without lie,
And thine own name also let me know shortly ;
For, my masters all, let me have the blame,
If this knave know his master or his own name.

---

[1] Blow.

CAREAWAY.

My master's name is Master Bongrace :
I have dwelled with him a long space ;
And I am Jenkin Careaway his page—

JACK JUGGLER.

What, ye drunken knave, begin you to rage !
Take that : art thou Master Bongrace's page ?
[Strikes him.

CAREAWAY.

It I be not, I have made a very good voyage—

JACK JUGGLER.

Darest thou to my face say thou art I ?

CAREAWAY.

I would it were true and no lie ;
For then thou shouldest smart, and I should bet,[1]
Where as now I do all the blows get.

JACK JUGGLER.

And is Master Bongrace thy master, doest you
    then say ?

CAREAWAY.

I woll swear on a book, he was once this day—

---

[1] Should do better.

JACK JUGGLER.

And for that thou shalt somewhat have,
Because thou presumest, like a saucy lying knave,
To say my master is thine.   Who is thy master
    now?   [*Strikes him again.*

CAREAWAY.

By my troth, sir, whosoever please you :
I am your own, for you beat me so,
As no man but my master should do.

JACK JUGGLER.

I woll handle thee better, if fault be not in fist—
                     [*Prepares to strike him.*

CAREAWAY.

Help! save my life, masters, for the passion of
    Christ !—

JACK JUGGLER.

Why, thou lousy thief, dost thou cry and roar ?—

CAREAWAY.

No, faith, I woll not cry one whit more :
Save my life, help, or I am slain—

JACK JUGGLER.

Yea, dost thou make a rumouring yet again ?
Did not I bid thee hold thy peace ?—

CAREAWAY.

In faith, now I leave crying: now I cease: help,
   help!

JACK JUGGLER.

Who is thy master?

CAREAWAY.

Master Bongrace—

JACK JUGGLER.

I woll make thee change that song, ere we pass this
   place;
For he is my master, and again to thee I say,
That I am his Jenkin Careaway.
Who art thou? now tell me plain.

CAREAWAY.

Nobody but whom please you, certain—

JACK JUGGLER.

Thou saidest even now thy name was Careaway?

CAREAWAY.

I cry you mercy, sir, and forgiveness pray:
I said amiss, because it was so to-day;
And thought it should have continued alway,
Like a fool as I am and a drunken knave.
But in faith, sir, ye see all the wit I have,
Therefore I beseech you do me no more blame,

But give me a new master and another name.
For it would grieve my heart, so help me God,
To run about the streets like a masterless nod.[1]

JACK JUGGLER.

I am he that thou saidest thou were,
And Master Bongrace is my master, that dwelleth
    here ;
Thou art no point, Careaway ; thy wits do thee
    fail.

CAREAWAY.

Yea, marry, sir, you have beaten them down into.
    my tail ;
But, sir, might I be bold to say one thing
Without any blows and without any beating ?

JACK JUGGLER.

Truce for a while ; say on what thee lust :

CAREAWAY.

May a man to your honesty by your word trust ?
I pray you swear by the mass you woll do me no
    ill—

JACK JUGGLER.

By my faith, I promise pardon thee I will—

CAREAWAY.

What, and you keep no promise ?

---

[1] *i.e.*, Noddy.

JACK JUGGLER.

Then upon Careaway [1]
I pray God light as much or more as hath on thee
  to-day.

CAREAWAY.

Now dare I speak, so mote I the,
Master Bongrace is my master, and the name of me
Is Jenkin Careaway !

JACK JUGGLER.

What, sayest thou so ?

CAREAWAY.

And if thou wilt strike me, and break thy promise,
    do,
And beat on me, till I stink, and till I die ;
And yet woll I still say that I am I !

JACK JUGGLER.

This Bedlam knave without doubt is mad—

CAREAWAY.

No, by God, for all that I am a wise lad,
And can call to remembrance every thing
That I did this day sith my uprising ;
For went not I with my master to-day
Early in the morning to the tennis-play ?
At noon, while my master at his dinner sat,
Played not I at dice at the gentleman's gate ?

---

[1] Original reads, ιρϳ cai.

Did not I wait on my master to supper-ward ?
And I think I was not changed the way homeward :
Or else, if thou think I lie,
Ask in the street of them that I came by ;
And sith that I came hither into your presence,
What man living could carry me hence ?
I remember I was sent to fetch my mistress,
And what I devised to save me harmless ;
Do not I speak now ? [is] not this my hand ?
Be not these my feet that on this ground stand ?
Did not this other knave here knock me about the
      head ?
And beat me, till I was almost dead ?
How may it then be, that he should be I ?
Or I not myself ?—it is a shameful lie.
I woll home to our house, whosoever say nay,
For surely my name is Jenkin Careaway.

JACK JUGGLER.

I woll make thee say otherwise, ere we depart, if we
      can—

JENKIN CAREAWAY.

Nay that woll I not in faith for no man,
Except thou tell me what thou hast done [1]
Ever sith five of the clock this afternoon :
Rehearse me all that without any lie,
And then I woll confess that thou art I.

JACK JUGGLER.

When my master came to the gentleman's place,
He commanded me to run home a great pace,

---

[1] Original reads, *I thou hast.*

To fet thither my mistress ; and by the way
I did a good while at the bucklers play ;
Then came I by a wife, that did costards sell,
And cast down her basket fair and well,
And gathered as many as I could get,
And put them in my sleeve : here they be yet !

CAREAWAY.

How the devil should they come there,
For I did them all in my own sleeve bear ?
He lieth not a word in all this,
Nor doth in any one point miss.
For ought I see yet between earnest and game
I must go seek me another name ;
But thou mightest see all this :—tell the rest that
    is behind,
And there I know I shall thee a liar find.

JACK JUGGLER.

I ran thence homeward a contrary way,
And whether I stopped there or nay,
I could tell, if me lusteth, a good token ;
But it may not very well be spoken.

JENKIN CAREAWAY.

Now, may I pray thee, let no man that hear,
But tell it me privily in mine ear.

JACK JUGGLER.

Ay, thou lost all thy money at dice, Christ give it
    his curse,
Well and truly picked before out of another man's
    purse !

JENKIN CAREAWAY.

God's body, whoreson thief, who told thee that
    same?
Some cunning devil is within thee, pain of shame!
In nomine patris, God and our blessed lady,
Now and evermore save me from thy company!

JACK JUGGLER.

How now, art thou Careaway or not?

CAREAWAY.

By the Lord, I doubt, but sayest thou nay to that!

JACK JUGGLER.

Yea, marry, I tell thee, Care-away is my name.

CAREAWAY.

And, by these ten bones, mine is the same!
Or else tell me, if I be not he,
What my name from henceforth shall be?

JACK JUGGLER.

By my faith, the same that it was before,
When I lust to be Careaway no more:
Look well upon me, and thou shalt see as now,
That I am Jenkin Careaway, and not thou:
Look well upon me, and by every thing
Thou shalt well know that I am not lesing.

CAREAWAY.

I see it is so without any doubt;
But how the devil came it about?

Whoso in England looketh on him steadily,
Shall perceive plainly that he is I:
I have seen myself a thousand times in a glass;
But so like myself, as he is, never was;
He hath in every point my clothing and my gear:
My head, my cap, my shirt, and knotted hair,
And of the same colour: my eyes, nose, and lips:
My cheeks, chin, neck, feet, legs, and hips:
Of the same stature, and height, and age:
And is in every point Master Bongrace page,
That if he have a hole in his tail,
He is even I mine own self without any fail!
And yet when I remember, I wot not how,
The same man that I have ever been me thinketh
    I am now:
I know my master and his house, and my five wits
    I have:
Why then should I give credence to this foolish
    knave,
That nothing intendeth but me delude and mock?
For whom should I fear at my master's gate to
    knock?

JACK JUGGLER.

Thinkest thou I have said all this in game?
Go, or I shall send thee hence in the devil's name!
Avoid, thou lousy lurden and precious stinking
    slave,
That neither thy name knowest nor canst any
    master have!
Wine-shaken pillory-peeper,[1] of lice not without a
    peck,
Hence, or by Gods precious,[2] I shall break thy
    neck!

---

[1] Original reads, *pilorye peepours.*
[2] [A common abbreviation, leaving its substantive to be
supplied at pleasure.]

CAREAWAY.

Then, master, I beseech you heartily take the pain,
If I be found in any place, to bring me to me
    again.
Now is not this a wonderful case,
That no man shall lese himself so in any place?
Have any of you heard of such a thing heretofore?
No, nor never shall, I daresay, from henceforth
    any more.

JACK JUGGLER [*Aside.*]

While he museth and judgeth himself upon,
I will steal away for a while, and let him alone.
                [*Exit Jack Juggler.*

CAREAWAY.

Good Lord of heaven, where did I myself leave?
Or who did me of my name by the way bereave?
For I am sure of this in my mind,
That I did in no place leave myself behind.
If I had my name played away at dice,
Or had sold myself to any man at a price,
Or had made a fray, and had lost it in fighting,
Or it had been stolen from me sleeping,
It had been a matter, and I would have kept
    patience;
But it spiteth my heart to have lost it by such
    open negligence.
Ah, thou whoreson, drowsy, drunken sot!
It were an alms-deed to walk [1] thy coat,
And I shrew him that would for thee be sorry,
To see thee well curried by and by;

---

[1] [Perhaps in our modern sense of *to walk into.*]

And, by Christ, if any man would it do,
I myself would help thereto.
For a man may see, thou whoreson goose,
Thou wouldest lese thine arse, if it were loose !
Albeit I would never the deed believe,
But that the thing itself doth show and preve.[1]
There was never ape so like unto an ape,
As he is to me in feature and shape ;
But what woll my master say, trow ye,
When he shall this gear hear and see ?
Will he know me, think you, when he shall see
    me ?
If he do not, another woll as good as he.
But where is that other I ? whither is he gone ?
To my master, by Cock's precious passion :
Either to put me out of my place,
Or to accuse me to my master Bongrace !
But I woll after, as fast as I can flee :
I trust to be there as soon as he.
That if my master be not ready home to come,
I woll be here again as fast as I can run.
In any wise to speak with my mistress,
Or else I shall never escape hanging doubtless.

DAME COY.

I shall not sup this night, full well I see ;
For as yet nobody cometh for to fet me.
But good enough, let me alone :
I woll be even with them every-chone.
I say nothing, but I think somewhat, i-wis :
Some there be that shall hear of this !
Of all unkind and churlish husbands this is the
    cast,
To let their wives sit at home and fast ;

---

[1] Prove.

While they be forth, and make good cheer :
Pastime and sport, as now he doth there.
But if I were a wise woman, as I am a mome,
I should make myself, as good cheer at home.
But if he have thus unkindly served me,
I woll not forget it this months three ;
And if I wist the fault were in him, I pray God I
        be dead,
But he should have such a curry,[1] ere he went to
        bed,
As he never had before in all his life,
Nor any man else have had of his wife !
I would rate him and shake him after such a sort,
As should be to him a corrosive full little to his
        comfort !

ALLISON TRIP-AND-GO.

If I may be so bold, by your mistress-ship's license,
As to speak and show my mind and sentence,
I think of this you may the boy thank ;
For I know that he playeth you many a like prank,
And that would you say, if you knew as much as
        we,
That his daily conversation and behaviour see ;
For if you command him to go speak with some
        one,
It is an hour, ere he woll be gone ;
Then woll he run forth, and play in the street,
And come again, and say that he cannot with him
        meet.

DAME COY.

Nay, nay, it is his master's play :
He serveth me so almost every third day ;

---

1 [Orig. *kyrie.*]

But I woll be even with him, as God give me joy,
And yet the fault may be in the boy—
As ungracious a graft, so mot I thrive,
As any goeth on God's ground alive !

CAREAWAY.

My wit is breeched in such a brake,
That I cannot devise what way is best to take.
I was almost as far as my master is ;
But then I began to remember this,
And to cast the worst, as one in fear :
If he chance to see me and keep me there,
Till he come himself, and speak with my mistress.
Then am I like to be in shrewd distress :
Yet were I better, thought I, to turn home again.
And first speak with her, certain—
Cock's body, yonder she standeth at the door !
Now is it worse than it was before.
Would Christ I could get again out of her sight ;
For I see by her look she is disposed to fight.
By the Lord, she hath there an angry shrew's look—

DAME COY.

Lo, yonder cometh that unhappy hook !

CAREAWAY.

God save me, mistress, do you know me well ?

DAME COY.

Come near [1] hither unto me, and I shall thee tell.
Why, thou naughty villain, is that thy guise,

---

[1] Nearer.

To jest with thy mistress in such wise?
Take that to begin with, and God before!
When thy master cometh home, thou shalt have
        more:
For he told me, when he forth went,
That thou shouldest come back again incontinent
To bring me to supper where he now is,
And thou hast played by the way, and they have
        done by this.
But no force I shall, thou mayest trust me,
Teach all naughty knaves to beware by thee.

CAREAWAY.

Forsooth, mistress, if ye knew as much as I,
Ye would not be with me half so angry;
For the fault is neither in my master, nor in me,
        nor you,
But in another knave that was here even now,
And his name was Jenkin Careaway—

DAME COY.

What, I see my man is disposed to play!
I ween he be drunken or mad, I make God a vow!

CAREAWAY.

Nay, I have been made sober and tame, I, now:—
I was never so handled before in all my life:
I would every man in England had so beaten [1] his
        wife!
I have forgotten with tousing by the hair,
What I devised to say a little ere.

----

[1] Original reads, *beat me.*

DAME COY.

Have I lost my supper this night through thy
negligence?

CAREAWAY.

Nay then were I a knave, mistress, saving your
reverence.

DAME COY.

Why, I am sure that by this time it is done—

CAREAWAY.

Yea, that it is more than an hour agone—

DAME COY.

And was not thou sent to fetch me thither?—

CAREAWAY.

Yea, and had come right quickly hither,
But that by the way I had a great fall,
And my name, body, shape, legs, and all:
And met with one, that from me did it steal;
But, by God, he and I some blows did deal!
I would he were now before your gate,
For you would pummel him jollily about the pate.

DAME COY.

Truly this wage-pasty[1] is either drunken or mad.

---

[1] [A term of contempt, perhaps of no very definite or clear
signification; but it does not seem to be glossed.]

CAREAWAY.

Never man suffered so much wrong as I had ;
But, mistress, I should say a thing to you :
Tarry, it woll come to my remembrance even now
I must needs use a substantial premeditation ;
For the matter lieth greatly me upon.
I beseech your mistress-ship of pardon and forgive-
    ness,
Desiring you to impute it to my simple and rude
    dulness :
I have forgotten what I had [1] thought to have said
And am thereof full ill-afraid ;
But when I lost myself, I knew very well,
I lost also that I should you tell.

DAME COY.

Why, thou wretched villain, doest thou me scorn
    and mock,
To make me to these folk a laughing-stock ?
Ere thou go out of my hands, thou shalt have
    something ;
And I woll reckon better in the morning.

CAREAWAY.

And if you beat me, mistress, avise you ;
For I am none of your servants now.
That other I is now your page,
And I am no longer in your bondage.

DAME COY.

Now walk, precious thief, get thee out of my sight !

---

[1] Original has *haue*.

And I charge thee come in my presence no more
    this night:
Get thee hence, and wait on thy master at once.

CAREAWAY.

Marry, sir, this is handling for the nonce:
I would I had been hanged, before that I was
    lost;
I was never this [1] canvassed and tossed:
That if my master, on his part also,
Handle me, as my mistress and the other I [2] do,
I shall surely be killed between them three,
And all the devils in hell shall not save me.
But yet, if the other I might have with me part,
All this would never grieve my heart.
                [Enter Jack Juggler.

JACK JUGGLER.

How say you, masters, I pray you tell,
Have not I requited my merchant well?
Have not I handled him after a good sort?
Had it not been pity to have lost this sport?
Anon his master, on his behalf,
You shall see how he woll handle the calf!
If he throughly angered be,
He woll make him smart, so mot I the.
I would not for a price of a new pair of shone,
That any part of this had been undone;
But now I have revenged my quarrel,
I woll go do off this mine apparel,
And now let Careaway be Careaway again;
I have done with that name now, certain,

---

[1] Thus.   [2] *i.e.,* Jack Juggler.

Except peraventure I shall take the self-same weed
Some other time again for a like cause and need.
                    [*Enter Bongrace and Careaway.*

BONGRACE.

Why, then, darest thou to presume to tell me,
That I know is no wise possible for to be ?

CAREAWAY.

Now, by my truth, master, I have told you no lie ;
And all these folks knoweth as well as I,
I had no sooner knocked at the gate,
But straightway he had me by the pate ;
Therefore, if you beat me, till I fart and shit again,
You shall not cause me for any pain ;
But I woll affirm, as I said before,
That when I came near, another stood at the door.

BONGRACE.

Why, thou naughty villain, darest thou affirm to me
That which was never seen nor hereafter shall be ?
That one man may have two bodies and two faces,
And that one man at one time may be in two
    places ?
Tell me, drankest thou anywhere by the way ?

CAREAWAY.

I shrew me, if I drank any more than twice to-day,
Till I met even now with that other I,
And with him I supped and drank truly ;
But as for you, if you gave me drink and meat,
As oftentimes as you do me beat,
I were the best-fed page in all this city.

But, as touching that, you have on me no pity,
And not only I, but all that do you serve,
For meat and drink may rather starve.

BONGRACE.

What, you saucy malapert knave,
Begin you with your master to prate and rave ?
Your tongue is liberal and all out of frame :
I must needs conjure it, and make it tame.
Where is that other Careaway that thou said was
    here ?

CAREAWAY.

Now, by my christendom, sir, I wot ne'er ?

BONGRACE.

Why, canst thou find no man to mock but me ?

CAREAWAY.

I mock you not, master, so mot I the,
Every word was true that I you told.

BONGRACE.

Nay I know toys and pranks of old,
And now thou art not satisfied nor content,
Without regard of my biddings and command-
    ment,
To have played by the way as a lewd knave and
    negligent,
When I thee on my message home sent,
But also wouldest willingly me delude and mock,
And make me to all wise men a laughing-stock :
Showing me such things as in no wise be may,

To the intent thy lewdness may turn to jest and
     play ;
Therefore if thou speak any such thing to me again,
I promise it shall be unto thy pain.

CAREAWAY.

Lo, is not he in miserable case,
That serveth such a master in any place ?
That with force woll compel him that thing to deny,
That he knoweth true, and hath seen with his
     eye ?

BONGRACE.

Was it not, trowest thou, thine own shadow ?

CAREAWAY.

My shadow could never have beaten me so !

BONGRACE.

Why, by what reason possible may such a thing be ?

CAREAWAY.

Nay, I marvel and wonder at it more than ye ;
And at the first it did me curstly meve [1]
Nor I would mine own eyes in no wise believe,
Until that other I beat me so,
That he made me believe it, whether I would or no.
And if he had yourself now within his reach,
He would make you say so too, or else beshit your
     breech.

----

[1] Move.

MASTER BONGRACE.

I durst a good meed and a wager lay,
That thou layest down and slepst by the way,
And dreamed all this, that thou hast me told.

CAREAWAY.

Nay, there you lie, master, if I might be so bold ;
But we rise so early that, if I had,
I had done well, and a wise lad.
Yet, master, I would you understood,
That I have always been trusty and good,
And fly as fast as a bear in a cage,
Whensoever you send me in your message ;
In faith, as for this that I have told you,
I saw and felt it as waking as I am now :
For I had no sooner knocked at the gate,
But the other-I knave had me by the pate ;
And I durst to you on a book swear,
That he had been watching for me there,
Long ere I came, hidden in some privy place,
Even for the nonce to have me by the face.

MASTER BONGRACE.

Why, then, thou spakest not with my wife ?

CAREAWAY.

No, that I did not, master, by my life,
Until that other I was gone,
And then my mistress sent me after anon,
To wait on you home in the devil's name :
I ween the devil never so beat his dame !

MASTER BONGRACE.

And where became that other Careaway ?

CAREAWAY.

By mine honesty, sir, I cannot say ;
But I warrant he is now not far hence ;
He is here among this company, for forty pence.

MASTER BONGRACE.

Hence, at once seek and smell him out ;
I shall rap thee on the lying knave's snout :
I woll not be deluded with such a glossing lie,
Nor give credence, till I see it with my own eye.

CAREAWAY.

Truly, good sir, by your mastership's favour,
I cannot well find a knave by the savour ;
Many here smell strong, but none so rank as he :
A stronger-scented knave than he was cannot be.
But, sir, if he be haply found anon,
What amends shall I have for that you have me
   done ?

MASTER BONGRACE.

If he may be found, I shall walk his coat.

CAREAWAY.

Yea, for our lady's sake, sir, I beseech you spare
   him not,
For it is some false knave withouten doubt.
I had rather than forty pence we could find him
   out ;
For, if a man may believe a glass,
Even my very own self it was.
And here he was but even right now,
And stepped away suddenly, I wot not how.

Of such another thing I have neither heard ne seen,
By our blessed lady, heaven queen !

MASTER BONGRACE.

Plainly it was thy shadow, that thou didst see ;
For, in faith, the other thing is not possible to be.

CAREAWAY.

Yes, in good faith, sir, by your leave,
I know it was I by my apples in my sleeve,
And speaketh as like me as ever you heard : [1]
Such hair, such a cap, such hose and coat,
And in everything as just as fourpence to a groat.
That if he were here, you should well see,
That you could not discern nor know him from
    me ;
For think you, that I do not myself know ?
I am not so foolish a knave, I trow.
Let who woll look him by and by,
And he woll depose upon a book that he is I ;
And I dare well say you woll say the same ;
For he called himself by my own name.
And he told me all that I have done,
Sith five of the clock this afternoon,
He could tell when you were to supper set
[When] you send me home my mistress to fet,
And showed me all things that I did by the way—

BONGRACE.

What was that ?

---

[1] [A line seems to have dropped out here.]

CAREAWAY.

How I did at the bucklers play ;
And when I scattered a basket of apples from a
  stall,
And gathered them into my sleeve all,
And how I played after that also—

BONGRACE.

Thou shalt have, boy, therefore,[1] so mote I go ;
Is that the guise of a trusty page,
To play, when he is sent on his master's message ?

DAME COY.

Lay on and spare not, for the love of Christ,
Joll his head to a post,[2] and favour your fist !
Now for my sake, sweetheart, spare and favour
  your hand,
And lay him about the ribs with this wand.

CAREAWAY.

Now mercy that I ask of you both twain :
Save my life, and let me not be slain.
I have had beating enough for one day :
That a mischief take the other-me Careaway !
That if ever he come to my hands again,
I-wis it shall be to his pain.
But I marvel greatly, by our Lord Jesus,
How he-I escaped, I-me beat me thus.
And is not he-I an unkind knave,
That woll no more pity on myself have ?

---

[1] [Original reads *have by therefore.*]
[2] [Beat his head against a post.]

Here may you see evidently, i-wis,
That in him-me no drop of honesty is.
Now a vengeance light on such a churlish knave
That no more love toward myself have !

DAME COY.

I knew very,[1] sweet-heart, and said right now,
That no fault thereof should be in you.

BONGRACE.

No, truly, good bedfellow, I were then much unkind,
If you at any time should be out of my mind.

DAME COY.

Surely, I have of you a great treasure,
For you do all things which may be to my pleasure.

BONGRACE.

I am sorry that your chance hath now been so ill:
I would gladly been unsupped, so you had your
    fill;
But go we in, pigsnie, that you may sup;
You have cause now to thank this same hang-up
For had not he been, you had fared very well.

DAME COY.

I bequeath him with a hot vengeance to the devil
    of hell,
And heartily I beseech him that hanged on the
    rood,

---

[1] Verily.

That he never eat nor drink that may do him
    good,
And that he die a shameful death, saving my
    charity !

CAREAWAY.

I pray God send him such prosperity,
That hath caused me to have all this business.
But yet, sirs, you see the charity of my mistress :
She liveth after a wonderful charitable fashion ;
For I assure you she is always in this passion,
And scarcely one day throughout the whole year
She woll wish any man better cheer,
And some time, if she well-angered be,
I pray God (woll she say) the house may sink
    under me !
But, masters, if you happen to see that other I,
As that you shall, it is not very likely,
Nor I woll not desire you for him purposely to
    look,
For it is an uncomparable unhappy hook ;
And if it be I, you might happen to seek,
And not find me out in an whole week.
For when I was wont to run away,
I used not to come again in less than a month or
    tway :
Howbeit, for all this I think it be not I ;
For, to show the matter indeed truly,
I never use to run away in winter nor in vere,[1]
But always in such time and season of the year,
When honey lieth in the hives of bees,
And all manner fruit falleth from the trees :
As apples, nuts, pears, and plums also,
Whereby a boy may live abroad a month or two.

---

[1] Spring.

This cast do I use, I woll not with you feign ;
Therefore I wonder if he be I, certain.
But, and if he be, and you meet me abroad by
    chance,
Send me home to my master with a vengeance !
And show him, if he come not here to-morrow
    night,
I woll never receive him again, if I might ;
And in the meantime I woll give him a groat,
That woll well and thriftily walk his coat ;
For a more ungracious knave is not even now
Between this place and Calicow.[1]
Nor a more frantic-mad knave in Bedlam,
Nor a more fool hence to Jerusalem.
That if to come again percase he shall refuse,
I woll continue as I am, and let him choose ;
And but he come the sooner, by our lady bright,
He shall lie without the doors all night.
For I woll shit[2] up the gate, and get me to-
    bed,
For I promise you I have a very giddy head.
I need no supper for this night,
Nor would eat no meat, though I might ;
And for you also, master, I think it[1] best
You go to-bed, and take your rest.
For who of you had been handled as I have
    been,
Would not be long out of his bed, I ween ;
No more woll I, but steal out of sight :
I pray God give you all good night !
And send you better hap and fortune,
Than to lese yourself homeward as I have done.
                              [*Exit Careaway.*

---

[1] Calicow or Calicut, *i.e.*, Calcutta.
[2] Shut.
[3] Original has *I.*

Somewhat it was, saith the proverb old,
That the cat winked when her eye was out,
That is to say, no tale can be told,
But that some English may be picked thereof out
If so to search the Latin and ground of it men will
    go about,
As this trifling enterlude that before you hath been
    rehearsed,
May signify some further meaning, if it be well
    searched.

Such is the fashion of the world now-a-days,
That the simple innocents are deluded,
And an hundred thousand divers ways
By subtle and crafty means shamefully abused,
And by strength, force, and violence ofttimes com-
    pelled
To believe and say the moon is made of a green
    cheese
Or else have great harm, and percase their life
    lese.

And an old saying it is, that most times might,
Force, strength, power, and colourable subtlety
Doth oppress, debar, overcome, and defeat right,
Though the cause stand never so greatly against
    equity,
And the truth thereof be knowen for never so perfit
    certainty :
Yea, and the poor simple innocent that hath had
    wrong and injury,
Must call the other his good master for showing
    him such mercy.

And as it is daily seen, for fear of further disprofit,
He must that man his best friend and master call,
Of whom he never received any manner benefit,

And at whose hand he never han any good at all ;
And must grant, affirm, or deny, whatsoever he
  shall.
He must say the crow is white, if he be so commanded,
Yea, and that he himself is into another body
  changed.

He must say he did amiss, though he never did
  offend ;
He must ask forgiveness, where he did no trespass,
Or else be in trouble, care, and misery without end,
And be cast in some arrearage without any grace ;
And that thing he saw done before his own face
He must by compulsion stiffly deny,
And for fear, whether he woll or not, say *tongue,
  you lie !*

And in every faculty this thing is put in ure,
And is so universal that I need no one to name,
And, as I fear, is like evermore to endure ;
For it is in all faculties a common sport and game,
The weaker to say as the stronger biddeth, or to
  have blame,
As a cunning sophist woll by argument bring to
  pass,
That the rude shall confess, and grant himself an
  ass.

And this is the daily exercise and practise of their
  schools,
And not among them only, but also among all
  others :
The stronger to compel, and make poor simple
  fools

To say as they command them in all manner
    matters.
I woll name none particular, but set them all
    together
Without any exception; for I pray you show me
    one
Amongst all in the world that seeth not such
    fashion.

He that is stronger and more of power and might,
If he be disposed to revenge his cause,
Woll soon pick a quarrel, be it wrong or right,
To the inferior and weaker for a couple of straws,
And woll against him so extremely lay the laws,
That he woll put him to the worse, either by false
    injury,
Or by some craft and subtlety, or else by plain
    tyranny.

As you saw right now by example plain
Another fellow, being a counterfeit page,
Brought the gentleman's servant out of his brain,
And made him grant that himself was fallen in
    dotage
Bearing himself in hand that he did rage,
And when he could not bring that to pass by
    reason,
He made him grant it, and say by compulsion.

Therefore happy are they, that can beware
Into whose hands they fall by any such chance;
Which if they do, they hardly escape care,
Trouble, misery, and woeful grievance,
And thus I make an end, committing you to his
    guidance,

That made and redeemed us all, and to you that
    be now here
I pray God grant and send many a good new year !

FINIS.[1]

---

[1] [The colophon is : Imprinted at London in Lothbury by
me Wyllyam Copland. The only copy known, formerly
Inglis's and Heber's, is now in the Devonshire collection.

The piece is undated, but it was licensed for the press in
1562-3.]

A PRETTY INTERLUDE,

CALLED

NICE WANTON.

[Of this interlude only two copies have hitherto been discovered, one in the Devonshire collection, the second in the King's Library, British Museum, from the Roxburghe sale. An account of the piece, which has never been reprinted before, is given by Collier ("History of Dramatic Poetry," ii. 381–3). Considering its rarity, early date, and curiosity, it is remarkable that "Nice Wanton" should have escaped Dodsley and his editors.]

A PRETTY INTERLUDE,

CALLED

NICE WANTON.

⁋ Wherein ye may see
Three branches of an ill tree :
The mother and her children three,
Two naught, and one godly.

Early sharp, that will be thorn,
Soon ill, that will be naught :
To be naught, better unborn,
Better unfed than naughtily taught.

Ut magnum magnos, pueros puerilia doctus.

PERSONAGES.

The Messenger.

Barnabas.	}	{	*Iniquity.*
Ismael.	}	{	*Baily errand.*
Dalilah.	}	{	*Xantippe.*
Eulalia.	}	{	*Worldly Shame.*

Daniel the Judge.

Anno Domini, M.D.LX.

THE PROLOGUE.

The Messenger. The prudent Prince Solomon
    doth say,
He that spareth the rod, the child doth hate,
He would youth should be kept in awe alway
By correction in time at reasonable rate :
    To be taught to fear God, and their parents
    obey,
To get learning and qualities, thereby to maintain
An honest quiet life, correspondent alway
To God's law and the king's, for it is certain,
    If children be noseled [1] in idleness and ill,
And brought up therein, it is hard to restrain,
And draw them from natural wont evil,
As here in this interlude ye shall see plain :
    By two children brought up wantonly in play,
Whom the mother doth excuse, when she should
    chastise ;
They delight in dalliance and mischief alway,
At last they end their lives in miserable wise.
    The mother persuaded by worldly shame,
That she was the cause of their wretched life,
So pensive, so sorrowful, for their death she be-
    came,
That in despair she would sle herself with a knife.
    Then her son Barnabas (by interpretation
The son of comfort), her ill-purpose do[th] stay,
By the scriptures he giveth her godly consolation,
And so concludeth ; all these parts will we play.

---

[1] Nursled.

BARNABAS cometh.

BARNABAS. My master, in my lesson yesterday,
Did recite this text of Ecclesiasticus :
Man is prone to evil from his youth, did he say,
Which sentence may well be verified in us.
Myself, my brother, and sister Dalilah,
Whom our parents to their cost to school do find.
I tarry for them here, time passeth away,
I lose my learning, they ever loiter behind.
    If I go before, they do me threat
To complain to my mother : she for their sake,
Being her tender tidlings,[1] will me beat :
Lord, in this perplexity, what way shall I take ?
What will become of them ? grace God them send
To apply their learning, and their manners amend !

ISMAEL and DALILAH come in singing.

Here we comen, and here we lonen,[2]
And here we will abide abide-a.

BARNABAS. Fye, brother, fye, and specially you,
    sister Dalilah,
Soberness becometh maids alway.
    DALILAH. What, ye dolt, ye be ever in one song !
    ISMAEL. Yea, sir, it shall cost you blows, ere it
    be long.
    BARNABAS. Be ye not ashamed the truands to
    play,
Losing your time and learning, and that every day ?
Learning bringeth knowledge of God and honest
    living to get.
    DALILAH. Yea, marry, I warrant you, master
    hoddypeak.

---

[1] [Pets. See Halliwell's "Dictionary," v. Tiddle.]
[2] [I do not find this word in any other glossaries ; but it occurs again below.]

BARNABAS. Learn apace, sister, and after to
    spin and sew,
And other honest housewifely points to know.
    ISMAEL. Spin, quod-a? yea, by the mass, and
    with your heels up-wind,
For a good mouse-hunt is cat after Saint Kind.[1]
    BARNABAS. Lewd speaking corrupteth good
    manners, Saint Paul doth say;
Come, let us go, if ye will, to school this day;
I shall be shent for tarrying so long,
                    [Barnabas goeth out.
    ISMAEL. Go, get thee hence, thy mouth full of
    horse-dung!
Now, pretty sister, what sport shall we devise?
Thus palting[2] to school, I think us unwise:
In summer die for thrist,[3] in winter for cold,
And still to live in fear of a churl who would?
    DALILAH. Not I, by the mass, I had rather he
    hanged were,
Than I would sit quaking like a mome for fear.
I am sun-burned in summer, in winter the cold
Maketh my limbs gross, and my beauty decay;
If I should use it, as they would I should,
I should never be fair woman, I dare say.
    ISMAEL. No, sister, no, but I can tell,
Where we shall have good cheer,
Lusty companions two or three,
At good wine, ale, and beer.
    DALILAH. O good brother, let us go,
I will never go more to-to[4] school.
Shall I never know,

---

[1] Old copy, *Kynge.*
[2] Trudging.
[3] Thirst.
[4] So in old copy, which is perhaps right. *To-to,* as an
intensitive, is a common form.

What pastime meaneth?
Yes, I will not be such a fool.
  ISMAEL. Have with thee, Dalilah :
Farewell our school !
Away with books and all,
                    [*They cast away their books.*
I will set my heart
On a merry pin,
Whatever shall befall.
  EULALIA. Lord, what folly is in youth !
How unhappy be children now-a-days ?
And the more pity, to say the truth,
Their parents maintain them in evil ways :
Which is a great cause that the world decays,
For children, brought up in idleness and play,
Unthrifty and disobedient continue alway.
  A neighbour of mine hath children hereby,
Idle, disobedient, proud, wanton, and nice.
As they come by, they do shrewd turns daily ;
Their parents so to suffer them surely be not wise.
They laugh me to scorn, when I tell them mine
    advice ;
I will speak with their elders and warn them
    neighbourly :
Never in better time, their mother is hereby.
                    [*Enter Xantippe.*
God save you, gossip, I am very fain,
That you chance now to come this way ;
I long to talk with you a word or twain,
I pray you take it friendly that I shall say :
Ismael your son and your daughter Dalilah
Do me shrewd turns daily more and more,
Chide and beat my children, it grieveth me sore.
  They swear, curse, and scold, as they go by the
    way,
Giving other ill ensample to do the same,
To God's displeasure and their hurt another day,

Chastise them for it, or else ye be to blame.
  XANTIPPE. Tush, tush, if ye have no more
    than that to say,
Ye may hold your tongue and get ye away,
Alas, poor souls, they sit a-school all day
In fear of a churl; and if a little they play,
He beateth them like a devil; when they come
    home,
Your mistress-ship would have me lay on.
If I should beat them, so oft as men complain,
By the mass, within this month I should make them
    lame.
  EULALIA. Be not offended, I pray you, I must
    say more,
Your son is suspect light-fingered to be :
Your daughter hath nice tricks three or four;
See to it in time, lest worse ye do see;
He that spareth the rod, hateth the child truly.
Yet Salomon sober correction doth mean,
Not to beat and bounce them, to make them lame.
  XANTIPPE. God thank you, mistress, I am well
    at ease :
Such a fool to teach me, preaching as she please !
Dame, ye belie them deadly, I know plain;
Because they go handsomely, ye disdain.[1]
  EULALIA. Then on the other[2] as well would I
    complain,
But your other son is good, and no thanks to
    you !
These will ye make nought, by sweet Jesu.
  XANTIPPE. Gup, liar,[3] my children nought ye lie :
By your malice they shall not set a fly ;
I have but one mome in comparison of his brother :
Him the fool praiseth, and despiseth the other.

---

[1] Are jealous of them.   [2] Barnabas.
[3] Old copy, *Gupliade.*

EULALIA. Well, Xantippe, better in time than
    too late,
Seeing ye take it so, here my leave I take.   [*Exit.*
    XANTIPPE. Marry, good leave have ye, the great
    God be with you!
My children or I be cursed, I think;
They be complained on, wherever they go,
That for their pleasure they might drink.
Nay, by this the poor souls be come from school
    weary;
I will go get them meat to make them merry.

INIQUITY, ISMAEL, *and* DALILAH *come in together.*

    INIQUITY. *Lo, lo, here I bring-a.*
    ISMAEL. *What is she, now ye have her?*
    DALILAH. *A lusty minion loner.*[1]
    INIQUITY. *For no gold will I give her—*
    ALL TOGETHER. *Welcome, my honey-a!*
    INIQUITY. O my heart!   [*Here he speaketh.*
This wench can sing,
And play her part.
DALILAH. I am yours, and you mine, with all my
    heart.
    INIQUITY. By the mass, it is well sung;
Were ye not sorry ye were a maid so long?
    DALILAH. Fie, master Iniquity, fie, I am a maid
    yet.
    ISMAEL. No, sister, no, your maidenhead is sick.
    INIQUITY. That knave your brother will be a
    blab still,
I-wis, Dalilah, ye can say as much by him, if ye will.
    DALILAH. By him, quod-a? he hath whores two
    or three,

---

[1] This word, as a verb, has occurred above. It is evidently
used in a bad sense, to signify an idle, *loafing* person.

But ich tell your minion doll,[1] by Gog's body :
It skilleth not she doth hold you as much.
   ISMAEL. Ye lie falsely, she will play me no such
     touch.
   DALILAH. Not she? Yes, to do your heart good,
I could tell you who putteth a bone in your hood !
   ISMAEL. Peace, whore, or ye bear me a box on[2]
     there—
   DALILAH. Here is mine ear, knave ; strike, and
     thou dare !
To suffer him thus ye be no man,
If ye will not revenge me, I will find one ;
To set so little by me ye were not wont—
Well, it is no matter ;
Though ye do, *ceteri nolunt.*
   INIQUITY. Peace, Dalilah ; speak ye Latin, poor
     fool?
   DALILAH. No, no, but a proverb I learned at
     school—
   ISMAEL. Yea, sister, you went to school, till ye
     were past grace ;—
   DALILAH. Yea, so didst thou, by thy knave's
     face !
   INIQUITY. Well, no more a-do, let all this go,
We kinsfolk must be friends, it must be so.
Come on, come on, come on,
               [*He casteth dice on the board.*
Here they be that will do us all good.
   ISMAEL. If ye use it long, your hair will grow
     through your hood.
   INIQUITY. Come on, knave, with Christ's curse,
I must have some of the money
Thou hast picked out of thy father's purse !
   DALILAH. He, by the mass, if he can get his
     purse,

---

    [1] Mistress.   [2] Old copy, *an.*

Now and then he maketh it by half the worse.

ISMAEL. I defy you both, whore and knave—

INIQUITY. What, ye princocks, begin ye to rave?
Come on—

DALILAH. Master Iniquity, by your leave,
I will play a crown or two here by your sleeve.

ISMAEL. Then be ye servant to a worshipful
man,
Master Iniquity—a right name, by Saint John!

DALILAH. What can ye say by Master Iniquity?
I love him and his name most heartily.

INIQUITY. God-a-mercy, Dalilah, good luck, I
warrant thee,
I will shrive you both by and by.   [*He kisseth her.*

ISMAEL. Come on, but first let us have a song.

DALILAH. I am content, so that it be not long.
                    [*Iniquity and Dalilah sing :*
          INIQUITY. *Gold locks,*
She must have knocks,
Or else I do her wrong.
          DALILAH. *When ye have your will*
Ye were best lie still,
The winter nights be long.
          INIQUITY. *When I ne may,*
Another assay ;
I will take it for no wrong :
          DALILAH. *Then, by the rood,*
A bone in your hood
I shall put, ere it be long.

ISMAEL. She matcheth you, sirrah!

INIQUITY. By Gog's blood, she is the best whore
in England.

DALILAH. It is knavishly praised ; give me your
hand.

INIQUITY. I would thou hadst such another.

ISMAEL. By the mass, rather than forty pound,
brother.

INIQUITY. Here, sirs, come on; seven—
[*They set him.*
Eleven [1] at all [2]—
    ISMAEL. Do ye nick us? [3] beknave your noly!—
    INIQUITY. Ten mine—
    ISMAEL (*casteth dice*). Six mine,
Have at it, and it were for all my father's kine.
It is lost by his wounds, [4] and ten to one!
    INIQUITY. Take the dice, Dalilah, cast on—
[*She casteth, and they set.*
    DALILAH. Come on; five!
Thrive at fairest—
    ISMAEL. Gup, whore, and I at rest [*he loseth*].
By Gog's blood, I ween God and the devil be
      against me—
    INIQUITY. If th' one forsake thee, th' other will
      take thee!
    ISMAEL. Then is he a good fellow; I would not
      pass, [5]
So that I might bear a rule in hell, by the mass:
To toss firebrands at these pennyfathers' [6] pates;
I would be porter, and receive them at the gates.
In boiling lead and brimstone I would seeth them
      each one:
The knaves have all the money, good fellows have
      none.
    DALILAH. Play, brother, have ye lost all your
      money now?
    ISMAEL. Yea, I thank that knave and such a
      whore as thou.
'Tis no matter, I will have money, or I will sweat;

---

[1] Old copy, *a leaven.*
[2] Altogether.
[3] *i.e.,* Do ye nick a cast? See Halliwell, *v. Nick*, No. 6.
[4] *i.e.,* By God's wounds, a common phrase.
[5] Care.
[6] A term of contempt. A skinflint, a curmudgeon.

By Gog's blood, I will rob the next I meet—
Yea, and it be my father.   [*He goeth out.*
   INIQUITY. Thou boy, by the mass, ye will climb
     the ladder,
Ah, sirrah, I love a wench that can be wily,
She perceived my mind with a twink of mine eye,
If we two play boody on any man,
We will make him as bare as Job anon,
Well, Dalilah, let see what ye have won.
                        [*They tell.*
   DALILAH. Sir, I had ten shillings when I begon,
And here is all—every farthing.
   INIQUITY. Ye lie like a whore, ye have won a
     pound !
   DALILAH. Then the devil strike me to the ground !
   INIQUITY. I will feel your pocket, by your leave,
     mistress—
   DALILAH. Away, knave, not mine, by the mass—
   INIQUITY. Yes, by God, and give you this to
     boot—   [*He giveth her a box.*
   DALILAH. Out, whoreson knave, I beshrew thy
     heart-root !
Wilt thou rob me and beat me too ?
   INIQUITY. In the way of correction, but a blow
     or two !
   DALILAH. Correct thy dogs, thou shalt not beat
     me,
I will make your knave's flesh cut, I warrant thee.
Ye think I have no friends ; yes, I have in store
A good fellow or two, perchance more.
Yea, by the mass, they shall box you for this gear,
A knave I found thee, a knave I leave thee here.
                     [*She goeth out.*
   INIQUITY. Gup, whore ; do ye hear this jade ?
Loving, when she is pleased :
When she is angry, thus shrewd :
Thief, brother : sister, whore ;

Two graffs of an ill tree,
I will tarry no longer here,
Farewell, God be with ye !   [*He goeth out.*

*DALILAH cometh in ragged, her face hid, or
disfigured, halting on a staff.*

Alas, wretched wretch that I am,
Most miserable caitiff that ever was born,
Full of pain and sorrow, crooked and lorn :
Stuff'd with diseases, in this world forlorn.
My sinews be shrunken, my flesh eaten with pox :
My bones full of ache and great pain :
My head is bald, that bare yellow locks ;
Crooked I creep to the earth again.
Mine eyesight is dim, my hands tremble and shake :
My stomach abhorreth all kind of meat :
For lack of clothes great cold I take,
When appetite serveth, I can get no meat.
Where I was fair and amiable of face,
Now am I foul and horrible to see ;
All this I have deserved for lack of grace ;
Justly for my sins God doth plague me.
   My parents did tiddle [1] me : they were to blame ;
Instead of correction, in ill did me maintain :
I fell to [2] naught, and shall die with shame ;
Yet all this is not half of my grief and pain.
   The worm of my conscience, that shall never die,
Accuseth me daily more and more :
So oft have I sinned wilfully,
That I fear to be damned evermore.

Enter BARNABAS.

BARNABAS. What woful wight art thou, tell
   me,

---

[1] Pet, spoil.   [2] Old copy, *no.*

That here most grievously dost lament?
Confess the truth, and I will comfort thee,
By the word of God omnipotent:
Although your time ye have misspent,
Repent and amend, while ye have space,
And God will restore you to health and grace.
  DALILAH. To tell you who I am, I dare not for
      shame;
But my filthy living hath brought me in this case,
Full oft for my wantonness you did me blame;
Yet to take your counsel I had not the grace.
To be restored to health, alas, it is past;
Disease hath brought me into such decay,
Help me with your alms, while my life doth last,
That, like a wretch as I am, I may go my way.
  BARNABAS. Show me your name, sister, I you
      pray,
And I will help you now at your need;
Both body and soul will I feed.
  DALILAH. You[1] have named me already, if I
      durst be so bold:
Your[2] sister Dalilah, that wretch I am;
My wanton nice toys ye knew of old.
Alas, brother, they have brought me to this shame.
  When you went to school, my brother and I
      would play,
Swear, chide, and scold with man and woman;
To do shrewd turns our delight was alway,
Yet were we tiddled, and you beaten now and then.
  Thus our parents let us do what we would,
And you by correction they kept thee under
      awe:
When we grew big, we were sturdy and bold;
By father and mother we set not a straw,
  Small matter for me; I am past;

---

[1] Old copy, *your*.   [2] Old copy, *you*.

But your brother and mine is in great jeo-
    pardy :
In danger to come to shame at the last,
He frameth his living so wickedly.
    BARNABAS. Well, sister,[1] I ever feared ye would
    be nought,
Your lewd behaviours sore grieve[d] my heart :
To train you to goodness all means have I sought,
But in vain ; yet will I play a brotherly part.
    For the soul is more precious, most dearly bought
With the blood of Christ, dying therefore :
To save it first a mean must be sought
At God's hand by Christ, man's only Saviour.
    Consider, Dalilah, God's fatherly goodness,
Which for your good hath brought you in this case.
Scourged you with his rod of pure love doubtless,
That, once knowing yourself, ye might call for grace.
    Ye seem to repent, but I doubt whether[2]
For your sins or for the misery ye be in :
Earnestly repent for your sin rather,
For these plagues be but the reward of sin.
    But so repent that ye sin no more,
And then believe with steadfast faith,
That God will forgive you for evermore,
For Christ's sake, as the scripture saith.
    As for your body, if it be curable,
I will cause to be healed, and[3] during your life
I will clothe you and feed you, as I am able.
Come, sister, go with me, ye have need of relief.
                           [*They go out.*
    DANIEL (*the judge*). As a judge of the country,
    here am I come,
Sent by the king's majesty, justice to do :

---

[1] Old copy, *siker*, *i.e.*, certainly, securely.
[2] Old copy, *whater*.   [3] Old copy, *or*.

Chiefly to proceed in judgment of a felon :
I tarry for the verdict of the quest,[1] ere I go.
　　　　　　　[*Iniquity, Baily errand, comes in ; the
　　　　　　　　　judge sitteth down.*
Go, Baily, know whether they be all agreed, or no ;
If they be so, bid them come away,
And bring their prisoner ; I would hear what they
　　　say.
　　[BAILY]. I go, my Lord, I go, too soon for one :
He is like to play a cast will break his neck-bone.
I beseech your lor'ship be good to him :
The man is come of good kin.
If your lordship would be so good to me,
　　　　　[*He telleth him in his ear the rest may not
　　　　　　　hear.*
As for my sake to set him free,
I could have twenty pound in a purse,　　　　　　{
Yea, and your lordship a right fair horse,
Well worth ten pound—
　　DANIEL (*the judge*). Get thee away, thou hell-
　　　hound !
If ye were well examined and tried,
Perchance a false knave ye would be spied.
　　　　　[*Iniquity goeth out ; the judge speaketh still.*
Bribes (saith Salomon) blind the wise man's sight,
That he cannot see to give judgment right.
Should I be a briber ?[2] nay, he shall have the law,
As I owe to God and the king obedience and awe.
　　　　[*They bring Ismael in, bound like a prisoner.*
INIQUITY (*aside*). Ye be tied fair enough for
　　running away !

---

[1] Jury.　Compare Hazlitt's "Popular Poetry," ii. 149.

[2] Here probably the word means literally *briber ;* but
bribour also means *a thief.*　See Way's edition of the
" Promptorium," p. 50, and Halliwell in *v. Brybe* and
brybour.

If ye do not after me, ye will be hanged, I dare
    say ;
If thou tell no tales, but hold thy tongue,
I will set thee at liberty, ere it be long,
Though thou be judged to die anon.
    JUDGE (*to the jury*). Come on, sirs, I pray you,
    come on,
Be you all agreed in one ?
    QU. Yea, my lord, everychone.
                [*One of them speaketh for the quest.*
    JUDGE. Where Ismael was indicted[1] by twelve
    men
Of felony, burglary, and murder,
As the indictment declareth how, where, and when,
Ye heard it read to you lately in order :
You, with the rest, I trust all true men,
Be charged upon your oaths to give verdit directly,
Whether Ismael thereof be guilty or not guilty.
    QU. Guilty, my lord, and most guilty.
                    [*One for the rest.*
    INIQUITY. Wilt thou hang, my lord, [this] whore-
    son noddy ?
    JUDGE (*to Iniquity*). Tush, hold thy tongue, and
    I warrant thee [2]—
    JUDGE (*to Ismael*). The Lord have mercy upon
    thee !
Thou shalt go to the place thou cam'st fro
Till to-morrow, nine of the clock, there to remain :
To the place of execution then shalt thou go,
There be hanged to death, and after again,
Being dead, for ensample to be hanged in a chain.
Take him away, and see it be done,
At your peril that may fall thereupon.

---

[1] Old copy, *intided*.

[2] In the old copy, this and the following line are trans-
posed, and some of the speeches are wrongly addressed.

ISMAEL. Though I be judged to die, I require
   respite,
For the king's advantage some [1] things I can recite.
   INIQUITY. Away with him, he will speak but of
   spite—
   JUDGE. Well, we will hear you say what you
   can,
But see that ye wrongfully accuse no man.
   ISMAEL. I will belie no man, but this I may
   say,
Here standeth he that brought me to this way :
   INIQUITY. My lord, he lieth like a damned knave,
The fear of death doth make him rave—
   ISMAEL. His naughty company and play at dice
Did me first to stealing entice :
He was with me at robberies, I say it to his face ;
Yet can I say more in time and space.
   INIQUITY. Thou hast said too much, I beshrew
   thy whoreson's face.   [*Aside.*
Hang him, my lord, out of the way,
The thief careth not what he doth say.
Let me be hangman, I will teach him a sleight ;
For fear of talking, I will strangle him straight ;
Tarry here that list, for I will go—   [*He would go.*
   JUDGE. No, no, my friend, not so ;
I thought always ye should not be good,
And now it will prove, I see, by the rood.
       [*They take him in a halter ; he fighteth with*
        them.
Take him, and lay him in irons strong,
We will talk with you more, ere it be long.
   INIQUITY. He that layeth hands on me in this
   place,
Ich lay my brawling iron on his face !
By Gog's blood, I defy thy worst ;

---

[1] Old copy, *in.*

If thou shouldest hang me, I were accurst.
I have been at as low an ebb as this,
And quickly aloft again, by Gis!
I have mo friends than ye think I have;
I am entertained of all men like no slave:
Yea, within this moneth, I may say to you,
I will be your servant and your master too.
Yea, creep into your breast, will ye have it so?
    JUDGE. Away with them both, lead them away
At his death tell me what he doth say,
For then belike he will not lie.
    INIQUITY. I care not for you both, no, not a fly!
                      [*They lead them out.*
    JUDGE. If no man have here more matter to say,
I must go hence some other way.   [*He goeth out.*

Enter WORLDLY SHAME.

WORLDLY SHAME. Ha, ha! though I come in
    rudely, be not aghast,
I must work a feat in all the haste;
I have caught two birds, I will set for the dame,
If I catch her in my clutch, I will her tame.
    Of all this while know ye not my name?
I am right worshipful master Worldly Shame;
The matter that I come now about,
Is even this, I put you out of doubt—
    There is one [1] Xantippe, a curst shrew,
I think all the world doth her know,
Such a jade she is, and so curst a quean,
She would out-scold the devil's dame, I ween.
    Sirs, this fine woman had babes three,
Twain the dearest darlings that might be,
Ismael and fair Dalilah these two:
With the lout Barnabas I have nothing to do.

---

[1] Old copy, *none.*

All was good, that these tiddlings do might :
Swear, lie, steal, scold, or fight :
Cards, dice, kiss, clip, and so forth :
All this our mammy would take in good worth.
　　Now, sir, Dalilah my daughter is dead of the pox,
And my son hang'th [1] in chains, and waveth his
　　　locks.
These news will I tell her, and the matter so frame,
That she shall be thine own, master Worldly
　　　Shame !
Ha, ha, ha !—

　　XANTIPPE. Peace, peace, she cometh hereby,
I spoke no word of her, no, not I,
　　O Mistress Xantippe, I can tell you news : [2]
The fair wench, your dear daughter Dalilah,
Is dead of the pox taken at the stews ;
And thy son Ismael, that pretty boy,
Whom I dare say you loved very well,
Is hanged in chains, every [3] man can tell.
Every man saith thy daughter was a strong whore,
And thy son a strong thief and a murderer.
It must needs grieve you wonderous,
That they died so shamefully both two :
Men will taunt you and mock you, for they say now
The cause of their death was even very you.
　　XANTIPPE. I the cause of their death ?
　　　　　　　　　　　　　　　[She would sowne. [4]

WORLDLY SHAME. Will ye sowne, the devil stop
　　　thy breath ?
Thou shalt die (I trow) with more shame ;
I will get me hence out of the way,
If the whore should die, men would me blame ;
That I killed her, knaves should say.　　　　[Exit.
　　XANTIPPE. Alas, alas, and well-away !

---

[1] Old copy, *hanged.*　　　　[2] Old copy, *neder.*
[3] Old copy, *ever.*　　　　[4] Swoon.

I may curse the time that I was born,
Never woman had such fortune, I dare say;
Alas, two of my children be forlorn.
My fair daughter Dalilah is dead of the pox:
My dear son Ismael hanged up in chains.
Alas, the wind waveth his yellow locks,[1]
It slayeth my heart, and breaketh my brains.
Why should God punish and plague me so sore?
To see my children die so shamefully!
I will never eat bread in this world more,
With this knife will I slay myself by and by.
     [She would stick herself with a knife.

Enter BARNABAS.

BARNABAS. Beware what ye do; fye, mother, fye!
Will ye spill yourself for your own offence,
And seem for ever to exclude God's mercy?
God doth punish you for your negligence:
Wherefore take his correction with patience,
And thank him heartily, that of his goodness
He bringeth you in knowledge of your trespass.
For when my brother and sister were of young
 age,
You saw they were given to idleness and play,
Would apply no learning, but live in outrage.
And men complained on them every day.
Ye winked at their faults, and tiddled them alway;
By maintenance they grew to mischief and ill,
So at last God's justice did [2] them both spill.
In that God preserved me, small thank to you:
If God had not given me special grace,
To avoid evil and do good, this is true,

---

[1] See Hazlitt's "Popular Poetry," iv. 239. The term
goldylocks, curiously enough, seems to have been in early
use in a contemptuous or bad sense.

[2] Old copy, *bid.*

I had lived and died in as wretched case,
As they did, for I had both suffrance and space;
But it is an old proverb, you have heard it, I think:
That God will have see, shall not wink.
　　Yet in this we may all take comfort:
They took great repentance, I heard say,
And as for my sister, I am able to report,
She lamented for her sins to her dying day:
To repent and believe I exhorted[1] her alway;
Before her death she believed, that God of his
　　　　mercy,
For Christ's sake would save her eternally.
If you do even so, ye need not despair,
For God will freely remit your sins all,
Christ hath paid the ransom, why should ye fear?
To believe this and do well, to God for grace call.
All worldly cares let pass and fall,
And thus comfort my father I pray you heartily,
　　　　　　　　　　　[*Xantippe goeth out.*
I have a little to say, I will come by and by.
　　Right gentle audience, by this interlude ye may
　　　　see,
How dangerous it is for the frailty of youth,
Without good governance, to live at liberty,
Such chances as these oft happen of truth:
Many miscarry, it is the more ruth,
By negligence of their elders and not taking pain,
In time good learning and qualities to attain.
　　Therefore exhort I all parents to be diligent
In bringing up their children aye[2] to be circumspect;
Lest they fall to evil, be not negligent;
But chastise them, before they be sore infect:
Accept their well-doing, in ill them reject.
A young plant ye may plant and bow as ye will;
Where it groweth strong, there will it abide still.

---

[1] Old copy, *exhorting.*　　　　　[2] Old copy, *yea.*

Even so by children : in their tender age
Ye may work them, like wax, to your own intent ;
But if ye suffer them long to live in outrage,
They will be sturdy and stiff, and will not relent.
O ye children, let your time be well-spent,
Apply your learning, and your elders obey ;
It will be your profit another day.
    Now, for the Queen's royal majesty let us pray,
[He kneeleth down.

That God (in whose hands is the heart of all queens),
May endue her highness with godly puissance
    alway :
That her grace may long reign and prosper in all
    things,
In God's word and justice may give light to all
    queens.
Let us pray for the honourable council and nobility,
That they may always counsel us[1] wisdom with
    tranquillity,
God save the Queen, the realm, and commonalty !
[He maketh courtesy and goeth out.

FINIS.

A SONG.

It is good to be merry
But who can be merry ?[2]
He that hath a pure conscience,
He may well be merry.[3]

---

[1] Old copy, is.   [2] Old copy, cam me mery !
This marginal note has partly been cut off by the binder : —

[3] resyng,
answer-
ing   other
t always
staff,
,   ysing to
other.

Who hath a pure conscience, tell me?
No man of himself, I ensure thee,
Then must it follow of necessity,
  That no man can be merry.

Purity itself may pureness give;
You must ask it of God in true belief:
Then will he give it, and none repreve:[1]
  And so we may be merry.

What is the practice of a conscience pure?
To love and fear God, and other allure,
And for his sake to help his neighbour:
  Then may he well be merry.

What shall we have, that can and will do this?
After this life everlasting bliss,
Yet not by desert, but by gift, i-wis:
  There God make us all merry!

FINIS.[2]

---

[1] Reprove.
[2] The colophon is: Imprinted at London, in Paules
Churche yearde at the Sygne of the Swane by John Kyng.

THE HISTORY

OF

JACOB AND ESAU.

EDITION.

A newe mery and wittie Comedie or Enterlude, newely imprinted, treating vpon the Historie of Iacob and Esau, taken out of the xxvij. Chap. of the first booke of Moses entituled Genesis. Imprinted at London by Henrie Bynneman, dwelling in Knight-rider Streate, at the signe of the Mermayde. Anno Domini. 1568. 4to.

This piece is placed earlier in the series than the mere date of publication given above would warrant, because the interlude was licensed in 1557-8, and probably published in pursuance of its registration at Stationers' Hall. The 4to of 1568 is, however, the only impression hitherto recovered, and it is of the greatest rarity. An account of this dramatic curiosity will be found in Collier's "History of English Dramatic Poetry," 1831. It is now for the first time reprinted.

THE PARTS AND NAMES OF THE PLAYERS

WHO ARE TO BE CONSIDERED TO BE HEBREWS, AND

SO SHOULD BE APPARELLED WITH ATTIRE.

1. THE PROLOGUE, *a Poet.*

2. ISAAC, *an old man, father to Jacob and Esau.*

3. REBECCA, *an old woman, wife to Isaac.*

4. ESAU, *a young man and a hunter.*

5. JACOB, *a young man of godly conversation.*

6. ZETHAR, *a neighbour.*

7. HANAN, *a neighbour to Isaac also.*

8. RAGAN, *servant unto Esau.*

9. MIDO, *a little boy, leading Isaac.*

10. DEBORAH, *the nurse of Isaac's tent.*

11. ABRA, *a little wench, servant to Rebecca.*

PROLOGUE OF THE PLAY.

In the book of Genesis it is expressed,
  That when God to Abraham made sure promise,
That in his seed all nations should be blessed :
  To send him a son by Sarah he did not miss.
  Then to Isaac (as there recorded it is)
By Rebecca his wife, who had long time been
      barren,
When pleased him, at one birth he sent sons twain.

But before Jacob and Esau yet born were,
  Or had either done good, or ill perpetrate :
As the prophet Malachi and Paul witness bear,
  Jacob was chosen, and Esau reprobate :
  Jacob I love (saith God) and Esau I hate.
For it is not (saith Paul) in man's renewing or will,
But in God's mercy, who chooseth whom he will.

But now for our coming we shall exhibit here,
  Of Jacob and Esau how the story was ;
Whereby God's adoption may plainly appear :
  And also that, whatever God's ordinance was,
  Nothing might defeat, but that it must come to
      pass.
That, if this story may your eyes or ears delight,
We pray you of patience, while we it recite.

ACTUS PRIMA.   SCÆNA PRIMA.

RAGAN, *the servant.*

ESAU, *a young man, his master.*

[*Ragan entereth with his horn at his back and his
hunting staff in his hand, and leadeth three
greyhounds, or one, as may be gotten.*

Now let me see what time it is by the starlight?
God's for his grace, man, why it is not yet mid-
    night!
We might have slept these four hours yet, I dare
    well say;
But this is our good Esau his common play:
   [*Here he counterfeiteth how his master calleth him
    up in the mornings, and of his answers.*
What the devil aileth him? now truly, I think
    plain,
He hath either some worms or botts in his brain.
He scarcely sleepeth twelve good hours in two
    weeks.
I wot well his watching maketh me have lean
    cheeks,
For there is none other life with him day by day,
But, up, Ragan! up, drowsy hogshead! I say:

Why, when? up, will it not be? up. I come anon.
Up, or I shall raise you in faith, ye drowsy
    whoreson.
Why, when? shall I fet you? I come, sir, by
    and by.
Up, with a wild wanion! how long wilt thou lie?
Up, I say, up, at once! up, up, let us go hence:
It is time we were in the forest an hour since.
Now the devil stop that same yalling throat
    (think I)
Somewhiles: for from the call [1] farewell all wink of
    eye!
Begin he once to call, I sleep no more that stound,
Though half an hour's sleep were worth ten thou-
    sand pound.
Anon, when I come in, and bid him good morrow:
Ah sir, up at last? the devil give thee sorrow!
Now the devil break thy neck (think I by and by),
That hast no wit to sleep, nor in thy bed to lie.
Then come on at once; take my quiver and my
    bow,
Fet Lovel my hound, and my horn to blow.
Then forth go we fasting an hour or two ere day,
Before we may well see either our hands or way,
And there range we the wild forest, no crumb of
    bread
From morning to stark night coming within our
    head;
Sometimes Esau's self will faint for drink and
    meat,
So that he would be glad of a dead horse to eat.
Yet of fresh the next morrow forth he will again,
And sometime not come home in a whole night or
    twain:
Nor no delight he hath, no appetite nor mind.

---

[1] From the time he calls.

But to the wild forest, to hunt the hart or hind,
The roebuck, the wild boar, the fallow-deer, or
  hare :
But how poor Ragan shall dine, he hath no care.
Poor I must eat acorns or berries from the tree.
But if I be found slack in the suit following,
Or if I do fail in blowing or hallooing ;
Or if I lack my staff or my horn by my side :
He will be quick enough to fume, chafe, and chide.
Am I not well at ease such a master to serve,
As must have such service, and yet will let me
  starve ?
But, in faith, his fashions displease mo than me,
And will have but a mad end one day, we shall see.
He passeth nothing on Rebecca his mother,
And much less passeth he on Jacob his brother.
But peace, mum, no more : I see master Esau.

> [*Here Esau appeareth in sight, and bloweth his
>   horn, ere he enter.*

ESAU. How now, are we all ready, servant
  Ragan ?
Art thou up for all day, man ? art thou ready now?
  RAGAN. I have been here this half-hour, sir,
    waiting for you,
  ESAU. And is all thing ready, as I bad, to my
    mind ?
  RAGAN. Ye have no cause, that I know, any
    fault to find :
Except that we disease our tent and neighbours
  all
With rising over early each day, when ye call.
  ESAU. Ah, thou drowsy draffsack, wouldest thou
    rise at noon ?
Nay, I trow the sixth hour with thee were over-
  soon.
  RAGAN. Nay, I speak of your neighbours, being
    men honest,

That labour all the day, and would fain be at rest :
Whom with blowing your horn ye disease all-
    abouts.

    ESAU. What care I for waking a sort of clubbish
      louts ?

    RAGAN. And I speak of Rebecca your mother,
      our dame.

    ESAU. Tut, I pass not, whether she do me praise
      or blame.

    RAGAN. And I speak of your good father, old
      Isaac.

    ESAU. Peace, foolish knave : as for my father
      Isaac,

In case he be asleep, I do him not disease,
And if he be waking, I know I do him please,
For he loveth me well from mine nativity,
          [*Here Esau bloweth his horn again.*
And never so as now for mine activity.
Therefore have at it : once more will I blow my
    horn
To give my neighbour louts an hail-peal in a morn.
          [*Here he speaketh to his dogs.*
Now, my master Lightfoot, how say you to this
    gear,
Will you do your duty to red or fallow deer ?
And, Swan, mine own good cur, I do think in my
    mind
The game shall run apace, if thou come far behind :
And ha, Takepart, come, Takepart, here : how say
    you, child,
Wilt not thou do thy part ? yes, else I am beguil'd.
But I shrew your cheeks, they have had too much
    meat.

    RAGAN. I blame not dogs to take it, if they may
      it get :
But as for my part, they could have, pardè,
A small remnant of that that ye give me.

They may run light enough for ought of me they
    got,
I had not a good meal's-meat this week, that I wot.
    ESAU. If we have luck this day to kill hare,
    teg,[1] or doe,
Thou shalt eat thy bellyful, till thou criest ho.
    RAGAN. I thank you, when I have it, Master
    Esau.
    ESAU. Well, come on, let us go now, servant
    Ragan.
Is there anything more, that I should say or do?
For perhaps we come not again this day or two.
    RAGAN. I know nothing, master, to God I make
    a vow,
Except you would take your brother Jacob with
    you :
I never yet saw him with you an hunting go,
Shall we prove him once, whether he will go or no?
    ESAU. No, no, that were in vain, alas, good
    simple mome :
Nay, he must tarry and suck mother's dug at home :
Jacob must keep home, I trow, under mother's
    wing ;
To be from the tents he loveth not of all thing.
Jacob loveth no hunting in the wild forest :
And would fear, if he should there see any wild
    beast.
Yea, to see the game run, Jacob would be in fear.
    RAGAN. In good sooth, I ween he would think
    each hare a bear.
    ESAU. What, brother mine, what a word call ye
    that?
    RAGAN. Sir, I am scarce waked : I spake, ere I
    wist what.

---

[1] A young deer. "Tegge or pricket, saillant"—Pals-
grave's *Eclaircissement*, 1530 (edit. 1852, p. 279).

ESAU. Come on your ways, my child, take the
    law of the game.
I will wake you, I trow, and set your tongue in
    frame.
    RAGAN. O, what have you done, Master Esau,
      God's apes?
    ESAU. Why can ye not yet refrain from letting
      such scapes?
Come on, ye must have three jerts[1] for the nonce.
One—   *[Beats him.*
    RAGAN. O, for God's love, sir, have done, dis-
      patch at once.
    ESAU. Nay there is no remedy but bide it—
      there is twain.   *[Gives him another jerk.*
    RAGAN. O, ye rent my cheverel; let me be past
      my pain.
    ESAU. Take heed of hunting terms fro hence-
      forth!—there is three.   *[Jerks him again.*
    RAGAN. Whoop! now a mischief on all moping
      fools for me!
Jacob shall keep the tents ten year for Ragan,
Ere I move again that he hunt with Esau.
    ESAU. Come on, now let us go. God send us
      game and luck,
And if my hand serve me well—
    RAGAN (*aside*).   Ye will kill a duck.
                         [Exeant ambo.

ACTUS PRIMI, SCÆNA SECUNDA.

HANAN, ZETHAR, *two of Isaac's neighbours.*

    HANAN. Ah, sir, I see I am an early man this
      morn,
I am once more beguil'd with Esau his horn.

---

[1] Jerks with the whip.

But there is no such stirrer as Esau is :
He is up day by day, before the crow piss :
Then maketh he with his horn such toohing and
    blowing,
And with his wide throat such shouting and
    hallooing,
That no neighbour shall in his tent take any rest,
From Esau addresseth him to the forest.
So that he maketh us, whether we will or no,
Better husbands than we would be, abroad to go
Each of us about our business and our wark.
But whom do I see yonder coming in the dark ?
It is my neighbour Zethar, I perceive him now.
    ZETHAR. What, neighbour Hanan, well met,
        good morrow to you.
I see well now I am not beguiled alone :
But what boot to lie still ? for rest we can take
        none ;
That I marvel much of old father Isaac,
Being so godly a man, why he is so slack
To bring his son Esau to a better stay.
    HANAN. What should he do in the matter, I you
        pray ?
    ZETHAR. O, it is no small charge to fathers, afore
        God,
So to train their children in youth under the rod
That, when they come to age, they may virtue
        ensue,
Wicked pranks abhor, and all lewdness eschew,
And me-thinketh Isaac, being a man as he is—
A chosen man of God, should not be slack in this.
    HANAN. Alack, good man, what should he do
        more than he hath done ?
I dare say no father hath better taught his son,
Nor no two have given better example of life
Unto their children than both he and his wife :
As by their younger son Jacob it doth appear.

He livéth no loose life : he doth God love and fear.
He keepeth here in the tents, like a quiet man :
He giveth not himself to wildness any when.
But Esau evermore from his young childhood
Hath been like to prove ill, and never to be good.
Young it pricketh (folks do say), that will be a
    thorn,
Esau hath been naught, ever since he was born.
And whereof cometh this? of education?
Nay, it is of his own ill inclination.
They were brought up both under one tuition ;
But they be not both of one disposition.
Esau is given to loose and lewd living.
    ZETHAR. In faith, I warrant him [to] have but
        shrewd thriving.
    HANAN. Neither see I any hope, that he will
        amend.
    ZETHAR. Then let him even look to come to an
        ill end.
For youth that will follow none but their own
    bridle,
That leadeth a dissolute life and an idle :
Youth, that refuseth wholesome documents,
Or to take example of their godly parents :
Youth, that is retchless, and taketh no regard,
What become of themself, nor which end go for-
    ward :
It is great marvel and a special grace,
If ever they come to goodness all their life space.
But why do we consume this whole morning in
    talk
Of one that hath no reck ne care, what way he
    walk,
We had been as good to have kept our bed still.
    HANAN. O, it is our part to lament them that do
        ill.
Like as very nature a godly heart doth move

Others' good proceedings to tender and to love :
So such as in no wise to goodness will be brought,
What good man but will mourn, since God us all
    hath wrought,
But ye have some business, and so have I.
    ZETHAR. And we have been long ; farewell,
    neighbour, heartily.

ACTUS PRIMI, SCÆNA TERTIA.

REBECCA, *the mother.*   JACOB, *the son.*

REBECCA. Come forth, son Jacob, why tarriest
    thou behind ?
JACOB. Forsooth, mother, I thought ye had said
    all your mind.
REBECCA. Nay, come, I have yet a word or two
    more to say.
JACOB. Whatsoever pleaseth you, speak to me
    ye may.
REBECCA. Seeing thy brother Esau is such an
    one,
Why rebukest thou him not, when ye are alone ?
Why dost thou not give him some good sad wise
    counsel ?
    JACOB. He lacketh not that, mother, if it would
    avail.
But when I do him any thing of his fault[s] tell,
He calleth me foolish proud boy, with him to mell.
He will sometime demand, by what authority
I presume to teach them which mine elders be ?
He will sometime ask, if I learn of my mother
To take on me teaching of mine elder brother ?
Sometime, when I tell him of his lewd behaviour,
He will lend me a mock or twain for my labour :
And sometime for anger he will out with his purse,

And call me, as please him, and swear he will do
    worse.
  REBECCA. O Lord, that to bear such a son it was
    my chance.
  JACOB. Mother, we must be content with God's
    ordinance.
  REBECCA. Or, if I should need have Esau to my
    son,
Would God thou, Jacob, haddest the eldership
    won.
  JACOB. Mother, it is too late to wish; for that
    is pass'd;
It will not be done now, wish ye never so fast.
And I would not have you to wish against God's
    will:
For both it is in vain, and also it is ill.
  REBECCA. Why did it not please God, that thou
    shouldest as well
Tread upon his crown, as hold him fast by the
    heel?
  JACOB. Whatsoever mystery the Lord therein
    meant,
Must be referred to his unsearched judgment.
And whatsoever he hath 'ppointed me unto,
I am his own vessel, his will with me to do.
  REBECCA. Well, some strange thing therein of
    God intended was.
  JACOB. And what he hath decreed, must sure
    come to pass.
  REBECCA. I remember, when I had you both
    conceived,
A voice thus saying from the Lord I received:
Rebecca, in thy womb are now two nations
Of unlike natures and contrary fashions.
The one shall be a mightier people elect:
And the elder to the younger shall be subject.
I know this voice came not to me of nothing:

Therefore thou shalt follow my counsel in one thing.

JACOB. So it be not displeasing to the Lord, I
    must.

REBECCA. I fear the Lorde eke, who is merciful
    and just :
And loth would I be his majesty to offend ;
But by me (I doubt not) to work he doth intend.
Assay, if thou canst at some one time or other,
To buy the right of eldership from thy brother :
Do thou buy the birthright, that to him doth
    belong,
So may'st thou have the blessing, and do him no
    wrong.
What thou hast once bought, is thine own of due
    right.

JACOB. Mother Rebecca, if withouten fraud I
    might,
I would your advice put in ure with all my heart,
But I may not attempt any such guileful part.
To buy my brother's eldership and his birth-
    right,
I fear, would be a great offence in God's sight.
Which thing, if I wist to redeem, I ne would,
Though I might get thereby ten millions of gold.

REBECCA. God who, by his word and almightiful
    decree,
Hath appointed thee Esau his lord to be,
Hath appointed some way to have it brought about ;
And that is this way, my sprite doth not doubt.

JACOB. Upon your word, mother, I will assay
    ere long ;
Yet it grudgeth my heart to do my brother wrong.

REBECCA. Thou shalt do no wrong, son Jacob,
    on my peril.

JACOB. Then, by God's leave, once assay I will.

REBECCA. Then farewell, dear son, God's bless-
    ing and mine with thee.

JACOB. I will again to the tent.   Well you be !
[*Exeat Jacob.*

REBECCA. Ah, my sweet son Jacob, good for-
tune God thee send !
The most gentle young man alive, as God me
mend !
And the most natural to father and mother :
O, that such a meek spirit were in thy brother ;
Or thy sire loved thee, as thou hast merited,
And then should Esau soon be disinherited.

ACTUS PRIMI, SCÆNA QUARTA.

ISAAC, *the husband.*   REBECCA, *the wife.*   MIDO,
the lad that leadeth blind Isaac.

ISAAC. Where art thou, my boy Mido, when I
do thee lack ?
MIDO. Who calleth Mido ? here, good master
Isaac.
ISAAC. Come, lead me forth of doors a little, I
thee pray.
MIDO. Lay your hand on my shoulder, and
come on this way.
REBECCA. Now, O Lord of heaven, the fountain
of all grace,
If it be thy good will, that my will shall take
place :
Send success to Jacob, according to thy word,
That his elder brother may serve him as his lord.
MIDO. Sir, whither would ye go, now that
abroad ye be ?
ISAAC. To wife Rebecca.
MIDO.   Yonder I do her see.
REBECCA. Lord, thou knowest Jacob to be thy
servant true,
And Esau all froward thy ways to ensue.

MIDO. Yonder she is speaking, whatever she
    doth say :
By holding up her hands, it seemeth she doth
    pray.
ISAAC. Where be ye, wife Rebecca ? where be
    ye, woman ?
REBECCA. Who is that calleth ? Isaac, my good
    man ?
ISAAC. Where be ye, wife Rebecca, let me
    understand ?
MIDO. She cometh to you apace.
REBECCA.   Here, my lord, at hand.
ISAAC. Saving that whatsoever God doth is all
    right,
No small grief it were for a man to lack his sight.
But what the Lord doth send or work by his high
    will—
REBECCA. Cannot but be the best, no such thing
    can be ill.
ISAAC. All bodily punishment or infirmity,
With all maims of nature, whatever they be,
Yea, and all other afflictions temporal :
As loss, persecution, or troubles mortal,
Are nothing but a trial or probation.
And what is he that firmly trusteth in the Lord,
Or steadfastly believeth his promise and word,
And knoweth him to be the God omnipotent,
That feedeth and governeth all that he hath sent :
Protecting his faithful in every degree,
And them to relieve in all their necessity ?
What creature (I say) that doth this understand,
Will not take all thing in good heart at God's
    hand ?
Shall we at God's hand receive prosperity,
And not be content likewise with adversity ?
We ought to be thankful whatever God doth send,
And ourselves wholly to his will to commend.

REBECCA. So should it be, and I thank my lord
    Isaac,
Such daily lessons at your hand I do not lack.
    ISAAC. Why, then, should not I thank the Lord,
    if it please him,
That I shall now be blind, and my sight wax all dim.
For whoso to old age will here live and endure,
Must of force abide all such defaults of nature.
    MIDO. Why, must I be blind too, if I be an old
    man ?
How shall I grope the way, or who shall lead me
    then ?
    ISAAC. If the Lord have appointed thee such old
    days to see,
He will also provide that shall be meet for thee.
    MIDO. I trow, if I were blind, I could go well,
    enou',
I could grope the way thus, and go as I do now.
I have done so ere now both by day and by night,
As I see you grope the way, and have hit it right.
    REBECCA. Yea, sir boy, will ye play any such
    childish knack
As to counterfeit your blind master Isaac ?
That is but to mock him for his impediment.
    MIDO. Nay, I never did it in any such intent.
    REBECCA. Nay, it is to tempt God, before thou
    have need,
Whereby thou may'st provoke him, in very deed,
With some great misfortune or plague to punish
    thee.
    MIDO. Then will I never more do so, while I
    may see :
But against I be blind, I will be so perfit
That, though no man lead me, I will go at mid-
    night.
    ISAAC. Now, wife, touching the purpose that I
    sought for you.

REBECCA. What say'th my lord Isaac to his
    handmaid now?
ISAAC. Ye have oft in covert words been right
    earnest
To have me grant unto you a boon and request:
But ye never told me yet plainly what it was;
Therefore I have ever yet let the matter pass.
And now of late, by oft being from me absent,
I have half suspected you to be scarce content.
But, wife Rebecca, I would not have you to mourn,
As though I did your honest petition scorn.[1]
For I never meant to deny in all my life
Any lawful or honest request to my wife.
But in case it be a thing unreasonable,
Then must I needs be to you untractable.
Now therefore say on, and tell me what is your
    case.
    REBECCA. I would, if I were sure in your heart
    to find grace;
Else, sir, I would be loth.
    ISAAC.   To speak do not refrain,
And if it be reasonable, ye shall obtain:
Otherwise, ye must pardon me, gentle sweet wife.
    REBECCA. Sir, ye know your son Esau, and see
    his life,
How loose it is, and how stiff he is and stubborn,
How retchlessly he doth himself misgovern:
He giveth himself to hunting out of reason,
And serveth the Lord and us at no time or season.
These conditions cannot be acceptable
In the sight of God, nor to men allowable.
Now his brother Jacob, your younger son and mine,
Doth more apply his heart to seek the ways divine.
He liveth here quietly at home in the tent,
There is no man nor child but is with him content.

---

[1] Old copy, *wourne.*

ISAAC. O wife, I perceive ye speak of affection ;
To Jacob ye bear love, and to his brother none.
  REBECCA. Indeed, sir, I cannot love Esau so
    well
As I do Jacob, the plain truth to you to tell.
For I have no comfort of Esau, God wot :
I scarce know whe'r I have a son of him or not.
He goeth abroad so early before daylight,
And returneth home again so late in the night ;
And unneth I set eye on him in the whole week :
No, sometime not in twain, though I do for him
    seek.
And all the neighbours see him as seldom as I ;
But when they would take rest, they hear him
    blow and cry.
Some see him so seldom, they ask if he be sick :
Sometimes some demand, whether he be dead or
    quick.
But, to make short tale, such his conditions be,
That I wish of God he had ne'er been born of me.
  ISAAC. Well, wife, I love Esau, and must for
    causes twain.
  REBECCA. Surely your love is bestowed on him
    in vain ?
  ISAAC. First, active he is, as any young man can
    be,
And many a good morsel he bringeth home to me.
Then he is mine eldest and first-begotten son.
  REBECCA. If God were so pleased, I would that
    were foredone.   [Aside.
  ISAAC. And the eldest son is called the father's
    might.
  REBECCA. If yours rest in Esau, God give us
    good night !
  ISAAC. A prerogative he hath in every thing.
  REBECCA. More pity he should have it without
    deserving.

ISAAC. Of all the goods his portion is greater.

REBECCA. That the worthy should have it, I think much better.

ISAAC. Among his brethren he hath the pre-eminence.

REBECCA. Where Esau is chief, there is a gay presence !

ISAAC. Over his brethren he is sovereign and lord.

REBECCA. Such dignity in Esau doth ill accord.

ISAAC. He is the head of the father's succession.

REBECCA. I would Esau had lost that possession.

ISAAC. And he hath the chief title of inheritance.

REBECCA. Wisdom would in Esau change that ordinance.

ISAAC. To the eldest son is due the father's blessing.

REBECCA. That should be Jacob's, if I might have my wishing.   [Aside.

ISAAC. And the chief endowment of the father's substance.

REBECCA. Which will thrive well in Esau his governance.

ISAAC. By title of eldership he hath his birthright.

REBECCA. And that would I remove to Jacob, if I might.   [Aside.

ISAAC. He must have double portion to another.

REBECCA. That were more fit for Jacob his younger brother.

ISAAC. In all manner of things divided by a rate.

REBECCA. Well given goods to him, that the Lord doth hate !

ISAAC. Why say ye so of Esau, mine eldest son ?

REBECCA. I say true, if he proceed, as he hath
  begun.
ISAAC. Is he not your son too, as well as he is
  mine?
Wherefore do ye then against him thus sore re-
  pine?
REBECCA. Because that in my spirit verily I
  know,
God will set up Jacob, and Esau down throw.
I have showed you many a time ere this day,
What the Lord of them being in my womb did say.
I use not for to lie, and I believe certain,
That the Lord spake not these words to me in vain.
And Jacob it is (I know), in whom the Lord will
His promises to you made and to your seed fulfil.
  ISAAC. I doubt not his promise made to me and
  my seed,
Leaving to his conveyance how it shall proceed.
The Lord after his way may change th'inheritance;
But I may not wittingly break our ordinance.
  REBECCA. Now would God I could persuade my
  lord Isaac
Jacob to prefer, and Esau to put back.
  ISAAC. I may not do it, wife, I pray you be con-
  tent :
The title of birthright, that cometh by descent,
Or the place of eldership coming by due course,
I may not change nor shift for better nor for worse.
Nature's law it is, the eldest son to knowledge,
And in no wise to bar him of his heritage :
And ye shall of Esau one day have comfort.
  REBECCA. Set a good long day then, or else we
  shall come short.
  ISAAC. I warrant you, he will do well enough at
  length.
  REBECCA. You must needs commend him, being
  your might and strength.

ISAAC. Well, now go we hence ; little Mido,
    where art thou ?
MIDO. I have stood here all this while, list'ning,
    how you
And my dame Rebecca have been laying the law ;
But she hath as quick answers as ever I saw.
Ye could not speak anything unto her so thick,
But she had her answer as ready and as quick.
    ISAAC. Yea, women's answers are but few times
    to seek.
    MIDO. But I did not see Esau neither all this
    same week.
Nor do I love your son Esau so well,
As I do love your son Jacob by a great deal.
    ISAAC. No, doest thou, Mido ? and tell me the
    cause why.
    MIDO. Why ? for I do not : And none other
    cause know I.
But everybody, as well one as other,
Do wish that Jacob had been the elder brother.
    ISAAC. Well, come on, let us go.
    MIDO. And who shall lead you ? I ?
    REBECCA. No, it is my office as long as I am by.
And I would all wives, as the world this day is,
Would unto their husbands likewise do their office.
    MIDO. Why, dame Rebecca, then all wedded
    men should be blind.
    REBECCA. What, thou foolish lad, no such thing
    was in my mind.

ACTUS SECUNDI, SCÆNA PRIMA.

RAGAN, *the servant of Esau.*

RAGAN. I have heard it oft, but now I feel a
    wonder,
In what grievous pain they die, that die for hunger.

O my greedy stomach, how it doth bite and gnaw?
If I were at a rack, I could eat hay or straw.
Mine empty guts do fret, my maw doth even tear,
Would God I had a piece of some horsebread here.
Yet is master Esau in worse case than I.
If he have not some meat, the sooner he will die :
He hath sunk for faintness twice or thrice by the
     way,
And not one seely bit we got since yesterday.
All that ever he hath, he would have given to-day
To have had but three morsels his hunger to allay.
Or in the field to have met with some hogs ;
I could scarcely keep him from eating of these dogs.
He hath sent me afore some meat for to provide,
And cometh creeping after, scarce able to stride.
But if I know where to get of any man,
For to ease mine own self, as hungry as I am,
I pray God I stink; but if any come to me,
Die who die will ; for sure I will first served be.
I will see, if any be ready here at home,
Or whether Jacob have any, that peakish mome.
But first I must put all my dogs up,
And lay up this gear, and then God send us the
     cup.

ACTUS SECUNDI, SCÆNA SECUNDA.

ESAU, *the master*.   RAGAN, *the servant*.

[*Esau cometh in so faint, that he can scarce go.*

ESAU. O, what a grievous pain is hunger to a
     man ?
Take all that I have for meat, help who that can.
O Lord, some good body, for God's sake, give me
     meat.
I force not what it were, so that I had to eat.

Meat or drink, save my life—or bread, I reck not
    what :
If there be nothing else, some man give me a cat.
If any good body on me will do so much cost,
I will tear and eat her raw, she shall ne'er be rost;
I promise of honesty I will eat her raw.
And what a noddy was I, and a whoreson daw,
To let Ragan go with all my dogs at once :
A shoulder of a dog were now meat for the nonce.
O, what shall I do? my teeth I can scarcely charm
From gnawing away the brawn of my very arm.
I can no longer stand for faint, I must needs lie.
And except meat come soon, remediless I die.
And where art thou, Ragan, whom I sent before?
Unless thou come at once, I never see thee more.
Where art thou, Ragan; I hear not of thee yet?
    RAGAN. Here, as fast as I can, but no meat can
      I get.
Not one draught of drink, not one poor morsel of
    bread.
Not one bit or crumb, though I should straight-
    way be dead.
Therefore ye may now see, how much ye are to
    blame,
That will thus starve yourself for following your
    game.
    ESAU. Ah, thou villain, tellest thou me this now?
If [I] had thee, I would eat thee, to God I vow.
Ah, meat, thou whoreson, why hast thou not
    brought me meat?
    RAGAN. Would you have me bring you that, I
    can nowhere get?
    ESAU. Come hither, let me tell thee a word in
    thine ear.
    RAGAN. Nay, speak out aloud : I will not come
    a foot near.
Fall ye to snatching at folks? adieu, I am gone.

Esau. Nay, for God's love, Ragan, leave me not
    alone :
I will not eat thee, Ragan, so God me help.
    Ragan. No, I shall desire you to choose some
    other whelp.
Being in your best lust, I would topple with ye,
And pluck a good crow, ere ye brake your fast
    with me.
What? are you mankin[1] now? I reckon it best, I,
To bind your hands behind you, even as ye lie.
    Esau. Nay, have mercy on me, and let me not
    perish.
    Ragan. In faith, nought could I get, wherewith
    you to cherish.
    Esau. Was there nothing to be had among so
    many?
    Ragan. I could not find one but Jacob that had
    any,
And no grant would he make for ought that I
    could say,
Yet no man alive with fairer words could him pray.
But the best red pottage he hath, that ever was.
    Esau. Go, pray him, I may speak with him once,
    ere I pass.
    Ragan. That message, by God's grace, shall not
    long be undone.
    Esau. Hie thee, go apace, and return again soon.
If Jacob have due brotherly compassion,
He will not see me faint after this fashion ;
But I daresay, the wretch had rather see me throst,
Than he would find in his heart to do so much cost.
For where is, between one fremman[2] and another,
Less love found than now between brother and
    brother?

---

[1] *i.e.*, Mankind, masculine, furious.
[2] Stranger. A more usual form is *fremed*.

Will Jacob come forth to shew comfort unto me ?
The whoreson hypocrite will as soon hanged be.
Yet, peace, methinketh Jacob is coming indeed :
And my mind giveth me at his hand I shall speed,
For he is as gentle and loving as can be,
As full of compassion and pity.
But let me see, doth he come ? no, I warrant you.
He come, quod I ? tush, he come ? then hang
    Esau !
For there is not this day in all the world round
Such another hodypeak wretch to be found,
And Ragan my man, is not that a fine knave ?
Have any mo masters such a man as I have ?
So idle, so loit'ring, so trifling, so toying ?
So prattling, so trattling, so chiding, so boying ?
So jesting, so wresting, so mocking, so mowing ?
So nipping, so tripping, so cocking, so crowing ?
So knappish, so snappish, so elvish, so froward ?
So crabbed, so wrabbed, so stiff, so untoward ?
In play or in pastime so jocund, so merry ?
In work or in labour so dead or so weary ?
O, that I had his ear between my teeth now,
I should shake him, even as a dog that lulleth a
    sow.
But in faith, if ever I recover myself,
There was never none trounced, as I shall trounce
    that elf.
He and Jacob are agreed, I daresay, I,
Not to come at all, but to suffer me here to die.
Which if they do, they shall find this same word
    true
That, after I am dead, my soul shall them pursue.
I will be avenged on all foes, till I die :
Yea, and take vengeance, when I am dead too, I.
For, I mistrust, against me agreed they have :
For thone is but a fool, and thother a stark knave.

Enter RAGAN *and* JACOB *behind, conversing.*

RAGAN. I assure you, Jacob, the man is very
    weak.
ESAU. But hark once again, methink I hear
    them speak!
RAGAN. I promise you, I fear his life be already
    pass'd.
JACOB. May God forbid!
ESAU. Lo, now they come at last.
RAGAN. If ye believe not me, see yourself, where
    he is.
JACOB. Fie, brother Esau, what a folly is this?
About vain pastime to wander abroad and peak,
Till with hunger you make yourself thus faint and
    weak.
ESAU. Brother Jacob, I pray you chide now no
    longer,
But give me somewhat, wherewith to slake mine
    hunger.
JACOB. Alack, brother, I have in my little cot-
    tage
Nothing but a mess of gross and homely pottage.
ESAU. Refresh me therewithall, and boldly ask
    of me
The best thing that I have, whatsoever it be.
I were a very beast, when thou my life dost save,
If I should stick with thee for the best thing I
    have.
JACOB. Can ye be content to sell your birthright
    to me?
ESAU. Hold, here is my hand, I do sell it here
    to thee.
With all the profits thereof henceforth to be thine,
As free, as full, as large, as ever it was mine.
JACOB. Then swear thou hand in hand before
    the living Lord

This bargain to fulfil, and to stand by thy word.
   ESAU. Before the Lord I swear, to whom each
      heart is known,
That my birthright that was from henceforth is
      thine own.
   JACOB. Thou shalt also with me by this promise
      indent,
With this bargain and sale to hold thyself content.
   ESAU. If each penny thereof might be worth
      twenty pound,
I willingly to thee surrender it this stound.
And if each cicle might be worth a whole talent,
I promise with this sale to hold me content.
   JACOB. Come, let us set him on foot, that he
      may go sup.
   RAGAN. Nay, first I will know a thing, ere I
      help him up,
Sirrah, will ye eat folk, when ye are long fasting?
   ESAU. No, I pray thee help me up, and leave thy
      jesting.
   RAGAN. No, trow, eat your brother Jacob now,
      if you lust;
For you shall not eat me, I tell you, that is just.
   JACOB. Come, that with my pottage thou may'st
      refreshed be.
   ESAU. There is no meat on earth, that so well
      liketh me.
   RAGAN. Yet I may tell you, it is pottage dearly
      bought.
   ESAU. No, not a whit, for my bargain take thou
      no thought.
I defy that birthright that should be of more price
Than helping of one's self: I am not so unwise.
   RAGAN. And how then, sir, shall poor Ragan
      have no meat?
   ESAU. Yes, and if thou canst my brother Jacob
      intreat.

JACOB. God grant I have enough for Esau alone.
RAGAN. Why then I perceive poor Ragan shall
    have none.

> *[Esau, entering into Jacob's tent, shaketh*
> *Ragan off.*

Well, much good do it you with your pottage of
    rice :
I would fast and fare ill, ere I ate of that price.
Would I sell my birthright, being an eldest son ?
Forsooth then were it a fair thread that I had
    spun.
And then to let it go for a mess of pottage !
What is that but both unthriftiness and dotage ?
Alack, alack, good blessed father Isaac,
That ever son of thine should play such a lewd
    knack !
And yet I do not think but God this thing hath
    wrought,
For Jacob is as good, as Esau is nought.
But forth cometh Mido, as fast as he can trot :
For a cicle, whether to call me in or not ?

ACTUS SECUNDI, SCÆNA TERTIA.

MIDO, *the boy.*   RAGAN.

> *[Mido cometh in clapping his hands and*
> *laughing.*

Ha, ha, ha, ha, ha, ha,
Now who saw e'er such another as Esau ?
By my truth, I will not lie to thee, Ragan,
Since I was born, I never see any man
So greedily eat rice out of a pot or pan.
He would not have a dish, but take the pot and
    sup.

Ye never saw hungry dog so stab[1] potage up.

RAGAN. Why, how did he sup it? I pray thee,
tell me, how?

MIDO. Marry, even thus, as thou shalt see me
do now.

[*Here he counterfeiteth supping out of the pot.*

O, I thank you, Jacob: with all my heart, Jacob.
Gently done, Jacob: a friendly part, Jacob!
I can sup so, Jacob!
Yea, then will I sup too, Jacob.
Here is good meat, Jacob!

RAGAN. As ere was eat, Jacob!

MIDO. As e'er I saw, Jacob!

RAGAN. Esau a daw, Jacob!

MIDO. Sweet rice pottage, Jacob!

RAGAN. By Esau's dotage, Jacob.

MIDO. Jolly good cheer, Jacob!

RAGAN. But bought full dear, Jacob!

MIDO. I was hungry, Jacob.

RAGAN. I was an unthrift, Jacob.

MIDO. Ye will none now, Jacob.

RAGAN. I cannot for you, Jacob.

MIDO. I will eat all, Jacob.

RAGAN. The devil go with all, Jacob.

MIDO. Thou art a good son, Jacob.

RAGAN. And would he never have done, Jacob?

MIDO. No, but still coggl'd[2] in, like Jackdaw
that cries *ka kob!*

That to be kill'd I could not laughing forbear:
And therefore I came out, I durst not abide there.

RAGAN. Is there any pottage left for me, that
thou wot?

---

[1] The meaning seems to be obvious enough; but the word
is not to be found in our glossaries.

[2] Halliwell mentions this word; but none of his interpre-
tations suits the present context.

MIDO. No, I left Esau about to lick the pot.

RAGAN. Lick, quod thou ? now a shame take
him that can all lick.

MIDO. The pot shall need no washing, he will it
so lick ;
And by this he is sitting down to bread and drink.

RAGAN. And shall I have no part with him, dost
thou think ?

MIDO. No, for he pray'd Jacob, ere he did begin,
To shut the tent fast, that no mo guests come in.

RAGAN. And made he no mention of me his
servant ?

MIDO. He said thou were a knave, and bad thee
hence avaunt :
Go shift, where thou couldest, thou gottest nothing
there.

RAGAN. God yield you, Esau, with all my
stomach cheer ! [1]

MIDO. I must in again, lest perhaps I be shent,
For I asked noboby licence, when I went.   [*Exeat.*

RAGAN. Nay, it is his nature, do what ye can for
him,
No thank at his hand ; but choose you, sink or
swim.
Then reason it with him in a meet time and place,
And he shall be ready to flee straight in your face.
This proverb in Esau may be understand :
Claw a churl by the tail, and he will file [2] your hand.
Well i-wis, Esau, ye did know well enou',
That I had as much need to be meated as you.
Have I trotted and trudged all night and all day,
And now leave me without door, and so go your
way ?
Have I spent so much labour for you to provide,
And you nothing regard what of me may betide ?

---

[1] Old copy, *stomachere.*   [2] Defile.

Have I run with you while I was able to go,
And now you purchase food for yourself and no
    mo?
Have I taken so long pain you truly to serve,
And can ye be content, that I famish and starve?
I must lacquey and come lugging greyhound and
    hound,
And carry the weight, I dare say, of twenty pound,
And to help his hunger purchase grace and favour,
And now to be shut out fasting for my labour!
By my faith, I may say I serve a good master,
Nay, nay, I serve an ill husband and a waster.
That neither profit regardeth nor honesty,
What marvel I then, if he pass so light on me?
But, Esau, now that ye have sold your birthright,
I commend me to you, and God give you good
    night.
And let a friend tell him his fau't at any time,
Ye shall hear him chafe beyond all reason or
    rhyme.
Except it were a friend or a very hell-hound,
Ye never saw the match of him in any ground.
When I shew him of good-will, what others do say,
He will fall out with me, and offer me a fray.
And what can there be a worser condition,
Than to do ill, and refuse admonition?
Can such a one prosper, or come to a good end?
Then I care not how many children God me send.
Once Esau shall not beguile me, I can tell:
Except he shall fortune to amend, or do well.
Therefore why do I about him waste thus much
    talk,
Whom no man can induce ordinately to walk?
But some man perchance doth not a little wonder,
How I, who but right now did roar out for hunger,
Have now so much vacant and void time of leisure,
To walk and to talk, and discourse all of pleasure.

I told you at the first, I would provide for one :
My mother taught me that lesson a good while
     agone.
When I came to Jacob, his friendship to require,
I drew near and near till I came to the fire :
There hard beside me stood the pottage-pot,
Even as God would have it, neither cold nor hot ;
Good simple Jacob could not turn his back so thick,
But I at the ladle got a gulp or a lick ;
So that, ere I went, I made a very good meal,
And din'd better cheap than Esau a good deal.
But here cometh now master Esau forth.

ACTUS SECUNDI, SCÆNA QUARTA.

ESAU and RAGAN.

Ah, sir, when one is hungry, good meat is much
     worth.
And well fare a good brother yet in time of need,
          [*Esau cometh forth, wiping his mouth.*
The world is now meetly well amended indeed,
  ESAU. By my truth, if I had bidden[1] from meat
     any longer,
I think my very maw would have fret asunder.
Then had I been dead and gone, I make God a
     vow.
  RAGAN. Surely then the world had had a great
     loss of you ;
For where should we have had your fellow in your
     place ?   [*Aside.*
  ESAU. What should I have done with my birth-
     right in this case ?
  RAGAN. Kept it still, and you had not been a
     very ass.   [*Aside.*

-----

¹ Abided.

ESAU. But the best pottage it was yet, that ever
    was.
It were sin not to sell one's soul for such gear.
    RAGAN. Ye have done no less in my conscience,
    I fear.   *[Aside.*
    ESAU. Who is this that standeth clattering at
    my back?
    RAGAN. A poor man of yours, sir, that doth his
    dinner lack.
    ESAU. Dinner, whoreson knave? dinner at this
    time a' day?
Nothing with thee but dinner and munching alway.
Why, thy whoreson villain slave, who is hungry
    now?
    RAGAN. Indeed, sir (as seemeth by your words)
    not you.
    ESAU. A man were better fill the bellies of some
    twelfe,
Than to fill the gut of one such whoreson elf;
That doth none other good but eat, and drink, and
    sleep.
    RAGAN. He shall do something else, whom ye
    shall have to keep.   *[Aside.*
    ESAU. And that maketh thee so slothful and so
    lither,
I dare say he was six hours coming hither,
When I sent him to make provision afore,
Not passing a mile hence or very little more.
And yet being so far pass'd the hour of dining,
See, and the knave be not for his dinner whining!
Fast a while, fast with a mischief, greedy slave,
Must I provide meat for every glutton knave?
    RAGAN. I may fast, for any meat that of you I
    have.   *[Aside.*
    ESAU. Or deserve thy dinner, before thou do't
    crave.
    RAGAN. If I have not deserved it at this season,

I shall never deserve it in mine own reason.
Ye promised I should eat, till I cried ho.
   ESAU. Yea, that was, if we took either hare,
    teg, or doe.
   RAGAN. But when yourself were hungry, ye said,
    I wot what ——
   ESAU. What, thou villain slave, tellest thou me
    now of that?
   RAGAN. Then, help, run apace, Ragan, my good
    servant.
   ESAU. Yea then was then, now is it otherwise:
    avaunt!
Have I nothing to do but provide meat for you?
   RAGAN. Ye might have given me some part,
    when ye had enough.
   ESAU. What, of the red rice pottage with Jacob
    I had?
Why, the crow would not give it her bird—thou
    art mad,
Is that meat for you? nay, it would make you too
    rank.
Nay, soft, brother mine, I must keep you more
    lank.
It hath made me ever[1] since so lusty and[2] fresh,
As though I had eaten all delicates of flesh.
I feel no manner faintness whereof to complain.
   RAGAN. Yet to-morrow ye must be as hungry
    again,
Then must ye and will ye wish again for good
    cheer:
And repent you, that ever ye bought this so
    dear.
   ESAU. Repent me? wherefore? then the Lord
    give me sorrow;
If it were to do, I would do it to-morrow.

---

[1] Old copy, *even*.   [2] Old copy, *as*.

For, thou foolish knave, what hath Jacob of me
    bought?
    RAGAN. But a matter of a straw and a thing of
    nought !
    ESAU. My birthright and whole title of mine
    eldership,
Marry, sir, I pray God much good do it his
    maship,
If I die to-morrow, what good would it do me?
If he die to-morrow, what benefit hath he?
And for a thing hanging on such casuality,
Better a mess of pottage than nothing, pardy !
If my father live long, when should I it enjoy?
If my father die soon, then it is but a toy.
For if the time were come, thinkest thou that
    Jacob
Should find Esau such a lout or such a lob
To suffer him to enjoy my birthright in rest ?
Nay, I will first toss him and trounce him of the
    best ;
I think to find it a matter of conscience,
And Jacob first to have a fart, sir reverence.
When my father Isaac shall the matter know,
He will not let Jacob have my birthright, I trow.
Or if he should keep it as his own, I pray you,
Might not I live without it, and do well enou' ?
Do none but men's eldest sons prosper well ?
How live younger brethren then, I beseech you,
    tell ?
Once, if anything be by the sword to be got,
This falchion and I will have part to our lot.
But now come on, go we abroad awhile and walk,
Let my birthright go, and of other matters talk.
    RAGAN. Who—I, walk? nay, I trow not, till I
    have better din'd.
It is more time to seek, where I may some meat
    find.

ESAU. What say'st thou, drawlatch? come forth,
   with a mischief!
Wilt thou not go with me? on, forward, whoreson
   thief?
Shall it be as pleaseth you, or as pleaseth me?
   RAGAN. Nay, as pleaseth you, sir, methink it
   must be.
   ESAU. And where be my dogs and my hound?
   be they all well?
   RAGAN. Better than your man, for they be in
   their kennel.
   ESAU. Then go see all be well in my part of the
   tent.
   RAGAN. With a right good will, sir, I go incontinent.
   ESAU. And I will to my field, the which I
   cleansed last,
To see what hope there is, that it will yield fruit
   fast.

ACTUS SECUNDI, SCÆNA QUARTA.

JACOB. MIDO. REBECCA. ABRA, *the handmaid.*

   JACOB. Thou knowest, little Mido, where my
   mother is.
   MIDO. I can go to her as straight as a thread,
   and not miss.
   JACOB. Go call her, and come again with her
   thine own self.
   MIDO. Yes, ye shall see me scud like a little elf.
   JACOB. Where I have, by the enticement of my
   mother,
Bargained and bought the birthright of my brother.
Turn it all to good, O Lord, if it be thy will:
Thou knowest my heart, Lord, I did it for no ill.
And whatever shall please thee to work or to do,

Thou shalt find me prest and obedient thereto.
But here is my mother Rebecca now in place.

    MIDO. How say you, master Jacob, ran not I
        apace?

    JACOB. Yes, and a good son to go quick on your
        errand.

    REBECCA. Son, how goeth the matter? let me
        understand.

    JACOB. Forsooth, mother, I did so, as ye me
        bad,
Esau to sell me all his birthright persuade.

    REBECCA. Hast thou bought it indeed, and he
        therewith content?

    JACOB. Yea, and have his promise, that he will
        never repent.

    REBECCA. Is the bargain through? hast thou
        paid him his price?

    JACOB. Yea, that I have, a mess of red pottage
        of rice,
And he ate it up every whit, well I wot.

    MIDO. When he had supp'd up all, I saw him
        lick the pot ;
Thus he licked, and thus he licked, and this way :
I thought to have lick'd the pot myself once to-day ;
But Esau beguil'd me, I shrew him for that,
And left not so much as a lick for puss our cat.

    REBECCA. Son Jacob, forasmuch as thou hast so
        well sped,
With an hymn or psalm let the Lord be praised.
Sing we all together, and give thanks to the Lord,
Whose promise and performance do so well accord.

    MIDO. Shall we sing the same hymn, that all
        our house doth sing?
For Abraham and his seed to give God praising.

    REBECCA. Yea, the very same.

    MIDO. Then must we all kneel down thus,
And Abra, our maid, here must also sing with us,

Kneel down, Abra ; what, I say, will ye not kneel
    down ?
Kneel, when I bid you, the slackest wench in this
    town !
    [*Here they kneel down to sing all four, saving that
        Abra is slackest, and Mido is quickest.*]

THE FIRST SONG.

Blessed be thou, O the God of Abraham,
    For thou art the Lord our God, and none but thou :
What thou workest to the glory of thy name,
    Passeth man's reason to search what way or how.
Thy promise it was Abraham should have seed
    More than the stars of the sky to be told ;
He believed, and had Isaac indeed,
    When both he and Sara seemed very old.
Isaac many years longed for a son,
    Rebecca, thy handmaid, long time was barren,
By prayer in thy sight such favour he won,
    That at one birth she brought him forth sons
        twain,
Wherefore, O Lord, we do confess and believe,
    That both thou canst and wilt thy promise fulfil :
But how it shall come, we can no reason give,
    Save all to be wrought according to thy will.
        Blessed be thou, O God of Abraham, &c.

REBECCA. Now, doubt not, Jacob, but God hath
    appointed thee
As the eldest son unto Isaac to be :
And now have no doubt, but thou art sure elected,
And that unthrift Esau of God is rejected.
And to sell thee his birthright since he was so
    mad,
I warrant thee the blessing that he should have had.

JACOB. Yea? how may that be wrought?
REBECCA. Yes, yes, let me alone.
Our[1] good old Isaac is blind, and cannot see,
So that by policy he may beguiled be,
I shall devise how for no ill intent ne thought,
But to bring to pass that I know God will have
    wrought,
And I charge you twain, Abra and little Mido.
    MIDO. Nay, ye should have set Mido before
    Abra, I trow,
For I am a man toward, and so is not she.
    ABRA. No, but yet I am more woman toward
    than ye.
    REBECCA. I charge you both that, whatever hath
    been spoken,
Ye do not to any living body open.
    ABRA. For my part it shall to no body uttered be.
    MIDO. And slit my tongue, if ever it come out
    for me :
But if any tell, Abra here will be prattling.
For they say, women will ever be clattering.
    ABRA. There is none here that prattleth so much
    as you.
    REBECCA. No mo words, but hence we altogether
    now.   [*Exeunt omnes.*

ACTUS TERTIJ, SCÆNA PRIMA.

ESAU. ISAAC. MIDO.

ESAU. Now, since I last saw mine old father
    Isaac,
Both I do think it long, and he will judge me slack,
But he cometh forth ; I will here listen and see,
Whether he shall chance to speak any word of me.
                    [*Steps aside.*

[1] Old copy, *once.*

ISAAC. On, lead me forth, Mido, to the bench
    on this hand,
That I may sit me down, for I cannot long stand.
    MIDO. Here, sir, this same way, and ye be at
    the bench now,
Where ye may sit down in God's name, if please
    you.
    ISAAC. I marvel, where Esau my son doth be-
    come,
That he doth now of days visit me so seldom.
But it is oft seen, whom fathers do best favour,
Of them they have least love again for their labour.
I think, since I saw him, it is a whole week.
In faith, little Mido, I would thou wouldest him
    seek.
    MIDO. Forsooth, Master Isaac, and I knew it
    where,
It should not be very long ere I would be there.
But shall I at adventure go seek where he is ?
    ESAU. Seek no farther, Mido : already here he is.
    ISAAC. Methinketh, I have Esau his voice per-
    ceived.
    ESAU. Ye guess truly, father, ye are not deceived.
    MIDO. Here he is come now invisible, by my
    soul :
For I saw him not, till he spake hard at my poll !
    ISAAC. Now, go thou in, Mido, let us two here
    alone.
    MIDO. Sir, if ye command me, full quickly I am
    gone.
    ISAAC. Yet, and if I call thee, see thou be not
    slack.
    MIDO. I come at the first call, good Master
    Isaac.
ISAAC. Son Esau.
ESAU. Here, father.
ISAAC. Is none here but we ?

ESAU. None to harken our talk, father, that I
do see.
      [*Rebecca entereth behind unseen, and listens.*
ISAAC. Son Esau, why hast thou been from me
so long ?
ESAU. I cry you mercy, father, if I have done
wrong.
But I am loth to trouble you, having nothing
To present you withal, nor venison to bring.
ISAAC. Son Esau, thou knowest that I do thee
love.
ESAU. I thank you for it, father, as doth me
behove.
ISAAC. And now thou seest my days draw towards
an end.
ESAU. That is to me great ruth, if I could it
amend.
ISAAC. I must go the way of all mortal flesh,
Therefore, while my memory and wit is yet fresh,
I would thee endow mine heritage to succeed :
And bless thee, as I ought, to multiply my seed.
The God of my father Abraham and of me
Hath promised, that our seed as the sand shall be.
He is a God of truth, and in his words just.
Therefore in my working shall be no fault, I trust.
Now, therefore, son Esau, get thee forth to hunt,
With thy bow and quiver, as erst thou hast been
wont ;
[And] bring me of thy venison that is good.
ESAU. Ye shall have of the best that runneth in
the wood.
ISAAC. When thou comest home, to dress it it
shall behove,
And to make for mine own tooth such meat as I
love.
Thus do, mine own dear son, and then I shall thee
kiss

With the kiss of peace, and thee for ever bless.
  ESAU. Your will t' accomplish, most dear father
    Isaac,
With all good haste and speed I shall not be found
  slack.
  ISAAC. Then help lead me home, in my tent that
    I were set,
And then go, when thou wilt.
  ESAU.   I shall withouten let.

ACTUS TERTIJ, SCÆNA SECUNDA.

REBECCA.

REBECCA. This talk of Isaac in secret have I
  heard,
And what end it should come to, my heart is afeard,
Ne'er had I so much ado to forbear to speak.
But the Lord, I trust, will Isaac's purpose break.
           [*Here she kneeleth down, and prayeth.*
O God of Abraham, make it of none effect :
Let Jacob have the blessing, whom thou hast elect.
I for my part shall work what may be wrought,
That it may to Jacob from Esau be brought,
And in will I go to see what I can devise,
That Isaac's intent may fail in any wise.

ACTUS TERTIJ, SCÆNA TERTIA.

RAGAN. ESAU.

RAGAN. Nay, we must on hunting go yet once
  more again,
      [*Here he cometh forth with his hunting staff
        and other things, and a bag of victuals.*
And never come home now, except we speed certain,
But I trow for hunger I have provided here :

That whatever befal, I, Ragan, shall have cheer.
I have no time to tell what delicates here be,
But (think this to be true) they're fit for better
    men than me.
And what? shall Esau hereof have any part?
Nay, I trust to convey it by such pretty art
That, till the bag be clear, he shall it never see.
I shall, and if he faint, feed him as he fed me:
I shall requite his shutting me out of the door
That, if he bid me run to get him meat afore,
I shall run as fast as my feet were made of lead,
And tell him there is none, though I may well be
    sped.
I will be even with him for my fare last day,
When he was with Jacob.
                    [*Esau enters suddenly behind him.*
ESAU.   What is it that thou dost say?
RAGAN. Sir, on your behalf I earnestly wish and
    pray
That, if like need chance, ye may fare as last day,
When ye were with Jacob.
ESAU.   Well, come on, let us go.
RAGAN. Even when ye will, is there let in me
    or no?   [*Exeunt ambo.*

ACTUS QUARTI, SCÆNA PRIMA.

REBECCA.   JACOB.

REBECCA. Son Jacob, even now is come the very
    hour
That, if thou have any grace, or heart, or power,
To play thy part well, and stick unto it through-
    out,
Esau his blessing will be thine without doubt.
    JACOB. Mother, I know your good-will to be
    unfeigned;

But I see not which way the thing may be attained.
   REBECCA. I have it contrived, how all things
     shall be done,
Do thou as I shall bid thee, and it will be won.
   JACOB. Mother, in me shall be no fault or negli-
     gence.
   REBECCA. Then harken very well unto this my
     sentence.
I heard old Isaac, in a long, solemn talk,
Bid thy brother Esau to the field to walk,
And there with his bow to kill him some venison,
Which brought and dressed, he is to have his benison.
For I am aged (said Isaac truly),
And would bless thee, dear son, before that I die.
Now is Esau gone to do it even so ;
But while he is away, I would have thee to go
Abroad unto the flock, and fetch me kids twain,
Of which I shall with a trice make such meat
     certain,
As shall say, *Come, eat me,* and shall make old Isaac
Lick his lips thereat, so toothsome shall it smack.
I shall make him thereof such as he doth love,
Which in thy brother's stead to bless thee shall him
     move.
   JACOB. O sweet and dear mother, this device is
     but vain,
For Esau is rough, and I am smooth certain.
And so, when I shall to my father bring this meat,
Perchance he will feel me, before that he will eat.
Old men be mistrustful : he shall the matter take,
That I went about my father a fool to make.
Mother, by such a prank the matter will be worse :
And I instead of blessing shall purchase me his
     curse.
   REBECCA. On me be thy curse, my son, let it
     light on me :
Only fetch thou the kids hither, as I bid thee,

Do thou thy true devoir, and let God work therein.
  JACOB. Upon your word, mother, I will the
    thing begin,
Send me little Mido to help me bear a kid.
  REBECCA. He shall come by and by, for so I
    shall him bid.
Now, Lord, and if thou please that this thing
    shall take place,
Further this our enterprise, helping with thy grace.
                                        [Exit.

ACTUS QUARTI, SCÆNA SECUNDA.

JACOB and MIDO.

  MIDO. Are ye here, master Jacob? I came you
    to look,
And here dame Rebecca hath sent you your sheep-
    crook;
And hath commanded me to wait on you this day,
But wherefore or why, she would nothing to me
    say.
  JACOB. Come on then, follow me, Mido, a little
    ways.
  MIDO. Whither ye shall lead me; I am at all
    assays.
  JACOB. And art thou able to bear a kid on thy
    back?
  MIDO. I am able, I trow, to bear a quarter-sack.
How say you to this corpse? is it not fat and round?
How say ye to these legs? come they not to the
    ground?
And be not here arms able your matter to speed?
Be not here likely shoulders to do such a deed?
Therefore come, master Jacob, if this your doubt
    be
For bringing home of kids, lay the biggest on me,

So that if we make a feast, I may have some part.
    JACOB. Yes, that shalt thou, Mido; right
      worthy thou art.

ACTUS QUARTI, SCÆNA TERTIA.

REBECCA.   ABRA.

REBECCA. I come to see, if Jacob be gone a-field
    yet ;
A little slacking may all our purpose let.
But now that he is gone, he will be here at once,
Therefore I will call my maid Abra for the nonce.
That all thing within may be in a readiness.
Abra, where be ye, Abra ?
    ABRA.   Here within, mistress.
    REBECCA. Come forth : when, Abra ? what,
      Abra, I say !
    ABRA. Anon.
    REBECCA. Must I call so oft ? why come ye not
      by and by ?
    ABRA. I was washing my vessel forsooth, mis-
      tress, I.
    REBECCA. And in very deed, look that all your
      vessels be clean.
    ABRA. There is not one foul piece in all our
      tent, I ween.
    REBECCA. Then make a great fire, and make
      ready your pot,
And see there be plenty of water, cold and hot ;
And see the spit be scoured as clean as any pearl.
    ABRA. If this be not quickly done, call me
      naughty girl.
    REBECCA. Nay, soft, whither away ? I have not
      yet all done.
    ABRA. I thought ye would have had me as quick
      to be gone,

As when ye call Abra, ye would have me to come.
  REBECCA. Then see ye have made ready cloves,
    mace, and cinnamon :
Pepper and saffron ; then fet herbs for the pot ;
  ABRA. We will have the best that by me can be
    got.
  REBECCA. And let no foul corner be about all
    the tent.
  ABRA. If ye find any fault, hardly let me be
    shent.
Is there anything else but that I may go now ?
  REBECCA. Nought but that, when I come, I find
    no fault in you.
  ABRA. No, I warrant you, I will not let my
    matters sleep.
  REBECCA. Any good wench will at her dame's
    bidding take keep.
Now, God of Abraham, as I trust in thy grace,
Send Jacob the blessing in Esau his place.
As thou hast ordained, right so must all thing be :
Perform thine own words, Lord, which thou
    spakest to me.
Now will I go in to see, that mine old husband
May of my secret working nothing understand.
Or in case he smell what we have thus far begun,
He may think it all for Esau to be done.

ACTUS QUARTI, SCÆNA QUARTA.

ABRA, *the maid.*   **DEBORAH,** *the nurse.*

  ABRA. He, that were now within, should find
    all thing, I ween,
As trim as a trencher, as trick, as sweet, as clean.
And seeing that my dame prepareth such a feast,
I will not, I trow, be found such a sluttish beast,

That there shall any filth about our tent be kept,
But that both within and without it shall be
    swept.
    [Then let her sweep with a broom, and while
        she doth it, sing this song, and when she
        hath sung, let her say thus : [1]

THE SECOND SONG.

It hath been a proverb, before I was born,
Young doth it prick, that will be a thorn.
Who will be evil, or who will be good;
Who given to truth, or who to falsehood.
Each body's youth showeth a great likelihood.
For young doth it prick, that will be a thorn.

Who so in youth will no goodness embrace,
But follow pleasure, and not virtue's trace,
Great marvel it is, if such come to grace.
For young doth it prick, that will be a thorn.

Such as in youth will refuse to be taught,
Or will be slack to work, as he ought,
When they come to age, their proof will be nought.
For young doth it prick, that will be a thorn.

If a child have been given to any vice,
Except he be guided by such as be wise,
He will thereof all his life have a spice.
For youny doth it prick, that will be a thorn.

It hath been a proverb, &c.

    ABRA. Now have I done, and, as it should be
        for the nonce,
My sweeping and my song are ended both at once.
Now but for fetting mine herbs I might go play.
Deborah, nurse Deborah, a word, I you pray.

---

[1] Referring to the speech below. In the old copy this
direction is printed in the margin, and such is, no doubt, its
most suitable position.

Enter DEBORAH.

DEBORAH. What is the matter? who calleth me
    Deborah ?
ABRA. Forsooth, gentle nurse, even I, little Abra,
I pray you, sweet Deborah, take in this same broom,
And look well to all thing, till I return home :
I must to the garden as fast as I can trot,
As I was commanded, to fet herbs for the pot.
But, in the meantime, I pray you, nurse, look
    about,
And see well to the fire, that it go not out ;
I will amble so fast, that I will soon be there,
And here again, I trow, ere an horse lick his ear.
                            [Exit.
DEBORAH. There is not a prettier girl within
    this mile,
Than this Abra will be within this little while.
As true as any steel, ye may trust her with gold.
Though it were a bushel, and not a penny told.
As quick about her work, that must be quickly
    sped
As any wench in twenty mile about her tread.
As fine a piece it is, as I know but a few,
Yet perchance her husband of her may have a
    shrew.
Cat after kind (say'th the proverb) sweet milk will
    lap ;
If the mother be a shrew, the daughter cannot
    'scape.
One sure[1] mark she hath : I marvel, if she slip :
For her nose is growing above her over lip.
But it is time, that I into the tent be gone,
Lest she come and chide me ; she will come now
    anon.

---

[1] Old copy, *once our*. Perhaps we ought to read *sour*.

ACTUS QUARTI, SCÆNA QUINTA.

ABRA.

ABRA. How say ye? have not I despatched me
    quickly?
A straw for that wench that doth not somewhat
    likely,
I have brought here good herbs, and of them plenty,
To make both broth and farcing,[1] and that full
    dainty,
I trust to make such broth that, when all things
    are in,
God Almighty self may wet his finger therein.
Here is thyme and parsley, spinach and rosemary.
Endive, succory, lacture, violet, clary,
Liverwort, marigold, sorrel, hart's-tongue, and sage:
Pennyroyal, purslane, bugloss, and borage,
With many very good herbs, mo than I do name.
But to tarry here thus long, I am much to blame.
For if Jacob should come, I not in readiness,
I must of covenant be shent of our mistress.
And I would not for twenty pound, I tell ye,
That any point of default should be found in me.
                               [Exit.

ACTUS QUARTI, SCÆNA SEXTA.

REBECCA.   MIDO.   JACOB.

REBECCA. I come to see, if Jacob do not return
    yet,
I cannot marvel enough what should be his let,
And greatly wonder he is away thus long.

---

[1] Stuffing or forcing, the same kind of thing as we now
know under the name of *forced* meat.

I fear much of his absence, lest something be wrong.
As well as heart can wish, all thing is ready here ;
And now to me each moment seemeth a whole year.
But hark, methinketh I hear a young kid blea !
It is so indeed ; I see Jacob ; well is me !
    MIDO. Hark, master Jacob, heard ye ever kid
      blea so ?
I ween she knoweth aforehand, whereto she shall go.
    JACOB. I would not my father Isaac should hear :
    MIDO. Nay, she will scarcely be still when she is
      dead, I do fear.
    JACOB. But lo, I see my mother stand before the
      tent.

Enter JACOB *and* MIDO.

REBECCA. O Lord, methinketh long, son Jacob,
    since thou went.
JACOB. And methinketh, mother, we have hied
    us well.
MIDO. I have made many feet to follow, I can
    tell.
REBECCA. Give me thy kid, my son, and now let
    me alone,
Bring thou in thine, Mido, and see thou be a stone.
    MIDO. A stone ? how should that be, mistress ?
      I am a lad,
And a boy alive, as good as e'er ye had :
And now, in bringing home this kid, I have, I trow,
Tried myself a man and a pretty fellow.
    REBECCA. I meant thou shouldest nothing say.
    MIDO. One warning is enough ; ye bad us so
      last day.
    REBECCA. Well, let me go in, and venison hereof
      make :
    JACOB. And hearest thou, Mido ? see that good
      heed thou take

In any wise to come in my father's sight.
   MIDO. Why, he seeth no better at noon than at
     midnight.
Is he not blind long since, and doth his eyes lack?
Therefore go in, dame, I bear an heavy pack.
   REBECCA. I leave you here, Jacob, and heartily
     you pray
That, when need shall require, you be not far away.
   JACOB. I shall be ready, mother, whensoe'er you
     call.   *[Exit Rebecca.*

ACTUS QUARTI, SCÆNA SEPTIMA.

JACOB. MIDO.

   JACOB. O, how happy is that same daughter or
     that son,
Whom the parents love with hearty affection!
And among all others how fortunate am I,
Whom my mother Rebecca tend'reth so greatly?
If it lay in her to do any good, ye see,
She would do her earnest devoir to prefer me.
But as for this matter, which she doth now intend,
Without thy aid, O Lord, how should it come to
     end?
Nevertheless, forasmuch as my said mother
Worketh upon thy word, O Lord, and none other,
It shall become me to show mine obedience,
And to thy promise, O Lord, to give due credence.
For what is so impossible to man's judgment,
Which thou canst not with a beck perform incon-
     tinent?
Therefore thy will, O Lord, be done for evermore.
   MIDO. O Jacob, I was never so afeard afore.
   JACOB. Why, what new thing is chanced, Mido,
I pray thee?

MIDO. Old Isaac, your father, heard your young
    kid blea.
He asked what it was : I said, a kid.
Who brought it from the fold ? I said you did.
For what purpose ? forsooth, sir, said I,
There is some matter that Jacob would remedy.
And where has thou been so long, little Mido,
    quod he,
That all this whole hour thou wert not once with
    me ?
Forsooth (quod I), when I went from you last of all,
You bad me be no more, but be ready at your
    call.
    JACOB. But of the kid's bleaing he did speak no
    more ?
    MIDO. No ; but, and if he had called me afore,
I must have told him all, or else I must have made
    a lie,
Which would not have been a good boy's part truly.
But I will to him, and no longer here remain,
Lest he should happen to call for Mido again.
                        [*Exit Mido.*

ACTUS QUARTI, SCÆNA OCTAVA.

JACOB. REBECCA. DEBORAH.

JACOB. I were best also to get me into the tent
That, if my mother need me, I may be present.
But I see her come forth, and nurse Deborah also,
And bring the gear with them, whatsoe'er it shall
    do.
    REBECCA. Where is my son Jacob? I do him
    now espy.
Come apace, Deborah, I pray thee let us hie,
That all thing were dispatched somewhat to my
    mind.

DEBORAH. It is happy, that Jacob ready here
    ye find.
JACOB. Mother, what have ye brought, and
    what things are those?
REBECCA. Gear that I have prepared to serve
    our purpose;
And because that Esau is so rough with hair,
I have brought sleeves of kid next to thy skin to
    wear.
They be made glovelike, and for each finger a
    stall :
So that thy father's feeling soon beguile they shall.
Then have I brought a collar of rough kid's hair,
Fast unto the skin round about thy neck to wear.
Come, let me do it on, and if Isaac feel,
He shall therewith be beguiled wondrous well.
       [Here she doth the sleeves upon Jacob's arms.
JACOB. And what shall this gear do, that ye
    have brought?
REBECCA. It shall serve anon, I warrant you,
    take no thought.
Now, thoroughly to ravish thy father Isaac,
Thou shalt here incontinent put upon thy back
Esau his best apparel, whose fragrant flavour
Shall conjure Isaac to bear thee his favour.
DEBORAH. Marry, sir, now is master Jacob trim
    indeed,
That is all tricksy and gallant, so God me speed :
Now I see apparel setteth out a man.
Doth it become Esau so? nay, beshrew me then.
REBECCA. Ye may now go in, nurse, and leave
    looking on him.
DEBORAH. I go ; marry, sir, Jacob is now gay
    and trim.
      [Jacob standeth looking on himself.
JACOB. No, forsooth, mother, this raiment liketh
    not me.

I could with mine own gear better contented be.
And, but for satisfying of your mind and will,
I would not wear it, to have it for mine own still.
I love not to wear another bird's feathers :
Mine own poor homely gear will serve for all
 weathers.
 REBECCA. Well, content thyself, and follow my
  mind this day.
Now the meat by this time is ready, I dare say.
Before that with too much *enough* it be all spilt,
Take thy time, and assail thy father, when thou
 wilt.
 JACOB. Yea, but have ye provided, mother, I
  you pray,
That nobody within may your counsel bewray ?
 REBECCA. I warrant the matter all safe from
  uttering,
I have stopped all mouths fro once muttering.
Therefore, while the time serveth, I thee warn ;
To slack, when all things are ready, may do harm.
 JACOB. Go before, and I follow : but my cheeks
  will blush red,
To be seen among our folk thus appareled.

ACTUS QUARTI, SCÆNA NONA.

ISAAC. MIDO. JACOB.

ISAAC. Come, Mido, for without thee I can
 nothing do.
MIDO. What is it, sir, that ye would have my
 help unto ?
ISAAC. Nothing but to sit abroad, and take
 th' open air.
MIDO. That shall be well done ; the weather is
 very fair.

ISAAC. Praised be the God of my father Abra-
   ham,
Who sendeth all thing needful for the use of man,
And most tenderly provideth he for me Isaac,
Better than I can feel or perceive what I lack.

Enter JACOB *disguised.*

JACOB. Where is my most dear father? as I
   would have it;
Taking the open air, here I see him sit.
O my most dear father Isaac, well thou be !
   ISAAC. Here I am, my sweet son, and who art
   thou, tell me ?
   JACOB. Dear father, I am Esau, thine eldest son,
According as thou badest me, so have I done.
Come in, dear father, and eat of my venison,
That thy soul may give unto me thy benison.
   ISAAC. But how hast thou sped so soon ? let me
   understand.
   JACOB. The Lord thy God at the first brought
   it to my hand.
   ISAAC. And art thou Esau, mine elder son
   indeed ?
   JACOB. To ask that question, father, what doth
   it need ?
   ISAAC. Come near, that I may feel, whether
   thou be he or not,
For Esau is rough of hair as any goat.
Let me feel thy hand; right ! Esau, by the hair :
And yet the voice of Jacob soconeth in mine ear.
God bless thee, my son, and so will I do anon,
As soon as I have tasted of thy venison.
Come on, lead me in ; I will eat a pittance :
A little thing, God wot, to me is suffisance.
                              [*They go in.*
   MIDO. I may now go play ; Jacob leadeth Isaac.

But I never saw such a pretty knack,
How Jacob beguiled his father, how sleightly :
Now I see it true, the blind eat many a fly !
I quaked once for fear, that Jacob would be caught,
But, as hap was, he had his lesson well taught.
But what will Esau say, when he cometh home ?
Choose him ; but for me to go in it is wisdom.

[Exit.

ACTUS QUARTI, SCÆNA DECIMA.

REBECCA.   ABRA.

REBECCA. Now I beseech the Lord prosper
    Jacob my son
In our hardy enterprise, which we have begun.
Isaac is eating such meat as he doth love,
Which thing to bless Jacob, I doubt not, will him
    move :
If he obtain the blessing, as I trust he shall,
Then shall my soul give to God laud perpetual.
But I will in to harken, how the thing doth frame.
    ABRA.[1] Come in, dame Rebecca.
    REBECCA. Who is it, that doth me name?
    ABRA. My master Isaac is coming forth straight-
    way.
    REBECCA. He shall not find me here in no wise,
    if I may.

ACTUS QUARTI, SCÆNA VNDECIMA.

ISAAC.   JACOB.

ISAAC. Set me down on the bench, where thou
    didst me first find :

---

[1] Old copy, *Mido.*

Now forsooth I have ate meat even to my mind.
It hath refreshed my soul wonderfully well.
Nor never drank I better wine that I can tell.
  JACOB. If it were to your liking, I am very glad.
  ISAAC. It was the best meat and wine that ever
    I had.
Come kiss me, son Esau, with the kiss of peace,
    [Jacob kisseth Isaac; and then kneeleth down
        to have his blessing.
That my love towards thee may the more increase.
I bless thee here for ever, my son, in this place,
The Lord my God of might endue thee with his
    grace.
What sweet flavour my son's raiment doth yield!
Even the fragrant smell that cometh from a field,
Which the Lord hath blessed, and the same Lord
    bless thee
With the dew of heaven! the Lord thy ground in-
    crease,
That the fatness of the earth may never cease!
The Lord send thee abundance of corn and wine,
And prosper continually all thing that is thine!
The Lord make great people servants unto thee:
And nations to do homage and fealty!
And here, to succeed my place, mine heir I thee
    make,
Of all things that I have possession to take.
Lord and ruler be thou over thy brethren all,
And bow to thee as head thy mother's children
    shall!
Cursed be that man, that shall thee curse or mis-
    say,
And who that blesseth thee, blessed be he for aye!
Thus here have I made my last will and testament,
Which the Lord God ratify never to repent.
Serve the Lord our God, and then well shalt thou
    speed,

And he shall keep promise to multiply thy seed.
My day draweth on ; for old and feeble I am.
When I die, put me to my father Abraham.
Now kiss me once again, my son, and then depart,
And enter upon all, whereof now lord thou art.
   Jacob. The Lord God reward your fatherly
     tenderness,
Which ye have here showed me of your mere good-
     ness.
   Isaac. Go in peace, my dear son, leaving me
     here alone :
And send little Mido to lead me in anon.
                     [*Exeat Jacob.*
Lord God, when thou shalt see time, as thou
     thinkest best,
Dissolve this feeble carcase, and take me to thy
     rest.

Enter Mido.

   Mido. How do ye, master Isaac ? I am here now.
For my master Jacob did bid me come to you.
   Isaac. Nay, boy, it was not Jacob, I dare well
     say so.
   Mido. Forsooth, it was Jacob, if my name be
     Mido.
   Isaac. If that be a true tale, somebody is come
     slack,
But, Lord, that I have done I will not now call
     back.
But yet I will go see, if I be deceived :
For indeed methought Jacob's voice I perceived.
                     [*Exeunt.*

ACTUS QUARTI, SCÆNA DUODECIMA.

REBECCA.

*[Then she speaketh kneeling, and holding up
her hands.*

REBECCA. O Lord, the God of Isaac and Abra-
ham,
I render thanks to thee, though a sinful woman,
Because of thy word and promise true art thou,
In sending Jacob the blessing of Esau ;
And for thus regarding a sinner, as I am,
I eftsoons thank thee, O Lord God of Abraham.
Thy mercy and wisdom shall I sing evermore :
And magnify thy name, for God's there is no more.
But I will to my husband Isaac, and see,
That for this matter he take no grief at me.

ACTUS QUINTI, SCÆNA PRIMA.

RAGAN.

[Ragan bringeth venison at his back.
Nay, now at last we have well sped, I warrant you :
Good luck is not evermore against Esau.
He coursed and coursed again with his dogs here :
But they could at no time take either hare or deer.
At last he killed this with his bow, as God would.
And to say that it is fat venison I be bold.
But dressed it must be at once in all the haste,
That old father Isaac may have his repast.
Then without delay Esau shall blessed be,
Then, faith, cock-on-hoop, all is ours ! then, who
but he ?
But I must in, that it may be dressed in time likely,
And I trow ye shall see it made ready quickly.
[Exit.

ACTUS QUINTI, SCÆNA SECUNDA.

MIDO.

MIDO. Nay now, old master Isaac (I warrant you)
Hath blessed Jacob in the place of Esau.
At home here with us it is judged no small change,
But a case wonderful, and also very strange.
The younger brother is made elder : and again
The elder must now serve the younger as his
    swain.[1]
And from henceforth we must all make courtesy
    and bow,
Unto master Jacob, and not to Esau now :
And Esau himself must under Jacob be,
At his commandment, even as well as we.
But I care not, I warrant you : for our household
Love Jacob better than Esau twentyfold.
None loveth Esau but for his father's sake :
But all good folks are glad Jacob's part to take.
And now by Esau no man will set a pin,
But yonder he cometh now ; I will get me in.

ACTUS QUINTI, SCÆNA TERTIA.

ESAU.

ESAU. I trow I have now won my spurs for ever ;
For once better venison killed I never,
And though it were somewhat long, ere I could it
    take,
Yet the goodness thereof doth some recompense
    make.
My father Isaac shall thereof have such meat,

---

[1] Servant.

As in all his life he hath not the better eat.
Whereupon, I doubt not, after tender kissing,
To be straight endowed with his godly blessing :
As his full and true heir in his place to succeed,
And t' enjoy the promise that God made to his seed,
And when I am once in my place of succession,
And have all manner things in full possession :
I shall wring all louts and make them stoop
    (I trow) ;
I shall make the slaves couch as low as dog, and
    bow.
I shall ruffle among them of another sort
Than Isaac hath done, and with another port.
But now will I go see, what haste within they make,
That part of my hunting my old father may take.
                             [*Exit.*

ACTUS QUINTI, SCÆNA QUARTA.

ISAAC. MIDO. ESAU.

ISAAC. Mido, come, Mido, where art thou, little
    Mido ?
MIDO. Here ready, master Isaac, what shall I do?
ISAAC. Come, lead me to mine old place, that I
    may sit down.
MIDO. That can I as well as any boy in this town.
ISAAC. O Lord my God, how deep and unsearch-
    able
Are all thy judgments, and how immutable ?
Of thy justice, whom it pleaseth thee, thou dost
    reject ;
Of thy mercy, whom it pleaseth thee, thou dost
    elect.
In my two sons, O Lord, thou hast wrought thy
    will,

And as thy pleasure hath wrought, so shall it stand
    still.
Since thou hast set Jacob in Esau his place,
I commit him to the governance of thy grace.

Enter ESAU.

ESAU. Now where is Isaac, that he may come
    and eat ?
Lo, where he is sitting abroad upon his seat.
Dear father Isaac, the Lord thy God thee save.
    ISAAC. Who art thou, my son ? what thing
    wouldest thou have ?
    ESAU. I am your eldest son, Esau by my name,
New come home from hunting, where I had joyly [1]
    game,
I have made meat thereof for your own appetite,
Meat for your own tooth, wherein you will much
    delight.
Come, eat your part, dear father, that, when ye
    have done,
Your soul may bless me as your heir and eldest
    son.
    ISAAC. Ah Esau, Esau, thou comest too late,
Another to thy blessing was predestinate,
And clean gone it is from thee, Esau.
    ESAU.   Alas !
Then am I the unhappiest that ever was,
I would the savage beasts had my body torn.
    ISAAC. The blessing that thou shouldest have
    had, another hath.
    ESAU. Alas, what wretched villain hath done
    me such scath ?
    ISAAC. Thy brother Jacob came to me by
    subtlety,

---

[1] Jolly, Fr. *joli*.

And brought me venison, and so prevented [1] thee.
I ate with him, ere thou cam'st, and with my good-
    will
Blessed him I have, and blessed he shall be still.
   Esau. Ah Jacob, Jacob, well may he be called
    so :
For he hath undermined me times two.
For first mine heritage he took away me fro,
And see, now hath he away my blessing also.
Ah father, father, though Jacob hath done this
    thing :
Yet let me Esau also have thy blessing.
Shall all my good huntings for thee be in vain ?
   Isaac. That is done and passed, cannot be called
    again.
Mine act must now stand in force of necessity.
   Esau. And hast thou never a blessing then left
    for me ?
   Isaac. Behold, I have made thy brother Jacob
    thy lord.
   Esau. A most poignant sword unto my heart is
    that word.
   Isaac. All his mother's children his servants
    have I made.
   Esau. That word is to me sharper than a razor's
    blade.
   Isaac. I have also 'stablished him with wine and
    corn.
   Esau. Woe be the day and hour that ever I was
    born !
   Isaac. What am I able to do for thee, my son ?
   Esau. Ah Jacob, Jacob, that thou hast me thus
    undone !
O unhappy hap : O misfortune ! well away !
That ever I should live to see this woful day.

---

[1] Forestalled.

But hast thou one blessing and no mo, my father?
Let me also have some blessing, good sweet father.
   Isaac. Well, nature pricketh me some remorse
     on thee to have.
Behold, thy dwelling-place the earth's fatness shall
     have,
And the dew of heaven, which down from above
     shall fall :
And with dint of sword thy living get thou shall,
And to thy brother Jacob thou shalt be servant.
   Esau. O, to my younger brother must I be
     servant?
O, that ever a man should be so oppressed !
   Isaac. Thine own fault it is, that thou art dis-
     possessed.
   Esau. Father, change that piece of thy sentence
     and judgment.
   Isaac. Things done cannot be undone ; there-
     fore be content,
Let me be in quiet, and trouble me no more.
Come, Mido, in God's name, lead me in at the door.
               [Exeunt Isaac and Mido.
   Esau. O, would not this chafe a man, and fret
     his guts out,
To live as an underling under such a lout?
Ah hypocrite, Ah hedgecreeper, Ah 'sembling
     wretch !
I will be even with thee for this subtle fetch.
O God of Abraham, what reason is herein,
That to sle one's enemy it should be made sin?
Were not one as good his part of heaven forego,
As not to be revenged on his deadly foe?
God was angry with Cain for killing Abel :
Else might I kill Jacob marvellously well.
I may fortune one day him to dispatch and rid :
The Lord will not see all things ; something may
     be hid.

But as for these misers [1] within my father's tent,
Which to the supplanting of me put their consent,
Not one, but I shall coil them, till they stink for
    pain,
And then for their stinking coil them off fresh
    again.
I will take no days [2]; but, while the matter is hot,
Not one of them shall 'scape, but they shall to the
    pot.

ACTUS QUINTI, SCÆNA QUINTA.

Ragan.

Where are we now become? marry, sir, here is
    array!
With Esau, my master, this is a black day.
I told you Esau one day would shit a rag,
Have we not well hunted, of blessing to come
    lag? [3]
Nay, I thought ever it would come to such a pass,
Since he sold his heritage like a very ass.
But, in faith, some of them, I dare jeopard a groat,
If he may reach them, will have on the petticoat. [4]

ACTUS QUINTI, SCÆNA SEXTA.

Esau.   Ragan.   Abra.   Mido.   Deborah.

Esau. Come out, whores and thieves; come out,
    come out, I say!

---

[1] Wretches.   [2] Lose no time.   [3] Late.

[4] *To have on the petticoat* is a phrase of very unusual occurrence, of which the sense may, without much difficulty or risk of error, be collected from the context.

RAGAN.[1] I told you, did I not, that there would
   be a fray?   *[Aside.*
ESAU. Come out, little whoreson ape, come out
   of thy den.
MIDO. Take my life for a penny, whither shall
   I ren?[2]
ESAU. Come out, thou little fiend, come out,
   thou skittish gill.
ABRA. Out, alas, alas! Esau will us all kill.
ESAU. And come out, thou mother Mab;[3] out,
   old rotten witch!
As white as midnight's arsehole or virgin pitch.
Where be ye? come together in a cluster.
   RAGAN. In faith, and these three will make a
   noble muster.
   ESAU. Ere ye escape my fingers, ye shall all
   be taught,
For these be they which have all this against me
   wrought.
   MIDO. I wrought not a stroke this day, but led
   Isaac :
If I wrought one stroke to-day, lay me on the jack.
   ESAU. Hence then, get thee in, and do against
   me no more.
   MIDO. I care as much for you now, as I did
   before.   *[Aside.*
   ESAU. What sayest thou, little thief? if I may
   thee catch.
   MIDO. Ye shall run apace then, I ween, so God
   me snatch.
   RAGAN. Now to go, Mido, ere thou art caught
   in a trip.   *[Exit* MIDO.

---

[1] Ragan and the others must be supposed to be at the back
of the stage, out of Esau's sight ; but they come forward
severally, and plead for themselves.

[2] Run.

[3] *i.e.*, Old witch. But compare Halliwell, *v. Mab.*

ESAU. Nay, for his sake, Abra, ye shall drink of
  the whip.
ABRA. Nay, for God's love, good sweet master
  Esau,
Hurt not me for Mido : speak for me, Ragan.
  RAGAN. Sir, spare little Abra, she hath done
  none evil.
  ESAU. A little fiend it is, and will be a right
  devil,
And she is one of them that love not me a deal.
  ABRA. If ye let me go, I will love you very well.
  ESAU. And never any more ado against me make?
  ABRA.   Ragan shall be surety.
  RAGAN.   Sir, I undertake.
  ESAU. Then hence, out of my sight at once, and
  get thee in.
  ABRA. Adieu, I set not a straw by you nor a pin.
  ESAU. What sayest thou, thou fib ? once ye shall
  have a rap.
  RAGAN. The best end of suretyship is to get a
  clap.   [*Aside.*
  ESAU. Now, come on, thou old hag, what shall
  I say to thee ?
  DEBORAH. Say what ye lust, so ye do not touch
  me.
  ESAU. Yes, and make powder of thee, for I dare
  say thou
Hast been the cause of all this feast to Esau.
  DEBORAH. No, it was Jacob's feast that I did
  help to dress.
  ESAU. Nay, I thought such a witch would do
  such business.
  DEBORAH.[1] But, by my truth, if I should die
  incontinent,
I knew not of the purpose, wherefore it was meant.

---

[1] Old copy, *Rebecca.*

ESAU. But wilt thou tell me truth, if I do forgive
  thee ?
DEBORAH. Yea, if I can, Master Esau, believe
  me.
ESAU. Is it true that, when I and my brother
  were first born,
And I by God's ordinance came forth him beforne,
Jacob came forthwith, holding me fast by the heel ?
  DEBORAH. It is true ; I was there, and saw it
  very well.
  ESAU. Is it true ? well, Jacob, I pray God I be
  dead,
But for my heel's sake, I will have thee by the
  head.
What devil was in me, that I had not the grace,
With kicking back my heel, to mar his mopish
  face ?
But my father Isaac will not long live now ;
If he were gone, Jacob, I would soon meet with
  you.
For my soul hateth Jacob even to the death,
And I will ne'er but hate him, while I shall have
  breath.
I may well dissemble, until I see a day,
But trust me, Jacob, I will pay thee when I may.
But if ever I hear that thou speak word of this,
I shall cut out thy tongue, I will not miss.
                    [*This he speaketh to Deborah.*
But come on, Ragan, with me : so mote I thrive,
I will get a good sword, for thereby must I live.
  RAGAN. Live, quod you ? we are like to live,
  God knoweth how.
  ESAU. What, ye saucy merchant,[1] are ye a prater
  now ?   [*Exeunt* ESAU *and* RAGAN.

---

[1] A word of contempt often used in our old comedies, as
we now employ *chap.*

ACTUS QUINTI, SCÆNA SEPTIMA.

DEBORAH. REBECCA.

DEBORAH. I am glad that Esau is now gone,
 certès.
For an evil-disposed man he is, doubtless.
Yet am I no gladder of his departure hence,
Than I am that Rebecca is come in presence.

Enter REBECCA.

REBECCA. Deborah, what doest thou, tarrying
 here so long ?
I came full ill afeard, lest something had been
 wrong ;
For Mido and Abra told me of Esau.
 DEBORAH. Indeed here he was, and departed
 hence but now :
And one thing I tell you, dame : let Jacob beware,
For Esau to mischief Jacob doth prepare.
 REBECCA. Call Jacob hither, that I may show
 him my mind.
Send him hither quickly, and tarry ye behind,
That he give place awhile, it is expedient,
And how he may be sure, I will the way invent.

ACTUS QUINTI, SCÆNA OCTAVA.

JACOB. REBECCA.

JACOB. Mother Rebecca, did ye send for me
 hither ?
REBECCA. Yea, and the cause is this, thou must
 go somewhither,
To hide thee from thy brother Esau a space.
 JACOB. Indeed, to men's malice we must some-
 time give place.
REBECCA. He lieth in await to sle thee, if he can :

Thou shalt therefore, by my reed, fle hence to
    Haran :
And lie with my brother Laban, a man aged,
Till Esau's wrath be somewhat assuaged.
When all things are forgotten, and his fury passed,
I shall send for thee again in all goodly haste.
    JACOB. Yea, but how will my father herewith
    be content?
    REBECCA. Thou shalt see me win him thereto
    incontinent.
And here he cometh happily : Jacob, hear me ;
Make a sign to Mido, that he do not name thee,
Then get thee in privily, till I do thee call.
    JACOB. As ye command me, mother Rebecca, I
    shall.

ACTUS QUINTI, SCÆNA NONA.

ISAAC. MIDO. REBECCA. JACOB.

ISAAC. Where be ye, good wife?
MIDO. My dame Rebecca is here.
REBECCA. I am glad, sweet husband, that I see
    you appear,
For [1] I have a word or two unto you to say.
    ISAAC. Whatsoever it be, tell it me, I you pray.
    REBECCA. Sir, ye know that now our life-days
    are but short,
And we had never so great need of comfort.
Now Esau his wives being Hittites both,
Ye know, to please us are much unwilling and loth.
That if Jacob eke would take any Hittite to wife,
Small joy should we both have or comfort of our
    life.

---

[1] In the old copy this line is improperly given to Isaac.

ISAAC. Wife, ye speak this well, and I will pro-
vide therefore,
Call Jacob quickly, that he appear me before.
MIDO. I can run apace for him, if ye bid me go.
REBECCA. Go, hie thee at once then, like a good
son, Mido.
    [Exit Mido, but returns directly with Jacob.
ISAAC. O Lord, save thou my son from mis-
carrying.
MIDO. Come, master Jacob, ye must make no
tarrying,
For I it is that shall be shent, if you be slack,
Here is your son Jacob now, master Isaac.
    ISAAC. Son Jacob, make thee ready, as fast [as]
thou can,
And in all haste possible get thee unto Laban.
He is thine own uncle, and a right godly man,
Marry of his daughters, and not of Canaan.
In Mesopotamia shalt thou lead thy life.
The Lord prosper thee here without debate or
strife ;
And the God of Abraham prosper thee in peace ;
He multiply thy seed, and make it to increase !
Now kiss me, dear son Jacob, and so go thy way.
REBECCA. Kiss me also, sweet son, and hence
without delay.
JACOB. Now, most tender parents, as well with
heart and word
I bid you well to fare, and leave you to the Lord.
MIDO. Nay, master Jacob, let me have an hand
also.
JACOB. Even with all my heart : farewell, little
Mido.   *[Exit Jacob.*
ISAAC. Now will I depart hence into the tent
again.
REBECCA. As pleaseth God and you, but I will
here remain.

ACTUS QUINTI, SCÆNA DECIMA.

ESAU. RAGAN. REBECCA. ISAAC. MIDO.

ESAU. And is he gone indeed to mine uncle
Laban,
In Mesopotamia at the town of Haran?
And is Jacob gone to the house of Bethuel?
The whirlwind with him, and flinging fiend of
hell!
But I shall meet with him yet one day well enough.
And who is this? my mother? whom I see here
now.
RAGAN. She stood here all this while, sir, did ye
not her see?
ESAU. Didst thou see her stand here, and
wouldest not warn me?
REBECCA. Son Esau, afore God, thou art much
to blame,
And to do, as I hear of thee, is a foul shame.
ESAU. Mother, what is it ye heard of me of late?
REBECCA. That thou dost thy brother Jacob
deadly hate.
ESAU. Hate Jacob? I hate him, and will do, till
I die,
For he hath done me both great wrong and villainy;
And that shall he well know, if the Lord give me
life.
REBECCA. Fie upon thee, to speak so, like a lewd
caitiff!
RAGAN. My master Esau is of nature much hot,
But he will be better than he saith, fear not.
ESAU. My birthright to sell did he not make me
consent?
REBECCA. But the same to do wert not thyself
content?

There is no man to blame for it but thine own
    self.
    ESAU. Yea, mother, I see that ye hold with that
       mopish elf.
It is your dainty darling, your prinkox, your
    golpol;
He can never be praised enough of your soul;
He must ever be extolled above the moon:
It is never amiss that he hath said or done.
I would he were rocked or dandled in your lap;
Or I would with this falchion I might give him
    pap.
I marvel why ye should so love him, and me not?
Ye groaned as well for the one as thother, I wot.
But Jacob must be advanced in any wise:
But I shall one day handle him of the new guise.[1]
    REBECCA. Both on thy father's blessing and
      mine, I charge thee,
That thy soul intend never such iniquity;
Beware by the example of Cain, I thee reed,
That thou bring not the Lord's curse upon thy head.
    ESAU. And what, should I take all this wrong
      at Jacob's hand?
    REBECCA. Forgive, and the Lord shall prosper
      thee in the land.
My son Esau, hear me; I am thy mother:
For my sake, let pass this grudge against thy
    brother.
    RAGAN. Sir, your mother's request is but reason-
      able,
Which for you to grant shall be much commend-
    able.

---

[1] The *new guise* is a term often met with in old plays, but
the application of it here is not very clear, although the
meaning of the writer—in a way that he (Jacob) little ex-
pected—is sufficiently intelligible.

ESAU. Mother, though it be a great thing that
 ye require :
Yet must all malice pass at your desire ;
And for your cause, mother, this mine anger shall
 slake.
  REBECCA. I thank thee, my son, that thou dost
 it for my sake.
  ESAU. For your sake, with Jacob I will be at
 accord.
  REBECCA. And shall I call thy father to be as
 record ?
  ESAU. As pleaseth you, mother, I can be well
 content.
  REBECCA. Then will I go call him hither incon-
 tinent.
And where he doth already love thee very well,
This will make him to love thee better a great deal.
  RAGAN. Truly, sir, this is of you a right gentle
 part :
At least, if it come from the bottom of your heart.
  ESAU. It must now be thus ; but when I shall
 Jacob find,
I shall then do as God shall put into my mind.

Enter ISAAC *and* MIDO *with* REBECCA.

  REBECCA. He hath at my word remitted all his
 quarrel.
  ISAAC. Forsooth, I love him the better a great deal.
And if he be here, I would commend his doing.
  ESAU.[1] All prest here, father, to tarry on your
 coming.
  ISAAC. Son Esau, thou hast thyself well ac-
 quitted,

---

[1] In the old copy this word is improperly placed opposite
the line, *That all quarrel, &c.*

That all quarrel to Jacob thou hast remitted.
It was the Lord's pleasure that it should thus be,
Against whose ordinance to stand is not for thee :
But now, to the intent it may please the Lord,
To knit your hearts one day in a perfect concord,
We shall first in a song give laud unto His name,
And then with all gladness within confirm the same.

    REBECCA. As ye think best, dear husband, I
      agree thereto.
    ESAU. Me ye may command to what ye will
      have me to do :
And so may ye do also Ragan my man.
    ISAAC. I see none ; but praise we the Lord the
      best we can,
Call forth all our household, that with one accord
We may all with one voice sing unto the Lord.
                    [Ragan calleth all to sing.

This song must be sung after the prayer.

O Lord, the God of our father Abraham,
How deep and unsearchable are thy judgments !
Thy almightiful hand did create and frame
Both heaven and earth, and all the elements.
Man of the earth thou hast formed and create ;
Some do thee worship, and some stray awry,
Whom pleaseth thee, thou dost choose or reprobate,
And no flesh can ask thee wherefore or why ?
Of thine own will thou didst Abraham elect,
Promising him seed as stars of the sky,
And them as thy chosen people to protect,
That they might thy mercies praise and magnify.
Perform thou, O Lord, thine eternal decree
To me and my seed, the sons of Abraham ;
And whom thou hast chosen thine own people to be,
Guide and defend to the glory of thy name.

FINIS.

*[Then entereth the Poet, and the rest stand still
till he have done.*

THE POET. When Adam, for breaking God's
   commandment,
Had sentence of death, and all his posterity :
Yet the Lord our God, who is omnipotent,
Had in his own self by his eternal decree
Appointed to restore man, and to make him free.
He purposed to save mankind by his mercy,
Whom he once had created unto his glory.
Yet not all flesh did he then predestinate,
But only the adopted children of promise :
For he foreknew that many would degenerate,
And wilfully give cause to be put from that bliss,
So on God's behalf no manner default there is ;
But where he chooseth, he showeth his great
   mercy :
And where he refuseth, he doth none injury,
But thus far surmounteth man's intellection,[1]
To attain or conceive, and (much more) to discuss :
All must be referred to God's election
And to his sacred judgment.   It is meet for us,
With Paul the apostle, to confess, and say thus :
O, the deepness of the riches of God's wisdom !
How unsearchable are his ways to man's reason ?
Our part therefore is first to believe God's word,
Not doubting but that he will his elected save :
Then to put full trust in the goodness of the Lord,
That we be of the number, which shall mercy
   have :
Thirdly, so to live, as we may his promise crave.
Thus if we do, we shall Abraham's children be,
And come with Jacob to endless felicity.
   [All the rest of the actors answer, Amen.

---

[1] Understanding.

Then followeth the prayer.

ISAAC. Now unto God let us pray for all the
    whole clergy,
To give them grace to advance God's honour and
    glory.
    REBECCA. Then for the Queen's majesty let us
    pray
Unto God to keep her in health and wealth night
    and day,
And that, of his mere mercy and great benignity,
He will defend and maintain her estate and dignity;
That she, being grieved with any outward hostility,
May against her enemies always have victory.
    JACOB. God save the Queen's councillors most
    noble and true,
And with all godliness their noble hearts endue.
    ESAU. Lord save the nobility and preserve them
    all :
And prosper the Queen's subjects universal.

AMEN.

*Thus endeth this Comedy or Enterlude of
Jacob and Esau.*

THE PLAYERS' NAMES.

<table>
<tr><td>THE PROLOGUE SPEAKER,</td><td>THE YOUNG WOMAN.</td></tr>
<tr><td>THE RICH MAN.</td><td>THE SERVINGMAN.</td></tr>
<tr><td>THE RICH MAN'S SON.</td><td>THE PRIEST.</td></tr>
<tr><td>THE MAN COOK.</td><td>THE DEVIL.</td></tr>
<tr><td>THE WOMAN COOK.</td><td>THE PERORATOR.</td></tr>
</table>

MR HALLIWELL'S PREFACE TO THE FORMER EDITION.[1]

So little is known respecting the history of the following tract, that it is rather from an unwillingness to
depart from the usual custom of affixing introductions
to our reprints, than from any expectation of satisfying
the slightest curiosity, that a few lines are here prefixed.
The interlude of "The Disobedient Child" was written
about the middle of the sixteenth century, by Thomas
Ingelend, who is described in the early printed copy as
"late student in Cambridge," and his fame seems to
rest entirely on that production, for he is not to be
traced in any other early literary record.[2] It has been
supposed by some writers, from a few indistinct allusions
in the play to Catholic customs, that it was composed
in the reign of Henry VIII. ; but if this be the case,
the notice of Queen Elizabeth, introduced towards the
close of the drama, must be an interpolation, a supposi-
tion not unlikely to be correct, for the audience are

---

[1] [The interlude of "The Disobedient Child," edited by
J. O. Halliwell. Percy Society, 1848.]

[2] [But see Cooper's "Cambridge Athenæ," i., 554.]

elsewhere reminded to " serve the king."   The printed
edition by Colwell is without date, but it was published
about the year 1560.   Two copies of this work which I
have collated differ in some slight particulars from each
other, but there is not sufficient reason for thinking that
there were two editions, for it was formerly a very
common practice to correct and alter the press whilst
the impression was being taken.[1]

[It is observable that the present interlude marks a
considerable advance, in point of literary merit, on those
which precede it in this collection.   The author was
evidently a man of taste and judgment, and many passages might be pointed out which possess no mean share
of picturesqueness, elegance, and dramatic propriety.

Contrary to the usual practice, in old as well as
modern pieces, "The Disobedient Child" concludes
unhappily, though without any attempt at a highly
wrought tragical catastrophe ; the Rich man persists in
his unrelenting conduct, and we are left to imagine that
his son returns to live and die in misery with his ter-
magant wife.]

---

[1] [The Bridgewater copy of the original edition was most
obligingly collated for the present writer by Mr Alexander
Smith, of Glasgow.   It affords numerous corrections of the
Percy Society's text.]

THE DISOBEDIENT CHILD.[1]

THE PROLOGUE.

THE PROLOGUE SPEAKER.

Now, forasmuch as in these latter days,
Throughout the whole world in every land,
Vice doth encrease, and virtue decays,
Iniquity having the upper hand;
We therefore intend, good gentle audience,
A pretty short interlude to play at this present:
Desiring your leave and quiet silence
To show the same, as is meet and expedient.[2]
The sum whereof, matter and argument,
In two or three verses briefly to declare,
Since that it is for an honest intent,
I will somewhat bestow my care.
In the city of London there was a rich man
Who, loving his son most tenderly,
Moved him earnestly now and then,

---

[1] [The full title is: *A pretie and mery new Enterlude,
called The Disobedient Child, compiled by Thomas Ingelend,
late Student in Cambridge. Imprinted at London, in Flete
strete, beneath the Conduit, by Thomas Colwell.* 4°.]

[2] These first eight lines are also found in the interlude
introduced into the play of *Sir Thomas More*, printed by
the Shakespeare Society, p. 60.—*Halliwell.*

That he would give his mind to study,
Saying that by knowledge, science and learning,
Is at the last gotten a pleasant life,
But through the want and lack of this thing
Is purchased poverty, sorrow and strife.
His son, notwithstanding this gentle monition,
As one that was clean devoid of grace,
Did turn to a mock and open derision
Most wickedly with an unshamefast[1] face ;
Insomuch that, contrary to his father's will,
Unto a young woman he did consent,
Whereby of lust he might have his fill,
And married the same incontinent.[2]
Not long after that, the child began
To feel his wife's great frowardness,
And called himself unhappy man,
Oppressed with pains and heaviness :
Who, before that time, did live blessedly,
Whilst he was under his father's wing ;
But now, being wedded, mourning and misery
Did him torment without ending.
But now it is time for me to be going,
And hence to depart for a certain space,
For I do hear the Rich Man coming
With the wanton boy into this place.

> *[Here the Prologue Speaker goeth out, and in*
> *cometh the Rich Man and his son.*

SON. Father, I beseech you, father, show me the
    way,
What thing I were best to take in hand,
Whereby this short life so spend I may,
That all grief and trouble I might withstand.

---

[1] Without shame—shameless.
[2] Immediately.   See " Othello," Act. iv. sc. 3.

FATHER. What is the meaning, my child, I thee
    pray,
This question to demand of me?
For that thing to do I am glad alway,
Which should not be grievous to thee.
SON. Marry, but therefore of you counsel I take,
Seeing now my childhood I am clean past,
That unto me ye plainly do make
What to a young man is best for to taste.
FATHER. I see nothing truly, my son, so meet,
And to prove so profitable for thee,
As unto the school to move thy feet,
With studious lads there for to be.
SON. What, the school! nay, father, nay!
Go to the school is not the best way.
FATHER. Say what thou list, for I cannot invent
A way more commodious to my judgment.[1]
SON. It is well known how that ye have loved
Me heretofore at all times most tenderly;
But now (me-think) ye have plainly showed
Certain tokens of hatred;
For if I should go to my book after your advice,
Which have spent my childhood so pleasantly,
I may then seem driven out of paradise,
To take pain and woe, grief and misery.
All things I had rather sustain and abide,
The business of the school once cast aside;
Therefore, though ye cry, till ye reve[1] asunder,
I will not meddle with such a matter.
FATHER. Why, cannot I thee thus much per-
    suade?
For that in my mind is the best trade.
SON. When all is said and all is done,

---

[1] That is, according to my judgment. See "Lear," Act
i. sc. 4.—*Halliwell.*
[1] To split, or burst. Generally spelt *rive.*

Concerning all things, both more and less,
Yet like to the school none under the sun
Bringeth to children so much heaviness.
    FATHER. What, though it be painful, what,
       though it be grievous,
For so be all things at the first learning,
Yet marvellous pleasure it bringeth unto us,
As a reward for such painstaking.
Wherefore come off, and be of good cheer,
And go to thy book without any fear,
For a man without knowledge (as I have read)
May well be compared to one that is dead.
    SON. No more of the school ; no more of the
      book ;
That woful work is not for my purpose,
For upon those books I may not look :
If so I did, my labour I should lose.
    FATHER. Why then to me thy fancy [doth] express,
That the school matters to thee are counted weari-
      ness.
    SON. Even as to a great man, wealthy and rich,
Service and bondage is a hard thing,
So to a boy, both dainty and nice,[1]
Learning and study is greatly displeasing.
    FATHER. What, my child, displeasing, I pray
      thee,
That maketh a man live so happily ?
    SON. Yea, by my troth, such kind of wisdom
Is to my heart, I tell you, very loathsome.
    FATHER. What trial thereof hast thou taken,
That the school of thee is so ill bespoken ?
    SON. What trial thereof would ye fain know?
Nothing more easy than this to show :

---

[1] Both tender and delicate. [Here, as pointed out in a note
to Heywood's "Four P.P." *supra*, the word *nice* is to be
pronounced *nich.*]

At other boys' hands I have it learned,
And that of those truly, most of all other,
Which for a certain time have remained
In the house and prison of a schoolmaster.

FATHER. I dare well say that there is no misery,
But rather joy, pastime and pleasure
Always with scholars keeping company :
No life to this, I thee well assure.

SON. It is not true, father, which you do say ;
The contrary thereof is proved alway,
For as the bruit goeth by many a one,
Their tender bodies both night and day
Are whipped and scourged, and beat[1] like a stone,
That from top to toe the skin is away.

FATHER. Is there not (say they) for them in this
  case
Given other while for pardon some place ?

SON. None, truly, none ; but that alas, alas,
Diseases among them do grow apace ;
For out of their back and side doth flow
Of very gore-blood marvellous abundance ;
And yet for all that is not suffered to go,
Till death be almost seen in their countenance.
Should I be content thither then to run,
Where the blood from my breech thus should
  spun,[2]
So long as my wits shall be mine own,
The schoolhouse for me shall stand alone.[3]

FATHER. But I am sure that this kind of fashion
Is not showed to children of honest condition.

SON. Of truth, with these masters is no differ-
  ence,

---

[1] Beaten.

[2] [Query same as *spwyn*, to burst or break out. See Way's
edit. of the " Promptorium," v. *Spwyn*.]

[3] Compare " Troilus and Cressida," i. 2.

For alike towards all is their wrath and violence.
  FATHER. Son, in this point thou art quite de-
    ceived,
And without doubt falsely persuaded,
For it is not to be judged that any schoolmaster
Is of so great fierceness and cruelty,
And of young infants so sore a tormentor,
That the breath should be about to leave the body.
  SON. Father, this thing I could not have believed,
But of late days I did behold
An honest man's son hereby buried,
Which through many stripes was dead and cold.
  FATHER. Peraventure, the child of some dis-
    ease did labour,
Which was the cause of his sepulture.[1]
  SON. With no disease, surely, was he disquieted,
As unto me it was then reported.
  FATHER. If that with no such thing he were
    infected,
What was the cause that he departed?
  SON. Men say that of[2] this man, his bloody
    master,
Who like a lion most commonly frowned,
Being hanged up by the heels together,
Was belly and buttocks grievously whipped;
And last of all (which to speak I tremble),[3]
That his head to the wall he had often crushed.[4]
  FATHER. Thus to think, son, thou art beguiled
    verily,
And I would wish thee to suppose the contrary,

---

[1] Burial. From the Latin.

[2] *i.e.*, By.

[3] [Original reads *trembled.*]

[4] [This account, if founded on fact, is a curious illustration
of the scholastic discipline of that period. We know that
Udall the dramatist was remarkable for his severity to his
pupils at Eton.]

And not for such tales my counsel to forsake,
Which only do covet thee learned to make.
　Son. If Demosthenes and Tully were present truly,
They could not print [1] it within my head [more]
　　deeply.
　Father. Yet, by thy father's will and intercession,
Thou shalt be content that thing to pardon.
　Son. Command what ye list, that only excepted,
And I will be ready your mind to fulfil,
But whereas I should to the school have resorted,
My hand to the palmer [2] submitting still,
I will not obey ye therein, to be plain,
Though with a thousand strokes I be slain.
　Father. Woe is me, my son, woe is me !
This heavy and doleful day to see.
　Son. I grant indeed I am your son ;
But you my father shall not be,
If that you will cast me into that prison,
Where torn in pieces ye might me see.
　Father. Where I might see thee torn and rent ?
O Lord, I could not such a deed invent !
　Son. Nay, by the mass, I hold [3] ye a groat,
Those cruel tyrants cut not my throat :
Better it were myself did slay,
Than they with the rod my flesh should flay.
Well, I would we did this talk omit,
For it is loathsome to me every whit.
　Father. What trade then, I pray thee, shall I
　　devise,
Whereof thy living at length may arise?

---

　[1] Impress.　Compare "Much Ado about Nothing," iv. 1.
—*Halliwell.*
　[2] [Query, the schoolmaster, so called from inflicting on
the pupil with a cane *cuts* on the hand.]
　[3] Bet.　See "Taming of the Shrew"—

　　　　"Now, by Saint Jamy,
　　　　　I hold you a penny."—*Halliwell.*

Wilt thou follow warfare, and a soldier be 'ppointed,
And so among Troyans and Romans be numbered ?
  SON. See ye not, masters, my father's advice ?
Have ye the like at any time heard ?
To will me thereto he is not wise,
If my years and strength he did regard ;
Ye speak worse and worse, whatsoever ye say ;
This manner of life is not a good way,
For no kind of office can me please,
Which is subject to wounds and strokes always.
  FATHER. Somewhat to do it is meet and con-
    venient ;
Wilt thou then give thy diligent endeavour
To let thy youth unhonestly be spent,
And do as poor knaves, which jaxes [1] do scour ?
For I do not see that any good art,
Or else any honest science or occupation,
Thou wilt be content to have a part,
After thy father's mind and exhortation.
  SON. Ha, ha, ha, ha, labour in very deed !
God send him that life which stands in need :
There be many fathers that children have,
And yet not make the worst of them a slave,
Might not you of yourself be well ashamed,
Which would have your son thither constrained ?
  FATHER. I would not have thee driven to that
    succour,
Yet for because the scriptures declare,
That he should not eat, which will not labour,
Some work to do it must be thy care.
  SON. Father, it is but a folly with you to strive,
But yet notwithstanding I hope to thrive.
  FATHER. That this thine intent may take good
    success,
I pray God heartily of his goodness.

---

[1] Jakes. Compare " Lear," ii. 2.—*Halliwell.*

SON. Well, well, shall I in few words rehearse
What thing doth most my conscience pierce.

FATHER. Therewith I am, son, very well contented.

SON. Yea, but I think that ye will not be pleased.

FATHER. Indeed, peradventure it may so chance.

SON. Nay, but I pray ye, without any perchance,
Shall not my request turn to your grievance?

FATHER. If it be just and lawful, which thou
dost require.

SON. Both just and lawful, have ye no fear.

FATHER. Now therefore ask; what is thy petition?

SON. Lo, this it is, without further dilation;[1]
For so much as all young men for this my beauty,
As the moon the stars, I do far excel,
Therefore out of hand[2] with all speed possibly
To have a wife, methink, would do well,
For now I am young, lively, and lusty,
And welcome besides to all men's company.

FATHER. Good Lord, good Lord, what do I hear!

SON. Is this your beginning to perform my
desire?

FATHER. Alas! my child, what meaneth thy
doting?
Why dost thou covet thy own undoing?

SON (*Aside*). I know not in the world how to
do the thing,
That to his stomach may be delighting.

FATHER. Why, foolish idiot, thou goest about a
wife,
Which is a burthen and yoke all thy life.

SON. Admit she shall as a burthen with me
remain,
Yet will I take one, if your good-will I attain.

---

[1] [Detail, or circumlocution.]   [2] At once.

FATHER. Son, it shall not be thus, by my
  counsel.
SON. I trust ye will not me otherwise compel.
FATHER. If thou were as wise as I have judged
  thee,
Thou wouldest in this case be ruled by me.
SON. To follow the contrary I cannot be turned ;
My heart thereon is stifly fixed.
FATHER. What, I say, about thine own destruc-
  tion ?
SON. No, no, but about mine own salvation :
For if I be helped, I swear by the mass,
It is only marriage that brings it to pass.
It is not the school, it is not the book :
It is not science or occupation,
It is not to be a barber or cook,
Wherein is now set my consolation ;
And since it is thus, be, father, content ;
For to marry a wife I am full bent.
FATHER. Well, if thou wilt not, my son, be ruled,
But needs will follow thine own foolishness,
Take heed hereafter, if thou be troubled,
At me thou never seek redress ;
For I am certain thou canst not abide
Any pain at all, grief or vexation.
Thy childhood with me so easily did slide,
Full of all pastime and delectation ;
And if thou wouldest follow the book and learning,
And with thyself also take a wise way,
Then thou mayst get a gentleman's living,
And with many other bear a great sway : [1]
Besides this, I would in time to come,
After my power and small hability,
Help thee and further thee, as my wisdom
Should me most counsel for thy commodity.

---

[1] Compare " Comedy of Errors," Act ii. sc. 1.—*Halliwell*.

And such a wife I would prepare for thee
As should be virtuous, wise, and honest,
And give thee with her after my degree,
Whereby thou mightest always live in rest.
    SON. I cannot, I tell ye again, so much of my
        life
Consume at my book without a wife.
    FATHER. I perceive therefore I have done too
        well,
And showed overmuch favour to thee,
That now against me thou dost rebel,
And for thine own furtherance wilt not agree;
Wherefore of my goods thou gettest not a penny,
Nor any succour else at my hands,
For such a child is most unworthy
To have any part of his father's lands.
    SON. I do not esteem, father, your goods or
        lands,
Or any part of all your treasure;
For I judge it enough to be out of bands,
And from this day forward to take my pleasure.
    FATHER. Well, if it shall chance thee thy folly
        to repent,
As thou art like within short space,
Think none but thyself worthy to be shent,[1]
Letting my counsel to take no place.
    SON. As touching that matter, I will no man
        blame :
Now, farewell, father, most heartily for the same.
    FATHER. Farewell, my son, depart in God's name!

---

[1] Blamed, scolded. See "Merry Wives of Windsor," i. 4.
The older meaning of the term is *ruined*, but Elizabethan
writers generally employ it in the sense here mentioned.—
Halliwell. [I do not agree. The older sense is, I think, the
only one admissible; yet, Nares cites a passage from Shakespeare which may shake this position. See *v. Shend*, No. 1,
second quotation.]

SON. Room,[1] I say ; room, let me be gone :
My father, if he list, shall tarry alone.
    [Here the Son goeth out, and the Rich
     Man tarrieth behind alone.

THE FATHER.

Now at the last I do myself consider,
How great grief it is and heaviness
To every man that is a father,
To suffer his child to follow wantonness :
If I might live a hundred years longer,
And should have sons and daughters many,
Yet for this boy's sake I will not suffer
One of them all at home with me to tarry ;
They should not be kept thus under my wing,
And have all that which they desire ;
For why it is but their only undoing,
And, after the proverb, we put oil to the fire.[2]
Wherefore we parents must have a regard
Our children in time for to subdue,
Or else we shall have them ever untoward,
Yea, spiteful, disdainful, naught and untrue.
And let us them thrust alway to the school,
Whereby at their books they may be kept under :
And so we shall shortly their courage cool,
And bring them to honesty, virtue and nurture.
But, alas, now-a-days (the more is the pity),
Science and learning is so little regarded,
That none of us doth muse or study
To see our children well taught and instructed.
We deck them, we trim them with gorgeous array,
We pamper and feed them, and keep them so gay,

---

[1] Compare the "Midsummer Night's Dream," ii. 1.—
Halliwell.
 [2] "Bring oil to fire" (*King Lear*, ii. 2). Compare also
" All's Well that ends Well," v. 3.—*Halliwell.*

That in the end of all this they be our foes.
We bass them, [we] kiss them, we look round about;
We marvel and wonder to see them so lean ;
We ever anon do invent and seek out
To make them go tricksy,[1] gallant, and clean :
Which is nothing else but the very provoking
To all unthriftiness, vice, and iniquity ;
It puffeth them up, it is an alluring
Their fathers and mothers at length to defy.
Which thing mine own son doth plainly declare,
Whom I always entirely have loved :
He was so my joy, he was so my care,
That now of the same I am despised.
And how he is hence from me departed,
He hath no delight with me to dwell ;
He is not merry, until he be married,
He hath of knavery took such a smell.[2]
But yet seeing that he is my son,
He doth me constrain bitterly to weep,
I am not (methink) well till I be gone ;
For this place I can no longer keep.

> *[Here the Rich Man goeth out, and the two*
> *Cooks cometh in ; first the one, and then*
> *the other.*

THE MAN-COOK.

Make haste, Blanche, blab it out, and come away,
For we have enough to do all this whole day ;
Why, Blanche, blab it out, wilt thou not come,
And knowest what business there is to be done ?
If thou may be set with the pot at thy nose,
Thou carest not how other matters goes ;

---

[1] "My tricksy spirit " (*Tempest,* v. 1).—*Halliwell.*
[2] "Smell of calumny " (*Measure for Measure,* ii. 4).—
Halliwell.

Come away, I bid thee, and tarry no longer,
To trust to thy help I am much the better !

THE MAID-COOK.

What a murrain, I say, what a noise dost thou
    make !
I think that thou be not well in thy wits !
I never heard man on this sort to take,
With such angry words and hasty fits.
  MAN. Why, dost thou remember what is to be
    bought
For the great bridal against to-morrow ?
The market must be in every place sought
For all kinds of meats, God give thee sorrow !
  MAID. What banging, what cursing, Long-tongue,
    is with thee !
I made as much speed as I could possibly ;
I-wis thou mightest have tarried for me,
Until in all points I had been ready ;
I have for thee looked full oft heretofore,
And yet for all that said never the more.
  MAN. Well, for this once I am with thee content,
So that hereafter thou make more haste ;
Or else, I tell thee, thou wilt it repent,
To loiter so long, till the market be past.
For there must be bought beef, veal and mutton,
And that even such as is good and fat,
With pig, geese, conies, and capon ;
How sayest thou, Blanche ? blab it out unto that ?
  MAID. I cannot tell, Long-tongue, what I should
    say ;
Of such good cheer I am so glad,
That if I would not eat at all that day,
My belly to fill I were very mad !
  MAN. There must be also pheasant and swan ;
There must be heronsew, partridge, and quail ;

And therefore I must do what I can,
That none of all these the gentleman fail.
I dare say he looks for many things mo,
To be prepared against to-morn ;
Wherefore, I say, hence let us go :
My feet do stand upon a thorn.

    MAID. Nay, good Long-tongue, I pray once again
To hear yet of my mind a word or twain.

    MAN. Come off, then : dispatch, and speak it
      quickly,
For what thing it is thou causest me tarry.

    MAID. Of whence is this gentleman that to-mor-
      row is married ?
Where doth his father and his mother dwell ?
Above forty miles he hath travelled,
As yesternight his servant did tell.

    MAN. In very deed he comes a great way,
With my master he may not long abide ;
It hath cost him so much on costly array,
That money out of his purse apace doth slide.
They say that his friends be rich and wealthy,
And in the city of London have their dwelling,
But yet of them all he hath no penny
To spend and bestow here at his wedding.
And if it be true that his servant did say,
He hath utterly lost his friends' good-will,
Because he would not their counsel obey,
And in his own country[1] tarry still ;
As for this woman, which he shall marry,
At Saint Albans always hath spent her life ;
I think she be a shrew, I tell thee plainly,
And full of debate, malice and strife.

    MAID. Though I never saw this woman before,
Which hither with him this gentleman brought,
Yet nevertheless I have tokens in store,

---

[1] Often used formerly for county.—*Halliwell.*

To judge of a woman that is forward and naught.
The tip of her nose is as sharp as mine,
Her tongue and her tune[1] is very shrill ;
I warrant her she comes of an ungracious kin,
And loveth too much her pleasure and will :
What though she be now so neat and so nice,
And speaketh as gentle as ever I heard :
Yet young men, which be both witty and wise,
Such looks and such words should not regard.
    MAN. Blanche, blab it out ; thou sayest very
      true ;
I think thou beginnest at length to preach :
This thing to me is strange and new,
To hear such a fool young men to teach.
    MAID. A fool ! mine own Long-tongue ! why,
      call'st thou me fool !
Though now in the kitchen I waste the day,
Yet in times past I went to school,
And of my Latin primer I took assay.
    MAN. Masters, this woman did take such assay,
And then in those days so applied her book,
That one word thereof she carried not away,
But then of a scholar was made a cook.
I dare say she knoweth not how her primer began,
Which of her master she learned then.
    MAID. I trow it began with *Domine labia, aperies.*
    MAN. What, did it begin with *butler de peas?*
    MAID. I tell thee again, with *Domine, labia*
      aperies,
If now to hear it be thine ease.
    MAN. How, how, with, *my madam lay in the*
      pease ?
    MAID. I think thou art mad ! with *Domine, labia*
      aperies.
    MAN. Yea, marry, I judged it went such ways ;

---

[1] Voice.

It began with, *Dorothy, lay up the keys!*
  MAID. Nay then, good night; I perceive by
    this gear,
That none is so deaf as who will not hear;
I spake as plainly as I could devise,
Yet me understand thou canst in no wise!
  MAN. Why, yet once again, and I will better
    listen,
And look upon thee how thy lips do open.
  MAID. Well, mark then, and hearken once for all,
Or else hear it again thou never shall;
My book, I say, began with *Domine, labia aperies.*
  MAN. Fie, fie, how slow am I of understanding!
Was it all this while, *Domine, labia aperies?*
Belike I have lost my sense of hearing,
With broiling and burning in the kitchen o' days.[1]
  MAID. I promise thee thou seemest to have done
    little better,
For that I wot in my life I never saw
One like to thyself in so easy a matter,
Unless he were deaf, thus play the daw.[2]
  MAN. Come on, come on, we have almost for-
    gotten
Such plenty of victuals as we should buy;
It were alms,[3] by my troth, thou were well beaten,
Because so long thou hast made me tarry.
  MAID. Tush, tush, we shall come in very good
    season,
If so be thou goest as fast as I;
Take up thy basket, and quickly have done,
We will be both there by and by.

---

  [1] In the daytime.—*Halliwell.* [Simply *o' days,* as printed
here.]
   [2] The simpleton. See 1, "Henry VI."—*Halliwell.*
   [3] A common phrase, equivalent to, it were a good thing.
See "Much Ado about Nothing," ii. 3.—*Halliwell.* [Not a
good thing, but *a charity.*]

MAN. I for my part will never leave running,
Until that I come to the sign of the Whiting.
   [*Here the two Cooks run out, and in cometh the
    Young Man and the Young Woman his lover.*

THE YOUNG WOMAN.

Where is my sweeting,[1] whom I do seek?
He promised me to have met me here :
Till I speak with him I think it a week,
For he is my joy, he is my cheer !
There is no night, there is no day,
But that my thoughts be all of him ;
I have no delight, if he be away :
Such toys in my head do ever swim.
But behold at the last, where he doth come.
For whom my heart desired long ;
Now shall I know, all and some,[2]
Or else I would say I had great wrong.

THE YOUNG MAN.

My darling, my coney,[3] my bird so bright of ble :[4]
Sweetheart, I say, all hail to thee !
How do our loves? be they fast asleep?
Or the old liveliness do they still keep?
   YOUNG WOMAN. Do ye ask, and[5] my love be
    fast asleep?
O, if a woman may utter her mind,
My love had almost made me to weep,

---

[1] "What, sweeting, all amort" (*Taming of the Shrew*).
—*Halliwell.*
  [2] Altogether, entirely.
  [3] Rabbit. A term of endearment.
  [4] My lady so fair in countenance. The expression is
common in our early romances.—*Halliwell.*
  [5] If.

Because that even now I did not you find ;
I thought it surely a whole hundred year,[1]
Till in this place I saw you here.
    YOUNG MAN. Alack, alack, I am sorry for
      this !
I had such business, I might not come ;
But ye may perceive what my wit is,
How small regard I have and wisdom.
    YOUNG WOMAN. Whereas ye ask me concerning
      my love,
I well assure you it doth daily augment ;
Nothing can make me start or move ;
You only to love is mine intent.
    YOUNG MAN. And as for my love it doth never
      relent,
For of you I do dream, of you I do think ;
To dinner and supper I never went,
But of beer and wine to you I did drink.
Now of such thinks [2] therefore to make an end,
Which pitiful lovers do cruelly torment,
To marriage, in God's name, let us descend,
As unto this hour we have been bent.
    YOUNG WOMAN. Your will to accomplish I am
      as ready
As any woman, believe me truly.
    YOUNG MAN. This ring then I give you as a
      token sure,
Whereby our love shall always endure.
    YOUNG WOMAN. With a pure pretence your
      pledge I take gladly,
For a sign of our love, faith, and fidelity.
    YOUNG MAN. Now I am safe, now I am glad,
Now I do live, now I do reign ;

---

[1] "Twelve years since " (*Tempest*).—*Halliwell.*
[2] A provincialism.—*Halliwell.*   [Rather, perhaps, a Cock-
neyism.]

Methought till now I was too sad,
Wherefore, sadness, fly hence again !
Away with those words which my father brought
    out !
Away with his sageness and exhortation !
He could not make me his fool or his lout,
And put me besides this delectation.
Did he judge that I would go to the school,
And might my time spend after this sort ?
I am not his calf,[1] nor yet his fool ;
This virgin I kiss is my comfort !
    YOUNG WOMAN. Well then, I pray you, let us
      be married,
For methink from it we have long tarried.
    YOUNG MAN. Agreed, my sweeting, it shall be
      then done,
Since that thy good-will I have gotten and won.
    YOUNG WOMAN. There would this day be very
      good cheer,
That every one his belly may fill,
And three or four minstrels would be here,
That none in the house sit idle or still.
    YOUNG MAN. Take ye no thought for abundance
      of meat,
That should be spent at our bridal,
For there shall be enough for all men to eat,
And minstrels besides thereto shall not fail.
The cooks, I dare say, a good while agone,
With such kind of flesh as I did them tell,
Are from the market both come home,
Or else, my own coney, they do not well.
I knew, before that I come to this place,
We should be married together this day,
Which caused me then forthwith in this case

---

[1] A term of contempt for a fool. See "Much Ado about
Nothing," iii. 3.—*Halliwell.*

To send for victuals, ere I came away.
  YOUNG WOMAN. Wherefore then (I pray ye)
    shall we go to our inn,
And look that everything be made ready?
Or else all is not worth a brass pin,[1]
Such haste is required in matrimony.
  YOUNG MAN. I think six o'clock it is not much
    past,
But yet to the priest we will make haste,
That according to custom we may be both coupled,
And with a strong knot for ever bound fast:
Yet, ere I depart, some song I will sing,
To the intent to declare my joy without fear,
And in the meantime you may, my sweeting,
Rest yourself in this little chair.

THE SONG.

Spite of his spite, which that in vain
Doth seek to force my fantasy,
I am professed for loss or gain,
To be thine own assuredly;
    Wherefore let my father spite[2] and spurn,
    My fantasy will never turn!
Although my father of busy wit
Doth babble still, I care not tho;
I have no fear, nor yet will flit,
As doth the water to and fro;
    Wherefore let my father spite and spurn,
    My fantasy will never turn!
For I am set and will not swerve,
Whom spiteful speech removeth nought;

---

[1] "At a pin's fee" (*Hamlet*).—*Halliwell.*
[2] Anger. "And that which spites me more than all these
wants" (*Taming of the Shrew*).—*Halliwell.*
  VOL. II.   T

And since that I thy grace deserve,
I count it is not dearly bought ;
> *Wherefore let my father spite and spurn,*
> *My fantasy will never turn !*
Who is afraid, let you him fly,
For I shall well abide the brunt :
Maugre to his lips that listeth to lie,
Of busy brains as is the wont ;
> *Wherefore let my father spite and spurn,*
> *My fantasy will never turn !*
Who listeth thereat to laugh or lour,[1]
I am not he that ought doth rech ;[2]
There is no pain that hath the power
Out of my breast your love to fetch ;
> *Wherefore let my father spite and spurn,*
> *My fantasy will never turn !*
For whereas he moved me to the school,
And only to follow my book and learning :
He could never make me such a fool,
With all his soft words and fair speaking ;
> *Wherefore let my father spite and spurn,*
> *My fantasy will never turn !*
This minion here, this mincing[3] *trull,*[4]
Doth please me more a thousand fold,
Than all the earth that is so full
Of precious stones, silver and gold ;
> *Wherefore let my father spite and spurn,*
> *My fantasy will never turn !*

---

[1] To look sad.   This term is often incorrectly explained.
" Fye, how impatience lowreth in your face " (*Com. Err.*), *i.e.*,
makes your face look sad, opposed to the " merry look."—
Halliwell.   [*Lour* is simply a contracted form of *lower*.]

[2] Care.

[3] Compare " Merchant of Venice," iii. 4.—*Halliwell*.

[4] Not a term of reproach.—Compare "1 Henry VI."—
Halliwell.

Whatsoever I did it was for her sake,
It was for her love and only pleasure;
I count it no labour such labour to take,
In getting to me so high a treasure;
> *Wherefore let my father spite and spurn,*
> *My fantasy will never turn!*
This day I intended for to be merry,
Although my hard father be far hence,
I know no cause for to be heavy,
For all this cost and great expense;
> *Wherefore let my father spite and spurn,*
> *My fantasy will never turn!*

YOUNG MAN. How like ye this song, my own
 sweet rose?
Is it well made for our purpose?
 YOUNG WOMAN. I never heard in all my life a
 better,
More pleasant, more meet for the matter;
Now let us go then, the morning is nigh gone,
We cannot any longer here remain:
Farewell, good masters every one,
Till from the church we come again.
  [*Here they go out, and in cometh the Priest*
   alone.
 PRIEST. Sirs, by my troth it is a world to see [1]
The exceeding negligence of every one,
Even from the highest to the lowest degree
Both goodness and conscience is clean gone.
There is a young gentleman in this town,
Who this same day now must be married:
Yet though I would bestow a crown,
That knave the clerk cannot be spied;
For he is safe, if that in the alehouse
He may sit tippling of nut-brown ale,

---

[1] Compare "Taming of the Shrew," ii. 1.—*Halliwell.*

That oft he comes forth as drunk as a mouse,
With a nose of his own not greatly pale ;
And this is not once, but every day
Almost, of my faith, throughout the whole year,
That he these tricks doth use to play,
Without all shame, dread and fear.
He knoweth himself, that yesternight
The said young gentleman came to me,
And then desired that he might
This morning betimes married be ;
But now I doubt it will be high noon,
Ere that his business be quite ended,
Unless the knavish fool come very soon,
That this same thing may be despatched ;
And therefore, since that this naughty pack
Hath at this present me thus served,
He is like henceforward my good-will to lack,
Or else unwise I might be judged.
I am taught hereafter how such a one to trust
In any matter concerning the church ;
For, if I should, I perceive that I must
Of mine own honesty lose very much.
And yet for all this, from week to week,
For his stipend and wages he ever[1] crieth,
And for the same continually doth seek,
As from time to time plainly appeareth ;
But whether his wages he hath deserved,
Unto you all I do me report,
Since that his duty he hath not fulfilled,
Nor to the church will scant resort ;
That many a time and oft[2] I am fain
To play the priest, clerk, and all,
Though thus to do it is great pain,
And my reward but very small.

---

[1] *Never* in the original copy.—*Halliwell.*
[2] Compare " The Merchant of Venice," i. 3.—*Halliwell.*

Wherefore (God willing) I will such order take,
Before that I be many days elder,
That he shall be glad this town to forsake,
And learn evermore to please his better,
And in such wise all they shall be used,
Which in this parish intend to be clerks ;
Great pity it were the church should be dis-
    ordered,
Because that such swillbowls[1] do not their works.
And to say truth, in many a place,
And other great towns beside this same,
The priests and parishioners be in the like case,
Which to the churchwardens may be a shame.
How should the priest his office fulfil,
Accordingly as indeed he ought,
When that the clerk will have a self-will,
And always in service-time must be sought ?
Notwithstanding at this present there is no re-
    medy,
But to take time, as it doth fall,
Wherefore I will go hence and make me ready,
For it helpeth not to chafe or brawl.
      *[Here the Priest goeth out, and in cometh the
      Rich Man.*

THE RICH MAN.

Coming this day forth of my chamber,
Even as for water to wash I did call,
By chance I espied a certain stranger,
Standing beneath within my hall ;
Who in very deed came from the innholder,
Whereas for a time my son did lie,
And said that his master had sent me a letter,
And bad him to bring it with all speed possible ;

---

[1] Drunkards.

Wherein he did write that as this day
That unthrift,[1] my son, to a certain maid
Should then be wedded without further delay,
And hath borrowed more than will be paid ;
And since that he heard he was my son
By a gentleman or two this other day,
He thought that it should be very well done
To let me have knowledge thereof by the way ;
And willed me, if that I would any thing
Of him to be done of me in this matter,
That then he his servant such word should bring,
As at his coming he might do hereafter :
I bad him thank his master most heartily,
And sent him by him a piece of venison,
For that he vouchsafed to write so gently,
Touching the marrying and state of my son ;
But notwithstanding I sent him no money
To pay such debts as my son did owe,
Because he had me forsaken utterly,
And me for his good father would not know ;
And said that with him I would not make
From that day forward during my life,
But as he had brewed, that so he should bake,
Since of his own choosing he gat him a wife.
Thus, when his servant from me departed,
Into my chamber I went again,
And there a great while I bitterly weeped :
This news to me was so great pain.
And thus with these words I began to moan,
Lamenting and mourning myself all alone :
O madness, O doting of those young folk !
O minds without wit, advice and discretion,
With whom their parents can bear no stroke
In their first matrimonial conjunction :
They know not what misery, grief and unquietness

---

[1] " Upstart unthrifts " (*Richard II.*)—*Halliwell.*

Will hereafter ensue of their extreme foolishness ;
Of all such labours they be clean ignorant,
Which, in the nourishing and keeping of children,
To their great charges it is convenient
Either of them henceforth to sustain :
Concerning expenses bestowed in a house,
They perceive as little as doth the mouse.
On the one side the wife will brawl and scold,
On the other side the infant will cry in the cradle :
Anon, when the child waxeth somewhat old,
For meat and drink he begins to babble :
Hereupon cometh it that at markets and fairs
A husband is forced to buy many wares.
Yet for all this hath my foolish son,
As wise [as] a woodcock,[1] without any wit,
Despising his father's mind and opinion,
Married a wife for him most unfit,
Supposing that mirth to be everlasting,
Which then at the first was greatly pleasing.
How they two will live, I cannot tell ;
Whereto they may trust, they have nothing.
My mind giveth me, that they will come dwell
At length by their father for want of living ;
But my son doubtless, for anything that I know,
Shall reap in such wise as he did sow ;
True he shall find, that Hipponax did write,
Who said with a wife are two days of pleasure ;
The first is the joy of the marriage-day and night,
The second to be at the wife's sepulture :
And this by experience he shall prove true,
That of his bridal great evils do ensue.
And (as I suppose) it will prove in his life,
When he shall wish that to him it may chance,
Which unto Eupolis and also his wife,

---

[1] Compare "Taming of the Shrew," i. 2 ; "O this woodcock, what an ass it is !"—*Halliwell.*

The night they were wedded, fell for a vengeance ;
Who with the heavy ruin of the bed were slain,
As the Poet Ovid in these two verses make plain :

> *Sit tibi conjugii nox prima novissimi vitæ,*
> *Eupolis hoc periit et nova nupta modo.*

Ovidius, writing against one Ibis his enemy,
That the first night of his marriage did wish
The last of his life might be certainly,
For so (quoth he) did Eupolis and his wife perish.
Yet to my son I pray God to send,
Because thereunto me nature doth bind,
Though he hath offended, a better end
Than Eupolis and his wife did find.
And now I shall long ever anon,
Till some of those quarters come riding hither,
Unto the which my son is gone,
To know how they do live together.
But I am fasting, and it is almost noon,
And more than time that I had dined :
Wherefore from hence I will go soon ;
I think by this time my meat is burned.
> [*Here the Rich Man goeth out, and in cometh the
> Young Man his son with the Young Woman, being
> both married.*

THE HUSBAND.

O my sweet wife, my pretty coney !

THE WIFE.

O my husband, as pleasant as honey.
   HUSBAND. O Lord, what pleasures and great
     commodity
Are heaped together in matrimony !
   WIFE. How vehement, how strong a thing
     love is !

How many smirks and dulsome [1] kisses!
   HUSBAND. What smiling, what laughing!
What sport, pastime, and playing!
   WIFE. What tickling, what toying!
What dallying, what joying!
   HUSBAND. The man with the wife is wholly de-
     lighted,
And with many causes to laughter enforced.
   WIFE. When they two drink, they drink to-
     gether;
They never eat but one with another.
   HUSBAND. Sometimes to their garden forth they
     walk,
And into the fields sometimes they go,
With merry tricks and gestures they talk,
As they do move their feet to and fro.
   WIFE. Sometimes they ride into the country,
Passing the time with mirth and sport;
And when with their friends they have been merry,
Home to their own house they do resort.
   HUSBAND. Sometimes abroad they go to see
     plays,
And other trim sights for to behold:
When often they meet in the highways
Much of their acquaintance they knew of old.
   WIFE. Sometimes to the church they do repair,
To hear the sermon that shall be made,
Though it to remember they shall have small care;
For why they be now but few of that trade.
   HUSBAND. Sometimes at home at cards they
     play,
Sometimes at this game, sometimes at that;
They need not with sadness to pass the day,
Nor yet to sit still, or stand in one plat.
   WIFE. And as for us wives, occasions do move

---

[1] [Rather, perhaps, *dulsum*, *i.e.*, sweet.]

Sometimes with our gossips to make good cheer,
Or else we did not, as did us behove,
For certain days and weeks in the year.
    HUSBAND. I think that a man might spend a
        whole day,
Declaring the joys and endless bliss,
Which married persons receive alway,
If they love faithfully, as meet it is.
    WIFE. Wives cannot choose but love earnestly,
If that their husbands do all things well ;
Or else, my sweetheart, we shall espy,
That in quietness they cannot dwell.
    HUSBAND. If they do not, it may be a shame,
For I love you heartily, I you assure :
Or else I were truly greatly to blame,
Ye are so loving, so kind and demure.
    WIFE. I trust that with neither hand or foot
Ye shall see any occasion by me :
But that I love you even from the heart-root,
And during my life so intend to be.
    HUSBAND. Who then merry marriage can dis-
        commend,
And will not with Aristotle in his Ethics [1] agree ?
But will say, that misery is the end,
When otherwise I find it to be :
A politic man will marry a wife,
As the philosopher makes declaration,
Not only to have children by his life,
But also for living, help, and sustentation.
    WIFE. Who will not with H'erocles plainly con-
        fess,
That mankind to society is wholly adjoining,

---

[1] This confirms in some measure a reading in the
"Taming of the Shrew"—"Or so devote to Aristotle's
Ethics."—*Halliwell.* [See Dyce's 2d edit. iii. 114, and the
note.]

And in this society nevertheless
Of worthy wedlock took the beginning :
Without the which no city can stand,
Nor household be perfect in any land ?

HUSBAND. Pythagoras, Socrates, and Crates also,
Which truly were men of very small substance,
As I heard my father tell long ago,
Did take them wives with a safe conscience ;
And dwelled together, supposing that they
Were unto philosophy nother stop nor stay.

WIFE. Yea, what can be more according to kind,
Than a man to a woman himself to bind ?

HUSBAND. Away with those therefore, that mar-
    riage despise,
And of dangers thereof invent many lies !

WIFE. But what is he that cometh yonder ?
Do ye not think it is our man ?
Somewhat there is that he hasteth hither,
For he makes as much speed as he can.

    [*Here the servant of the Rich Man's Son
      cometh in, with an errand to his master.*

SERVANT.

Master, there is a stranger at home,
He would very fain with you talk :
For until that to him ye do come,
Forth of the doors he will not walk.

HUSBAND. Come on then, my wife, if it be so,
Let us depart hence for a season :
For I am not well, till I do know
Of that man's coming the very reason.

    [*Here they both go out, and their Servant doth
      tarry behind alone.*

SERVANT.

Let them go both, and do what they will,
And with communication fill their belly :
For I, by Saint George, will tarry here still,
In all my life I was never so weary !
I have this day filled so many pots
With all manner wine, ale, and beer,
That I wished their bellies full of bots,[1]
Long of whom [2] was made such cheer.
What kinds of meat, both flesh and fish,
Have I, poor knave, to the table carried
From time to time, dish after dish ;
My legs from going never ceased !
What running had I for apples and nuts !
What calling for biscuits, comfits, and caraways ! [3]
A vengeance, said I, light on their guts,
That makes me to turn so many ways !
What crying was there for cards and dice !
What roisting,[4] what ruffling made they within !
I counted them all not greatly wise,
For my head did almost ache with din.
What babbling, what jangling [5] was in the house !
What quaffing, what bibbing with many a cup !
That some lay along as drunk as a mouse,
Not able so much as their heads to hold up !
What dancing, what leaping, what jumping about,
From bench to bench, and stool to stool,
That I wondered their brains did not fall out,

---

[1] "Begnaw with the bots" (*Taming of the Shrew*).—
Halliwell.

[2] Owing to whom.

[3] Caraway comfits. See "2 Henry IV." and the blun-
ders of the commentators corrected in my "Dictionary of
Archaisms," p. 231.—*Halliwell*.

[4] Compare "Troilus and Cressida," ii. 2.—*Halliwell*.

[5] "Good wits will be jangling" (*Love's Labour's Lost*).—
Halliwell.

When they so outrageously played the fool !
What juggling was there upon the boards !
What thrusting of knives through many a nose !
What bearing of forms, what holding of swords,
And putting of botkins [1] through leg and hose !
Yet for all that they called for drink,
And said they could not play for dry,
That many at me did nod and wink,
Because I should bring it by and by.
Howsoever they sported, the pot did still walk :
If that were away, then all was lost,
For ever anon the jug was their talk,
They passed [2] not who bare such charge and cost.
Therefore let him look his purse be right good,
That it may discharge all that is spent,
Or else it will make his hair grow through his hood, [3]
There was such havoc made at this present ;
But I am afeard my master be angry,
That I did abide thus long behind :
Yet for his anger I pass [4] not greatly,
His words they be but only wind !
Now that I have rested so long in this place,
Homeward again I will hie me apace.
> [*Here the Servant goeth out, and in cometh
> first the Wife, and shortly after the
> Husband.*

THE WIFE.

Where is my husband ? was he not here ?
I marvel much whither he is gone !
Then I perceive I am [not] much the near : [5]

---

[1] A dagger. See " Hamlet," iii. 1.—*Halliwell.*
[2] Cared.
[3] [A rather common phrase. See Hazlitt's "Proverbs,"
1869, p. 205.]
[4] Care.   [5] [Nearer.]

But lo, where he cometh hither alone!
Wot ye what, husband, from day to day
With dainty dishes our bodies have been filled?
What meat to-morrow next shall we assay,
Whereby we may then be both refreshed?
    HUSBAND. Do ye now provide and give a regard
For victuals hereafter to be prepared?
    WIFE. But that I know, husband, it lieth us in
      hand
Of things to come to have a consideration,
I would not once will you to understand
About such business my careful provision :
It is needful therefore to work we make haste,
That to get both our livings we may know the cast.
    HUSBAND. To trouble me now, and make me
      vexed,
This mischievous means hast thou invented.
    WIFE. What trouble for thee, what kind of
      vexation,
Have I to disquiet thee caused at this present ?
My only mind is thou make expedition
To seek for our profit, as is convenient.[1]
Wherefore to thee I say once again,
Because to take pains thou art so loth,
By Christ, it were best with might and main
To fall to some work, I swear a great oath !
    HUSBAND. Yet, for a time, if it may thee please,
Let me be quiet, and take mine ease.
    WIFE. Wilt thou have us then through hunger
      be starved ?
    HUSBAND. I would not we should for hunger be
      killed.
    WIFE. Then, I say then, this gear[2] go about,
And look that thou labour diligently,
Or else thou shalt shortly prove without doubt,

---

[1] Necessary, fit.   [2] Business.

Thy sluggishness will not please me greatly.
  HUSBAND. Beginnest thou even now to be painful
    and grievous,
And to thy husband a woman so troublous?
  WIFE. What words have we here, thou misbe-
    gotten :
Is there not already enough to be spoken?
  HUSBAND. O mirth, O joy, O pastime and
    pleasure,
How little a space do you endure!
  WIFE. I see my commandment can take no
    place;
Thou shalt aby therefore, I swear by the mass!
        [Here the Wife must strike her Husband
          handsomely about the shoulders with
          something.
  HUSBAND. Alas, good wife! good wife, alas,
    alas!
Strike not so hard, I pray thee heartily!
Whatsoever thou wilt have brought to pass,
It shall be done with all speed possible.
  WIFE. Lay these faggots, man, upon thy
    shoulder,
And carry this wood from street to street,
To sell the same, that we both together
Our living may get, as is most meet.
Hence, nidiot, hence without more delay!
What meanest thou thus to stagger and stay?
  HUSBAND. O Lord! what, how miserable men
    be those,
Which to their wives as wretches be wedded,
And have them continually their mortal foes,
Serving them thus, as slaves that be hired!
Now by experience true I do find,
Which oftentimes unto me heretofore
My father did say, declaring his mind,
That in matrimony was pain evermore;

What shall I do, most pitiful creature?
Just cause I have, alas, to lament:
That frantic woman my death will procure,
If so be this day without gain be spent:
For unless for my wood some money be taken,
Like a dog with a cudgel I shall be beaten!
Ho, thou good fellow, which standest so nigh,
Of these heavy bundles ease my sore back,
And somewhat therefore give me by and by,
Or else I die, for silver I do lack.
Now that I have some money received
For this my burthen, home I will go,
And lest that my wife be discontented,
What I have take, I will her show.
Wife, I am come: I went a long way,
And here is the profit and gains of this day!

 WIFE. Why, thou lout, thou fool, thou whore-
  son folt,[1]
Is this thy wood money, thou peevish[2] dolt?
Thou shalt smart for this gear, I make God a vow!
Thou knowest no more to sell wood than doth the
  sow!

 HUSBAND. By God's precious, I will not un-
  wisely suffer
To do as I have done any longer.

 WIFE. Why, dost thou rise against me, villain?
Take heed I scratch not out thy eyes twain!

 HUSBAND. Scratch, and thou dare, for I have a
  knife:
Perchance I will rid thee of thy life!

 WIFE. Slay me with thy knife, thou shitten
  dastard!
Dost thou think to find me such a dissard?

---

[1] Fool. "Folte, *stolidus*" (*Vocab. MS.*)—*Halliwell.*
[2] Foolish—"Our peevish opposition" (*Hamlet*).—*Halliwell.*

By Cock's bones, I will make thy skin to rattle,
And the brains in thy skull more deeply to settle.
    [*Here the Wife must lay on load upon her
     Husband.*
  HUSBAND. Good wife, be content! forgive me
   this fault!
I will never again do that which is naught.
  WIFE. Go to, foolish calf, go to, and uprise,
And put up thy knife, I thee advise.
  HUSBAND. I will do your commandments what-
   soever.
  WIFE. Hence away, then, and fill this with
   water.
  HUSBAND. O merciful God, in what lamentable
   state
Is he, of whom the wife is the master?
Would God I had been predestinate
On my marriage day to have died with a fever!
O wretched creature, what may I do?
My grievous wife shall I return unto?
Lo, wife, behold! without further delay
The water ye sent for here I do bring.
  WIFE. What, I say? what meaneth this weeping?
What aileth thee to make all this crying?
  HUSBAND. I weep not, forsooth, nor cry not as
   yet.
  WIFE. No, nor thou wilt not, if thou hast any
   wit;
It is not thy weeping that can ought avail,
And therefore this matter no longer bewail.
Come off, I say, and run by the river,
And wash these clothes in the water.
  HUSBAND. Wife, I will thither hie me fast.
  WIFE. Yet I advise thee, thou cullon,[1] make
   haste.

---

[1] Compare "Taming of the Shrew," iv. 2.—*Halliwell.*

HUSBAND. O, how unhappy and eke unfortunate
Is the most part of married men's condition !
I would to death I had been agate,[1]
When my mother in bearing me made lamentation.
What shall I do ? whither shall I turn ?
Most careful man now under the sky !
In the flaming fire I had rather burn,
Than with extreme pain live so heavily.
There is no shift ; to my wife I must go,
Whom that I did wed ; I am full wo !
Where are ye, wife ? your clothes are washed clean,
As white as a lily,[2] without spot or stain.

    WIFE. Thou thief, thou caitiff, why is not this
      place
Washed as fair as all the rest ?
Thou shalt for this gear now smoke apace !
By Jis,[3] I swear, thou brutish beast !

         [Here she must knock her Husband.

    HUSBAND. Alas, alas ! I am almost quite dead !
My wife so pitifully hath broken my head !

     [Here her Husband must lie along on the ground,
        as though he were sore beaten and wounded.

    WIFE. Well, I perceive the time will away,
And into the country to go I have promised ;
Look therefore thou go not from hence to-day,
Till home again I am returned.
Take heed, I say, this house thee retain,
And stir not for any thing out of my door,
Until that I come hither again,
As thou wilt be rewarded therefore.

     [Here his Wife goeth out, and the Husband
       tarrieth behind alone.

---

[1] [A-going, bound.]
[2] A common phrase. See "Two Gentlemen of Verona,"
ii. 3.—*Halliwell.*
[3] Compare the song in "Hamlet," iv. 5.—*Halliwell.*

HUSBAND. The flying fiend [1] go with my wife,
And in her journey ill may she speed !
I pray God Almighty to shorten her life !
The earth at no time doth bear such a weed !
Although that I be a gentleman born,
And come by my ancètors of a good blood,
Yet am I like to wear a coat torn,
And hither and thither go carry wood !
But rather than I this life will abide,
To-morrow morning I do intend
Home to my father again to ride,
If some man to me his horse will lend.
She is to her gossips gone to make merry,
And there she will be for three or four days :
She cares not, though I do now miscarry,
And suffer such pain and sorrow always.
She leaveth to me neither bread nor drink,
But such, as I judge, no body would eat :
I might by the walls lie dead and stink,
For any great wholesomeness in my meat.
She walketh abroad, and taketh her pleasure :
Herself to cherish is all her care :
She passeth not what grief I endure,
Or how I can live with noughty [2] fare :
And since it is so, without further delay
To my father to-morrow I will away.

      [*Here he goeth out, and in cometh the Devil.*[3]

SATAN THE DEVIL.

Ho, ho, ho, what a fellow am I !
Give room, I say, both more and less :

---

  [1] [Orig. has *flying and fiend.*]
  [2] Bad. " This is a noughty night" (*Lear*).—*Halliwell.*
  [3] The devil was generally attended by the Vice, but he is
here introduced by himself, and the exact meaning of his
part in this plot is somewhat a mystery.—*Halliwell.*

My strength and power, hence to the sky,
No earthly tongue can well express!
O, what inventions, crafts and wiles
Is there contained within this head!
I know that he is within few miles,
Which of the same is throughly sped.
O, it was all my study day and night
Cunningly to bring this matter to pass:
In all the earth there is no wight,
But I can make to cry alas.
This man and wife, that not long ago
Fell in this place together by the ears:
It was only I that this strife did sow,
And have been about it certain years.
For after that I had taken a smell
Of their good will and fervent love,
Me-thought I should not tarry in hell,
But unto debate them shortly move:
O, it was I that made him to despise
All wisdom, goodness, virtue, and learning,
That he afterward could in no wise
Once in his heart fancy teaching:
O, it was I that made him refuse
The wholesome monition of his father dear,
And caused him still of a wife to muse,
As though she should be his joy and cheer!
O, it was I that made him go hence,
And suppose that his father was very unkind;
It was I that did drive him to such expense.
And made him as bare as an ape is behind.
And now that I have this business ended,
And joined him and his wife together,
I think that I have my part well played:
None of you all would do it better.
Ho, ho, ho! this well-favoured head of mine,
What thing soever it hath in hand,
Is never troubled with ale or wine,

Neither by sea, nor yet by land.
I tell you I am a marvellous body,
As any is at this day living :
My head doth devise each thing so trimly,
That all men may wonder of the ending.
O, I have such fetches,[1] such toys in this head,
Such crafty devices and subtle train,
That whomsoever of you I do wed,
Ye are like at my hands to take small gain.
There is no gentleman, knight, or lord :
There is no duke, earl, or king,
But, if I list, I can with one word
Shortly send unto their lodging.
Some I disquiet with covetousness :
Some with wrath, pride and lechery ;
And some I do thrust into such distress,
That he feeleth only pain and misery.
Some I allure to have their delight
Always in gluttony, envy and murder,
And those things to practise with all their might,
Either by land or else by water.
Ho, ho, ho ! there is none to be compared
To me, I tell you, in any point :
With a great sort[2] myself I have tried,
That boldly ventured many a joint,
And when for a long time we had wrestled,
And showed our strength on either side,
Yet oftentimes a fall they received,
When through my policy their feet did slide.
Wherefore (my dear children) I warn ye all :
Take heed, take heed of my temptation,
For commonly at the last ye have the fall,
And also [be] brought to desperation.
O ! it is a folly for many to strive,
And think of me to get the upper hand,

---

[1] Tricks. See "King Lear."—*Halliwell.*
[2] Company.

For unless that God make them to thrive,
They cannot against me stick or stand :
And though that God on high have his dominion,
And ruleth the world everywhere,
Yet by your leave I have a portion
Of this same earth that standeth here.
The kingdom of God is above in heaven,
And mine is, I tell you, beneath in hell ;
But yet a greater place, if he had dealt even,
He should have given me and mine to dwell :
For to my palace of every nation,
Of what degree or birth soever they be,
Come running in with such festination,[1]
That otherwhiles they amazed me.
O, all the Jews and all the Turks,
Yea, and a great part of Christendom,
When they have done my will and my works,
In the end they fly hither all and some :[2]
There is no minute of the day,
There is no minute of the night,
But that in my palace there is alway
Crowding together a marvellous sight ;
They come on thicker than swarms of bees,
And make such a noise and crying out,
That many a one lieth on his knees,
With thousands kept under and closed about :
Not so much as my parlours, halls, and every
    chamber :
My porches, my galleries, and my court :
My entries, my kitchen, and my larder,
But with all manner people be filled throughout !
What shall I say more, I cannot tell,
But of this (my children) I am certain,
There comes more in one hour unto hell,
Than unto heaven in a month or twain.
And yet for all this my nature is such,

---

[1] Haste. *Lat.*   [2] Every one.

That I am not pleased with this company,
But out of my kingdom I must walk much,
That one or other I may take tardy.
Ho, ho, ho! I am never once afraid
With these my claws you for to touch,
For I will not leave, till you be paid
Such treasure as is within my pouch.
The world is my son, and I am his father,
And also the flesh is a daughter of mine;
It is I alone that taught them to gather
Both gold and silver that is so fine;
Wherefore I suppose that they love me well,
And my commandments gladly obey,
That at the last then unto hell
They may come all the ready way.
But now (I know), since I came hither,
There is such a multitude at my gate,
That I must again repair down thither
After mine old manner and rate.

> [*Here the Devil goeth out, and in cometh the Rich
> Man's Son alone.*

THE SON.

How glad am I that my journey is ended,
Which I was about this whole day!
My horse to stand still I never suffered,
Because I would come to the end of my way:
But yet I am sorry that I cannot find
My loving father at home at his place,
That unto him I may break my mind,
And let him know my miserable case.

> [*Here he confesseth his naughtiness, uttering the
> same with a pitiful voice.*

I have been wild, I have been wanton,
I have ever followed my fancy and will:
I have been to my father a froward son,
And from day to day continued still.

I have always proudly disdained those
That in my madness gave me good counsel :
I counted them most my mortal foes,
And stoutly against them did rebel.
The thing that was good I greatly hated,
As one which lacked both wit and reason ;
The thing that was evil I ever loved,
Which now I see is my confusion.
I could not abide of the school to hear ;
Masters and teachers my heart abhorred ;
Methought the book was not fit gear
For my tender fingers to have handled ;
I counted it a pleasure to be daintily fed,
And to be clothed in costly array :
I would most commonly slug in my bed,
Until it were very far-forth day.
And (to be short) anon after this,
There came such fancies in my brain,
That to have a wife, whom I might kiss,
I reckoned to be the greatest gain.
But yet, alas, I was quite deceived ;
The thing itself doth easily appear ;
I would, alas, I had been buried,
When to my father I gave not ear !
That which I had I have clean spent,
And kept so much riot with the same,
That now I am fain a coat that is rent,
Alas, to wear for very shame.
I have not a cross left in my purse
To help myself now in my need,
That well I am worthy of God's curse,
And of my father to have small meed.
　　[*Here the Rich Man must be as it were coming in.*
But except mine eyes do me beguile,
That man is my father, whom I do see :
And now that he comes, without craft or wile,
To him I will bend on either knee.
Ah, father, father, my father most dear !

FATHER. Ah! mine own child, with thee what
    cheer?
SON. All such sayings as in my mind
At the first time ye studied to settle,
Most true, alas, I do them find,
As though they were written in the Gospel.
    FATHER. Those words, my son, I have almost
    forgotten;
Stand up, therefore, and kneel no longer,
And what it was I spake so often,
At two or three words recite to thy father.
    SON. If that ye be, father, well remembered,
As the same I believe ye cannot forget,
You said that, so soon as I were married,
Much pain and trouble thereby I should get.
    FATHER. Hast thou by proof, son, this thing
    tried?
SON. Yea, alas, too much I have experienced:
My wife I did wed all full of frenzy.
My seely poor shoulders hath now so bruised,
That like to a cripple I move me weakly,
Being full often with the staff thwacked:
She spareth no more my flesh and bone,
Than if my body were made of stone!
Her will, her mind, and her commandment
From that day hither I have fulfilled,
Which if I did not, I was bitterly shent,
And with many strokes grievously punished:
That would God, the hour when I was married,
In the midst of the church I might have sinked.
I think there is no man under the sun,
That here on the earth beareth life,
Which would do such drudgery as I have done,
At the unkind words of such a wife;
For how I was used, and in what wise,
A day to declare will not suffice.
If this be not true, as I have spoken,
To my good neighbours I me report,

Who other whiles, when I was smitten,
My wife to be gentle did then exhort :
For glad I was to abide all labour,
Whereby the less might be my dolour.[1]
Wherefore, good father, I you humbly desire
To have pity of me and some compassion,
Or else I am like to lie fast in the mire,
Without any succour or consolation :
For at this hour I have not a penny,
Myself to help in this great misery.

    FATHER. For so much as by my advice and
        counsel
In no manner wise thou wouldest be ruled,
Therefore to thee I cannot do well,
But let thee still suffer as thou hast deserved,
For that thou hast suffered is yet nothing
To that tribulation which is behind coming.

    SON. Alas, father, what shall I do ?
My wits of themselves cannot devise
What thing I were best go unto,
Whereof an honest living may arise :
Wherefore, gentle father, in this distress,
Somewhat assuage mine heaviness.

    FATHER. What should I do, I cannot tell,
For now that thou hast taken a wife,
With me thy father thou mayest not dwell,
But always with her spend thy life.
Thou mayest not again thy wife forsake,
Which during life to thee thou didst take.

    SON. Alas, I am not able thus to endure,
Though thereunto I were never so willing ;
For my wife is of such a crooked nature,
As no woman else in this day living,
And if the very truth I shall confess,
She is to me an evil that is endless.

---

    [1] Grief. " My endless dolou " (*Two Gentlemen of Verona*).
—*Halliwell.*

FATHER. If that thou thinkest thyself alone
Only to lead this irksome life,
Thou may'st learn what grief, sorrow and moan,
Socrates had with Xantippe his wife[1];
Her husband full oft she taunted and checked,
And, as the book saith, unhonestly mocked.
    SON. I cannot tell what was Socrates wife,
But mine I do know, alas, too well;
She is one that is evermore full of strife,
And of all scolders beareth the bell.
When she speaketh best, then brawleth her tongue;
When she is still, she fighteth apace;
She is an old witch, though she be young:
No mirth with her, no joy or solace!
    FATHER. I cannot, my son, thy state redress;
Me thy father thou didst refuse;
Wherefore now help thy own foolishness,
And of thy wife no longer muse.
    SON. My wife went forth into the country
With certain gossips to make good cheer,
And bad me at home still to be,
That at her return she might find me there:
And if that she do take me from home,[2]
My bones, alas, she will make to crackle,
And me her husband, as a stark mome,[3]
With knocking and mocking she will handle;
And, therefore, if I may not here remain,
Yet, loving father, give me your reward,
That I may with speed ride home again,
That to my wife's words have some regard.
    FATHER. If that at the first thou wouldest have
        been ordered,
And done as thy father counselled thee,
So wretched a life had never chanced,

---

[1] Compare "Taming of the Shrew," i. 2.—*Halliwell.*
[2] [Catch me gone from home.]
[3] Fool.—See "Comedy of Errors, iii. 1."—*Halliwell.*

Whereof at this present thou complainest to me ;
But yet come on, to my house we will be going,
And there thou shalt see what I will give :—
A little to help thy need living,
Since that in such penury thou dost live ;
And that once done, thou must hence again,
For I am not he that will thee retain.
   [*Here the Rich Man and his Son go out, and in
      cometh the Perorator.*[1]

THE PERORATOR.

This Interlude here, good gentle audience,
Which presently before you we have played,
Was set forth with such care and diligence,
As by us truly might well be shewed.
Short it is, I deny not, and full of brevity,
But if ye mark thereof the matter,
Then choose ye cannot but see plainly,
How pain and pleasure be knit together.
By this little play the father is taught
After what manner his child to use,
Lest that through cockering[2] at length he be
    brought
His father's commandment to refuse ;
Here he may learn a witty [3] lesson
Betimes to correct his son being tender,
And not let him be lost and undone
With wantonness, of mischief the mother ;
For as long as the twig is gentle and pliant
(Every man knoweth this by experience),
With small force and strength it may be bent,
Putting thereto but little diligence ;
But after that it waxeth somewhat bigger,
And to cast his branches largely beginneth,

---

  [1] The person who spoke the Epilogue (Lat).
  [2] Indulgence.
  [3] Clever.—See "Taming of the Shrew."—*Halliwell.*

It is scant the might of all thy power,
That one bough thereof easily bendeth :
This twig to a child may well be applied,
Which, in his childhood and age of infancy,
With small correction may be amended,
Embracing the school with heart and body,
Who afterward, with overmuch liberty,
And ranging abroad with the bridle of will,
Despiseth all virtue, learning, and honesty,
And also his father's mind to fulfil :
Whereby at the length it so falleth out
That this the young stripling, after that day
Runs into confusion without any doubt,
And like for evermore quite to decay.
Wherefore take heed, all ye that be parents,
And follow a part after my counsel ;
Instruct your children and make them students,
That unto all goodness they do not rebel ;
Remember what writeth Solomon the wise :
Qui parcit virgæ, odit filium.
Therefore for as much as ye can devise,
Spare not the rod, but follow wisdom :
Further, ye young men and children also,
Listen to me and hearken a while,
What in few words for you I will show
Without any flattery, fraud, or guile.
This rich man's son whom we did set forth
Here evidently before our eyes,
Was (as it chanced) nothing worth :
Given to all noughtiness, vice, and lies.
The cause whereof was this for a truth :
His time full idly he did spend,
And would not study in his youth,
Which might have brought him to a good end ;
His father's commandment he would not obey,
But wantonly followed his fantasy,
For nothing that he could do or say
Would bring this child to honesty.

And at the last (as here ye might see)
Upon a wife he fixed his mind,
Thinking the same to be felicity,
When indeed misery came behind ;
For by this wife he carefully [1] lived,
Who under his father did want nothing,
And in such sort was hereby tormented,
That ever anon he went lamenting.
His father did will him lightness [2] to leave,
And only to give himself unto study,
But yet unto virtue he would not cleave,
Which is commodious for soul and body.
You heard that by sentences ancient and old,
He stirred his son as he best thought ;
But he, as an unthrift stout and bold,
His wholesome counsel did set at nought ;
And since that he despised his father,
God unto him did suddenly then send
Such poverty with a wife and grief together,
That shame and sorrow was his end.
Wherefore to conclude, I warn you all
By your loving parents always be ruled,
Or else be well assured of such a fall,
As unto this young man worthily chanced.
Worship God daily, which is the chief thing,
And his holy laws do not offend :
Look that ye truly serve the king,
And all your faults be glad to amend :
Moreover, be true of hand and tongue,
And learn to do all things that be honest,
For no time so fit, as when ye be young,
Because that age only is the aptest.
I have no more to speak at this season,
For very good will these things I did say,

---

[1] With care or sorrow.
[2] Levity.—Cf. "Taming of Shrew," iv. 2.—*Halliwell.*

Because I do see that virtue is geason [1]
With most men and children at this day.

> [*Here the rest of the Players come in, and
> kneel down all together, each of them
> saying one of these verses :*

And last of all to make an end,
O God, to thee we most humbly pray,
That to Queen Elizabeth thou do send
Thy lively path and perfect way !
Grant her in health to reign
With us many years most prosperously,
And after this life for to attain
The eternal bliss, joy, and felicity !
Our bishops, pastors, and ministers also,
The true understanding of thy word,
Both night and day, now mercifully show,
That their life and preaching may godly accord.
The lords of the council and the nobility,
Most heavenly father, we thee desire
With grace, wisdom, and godly policy
Their hearts and minds always inspire.
And that we thy people, duly considering
The power of our queen and great auctority,
May please thee and serve her without feigning,
Living in peace, rest, and tranquillity.

GOD SAVE THE QUEEN.

A SONG.

Why doth the world study vain glory to attain,
The prosperity whereof is short and transitory,
Whose mighty power doth fall down again,
Like earthen pots, that breaketh suddenly ?
Believe rather words that be written in ice,
Than the wretched world with his subtlety,

---

[1] Scarce.

Deceitful in gifts, men only to entice,
Destitute of all sure credence and fidelity.
Give credit more to men of true judgments
Than to the worldly renown and joys,
Replenished with dreams and vain intents,
Abounding in wicked and noughty toys.
Where is now Salomon, in wisdom so excellent ?
Where is now Samson, in battle so strong ?
Where is is now Absolom, in beauty resplendent ?
Where is now good Jonathas, hid so long ?
Where is now Cæsar, in victory triumphing ?
Where is now Dives, in dishes so dainty ?
Where is now Tully, in eloquence exceeding ?
Where is now Aristotle, learned so deeply ?
What emperors, kings, and dukes in times past,
What earls and lords, and captains of war,
What popes and bishops, all at the last
In the twinkling of an eye are fled so far ?
How short a feast is this worldly joying ?
Even as a shadow it passeth away,
Depriving a man of gifts everlasting,
Leading to darkness and not to day !
O meat of worms, O heap of dust,
O like to dew, climb not too high !
To live to-morrow thou canst not trust,
Therefore now betime help the needy.
The fleshly beauty, whereat thou dost wonder,
In holy Scripture is likened to hay,
And as a leaf in a stormy weather,
So is man's life blowen clean away.
Call nothing thine that may be lost :
The world doth give and take again,
But set thy mind on the Holy Ghost ;
Despise the world that is so vain !

FINIS.

THE MARRIAGE

OF

WIT AND SCIENCE.

VOL. II.   X

[The title of the old copy is : *A new and Pleasaunt
enterlude intituled the mariage of Witte and Science.
Imprinted at London in Flete Streete, neare vnto sainct
Dunstones churche by Thomas Marshe. 4°, black letter.

There is no date, but the size is a small 4to, and it
probably appeared in 1570, having been licensed in
1569–70 to Marsh.   Some further particulars of the
play, now first reprinted from the only known copy in
the Malone collection at Oxford, may be found in Hazlitt's "Handbook," 1867, p. 465 ; Collier's " Extr. from
the Stat. Reg.," i. 204 ; and Collier's "Hist. Engl.
Dram. Poetry," ii. 341–7, where there is a somewhat
long review of the piece, with extracts.   Mr Collier,
who bestows considerable praise on this interlude, observes :—"The moral play of ' The Marriage of Wit
and Science' contains a remarkable external feature
not belonging to any other piece of this class that I
remember to have met with : it is regularly divided
into five acts, and each of the scenes is also marked."
The anonymous author appears to have borrowed to
some extent from the older performance by John
Redford, printed from a MS. by the Shakespeare Society
in 1848 ; but the two productions must, nevertheless,
be regarded as distinct and independent.]

THE PLAYERS' NAMES.

Nature.	Science.	Shame.
Wit.	Reason.	Idleness.
Will.	Experience.	Ignorance.
Study.	Recreation.	Tediousness.

Diligence, *with three other women singers.* Instruction.

THE

MARRIAGE OF WIT AND SCIENCE.

——◆——

[ACT I.]

GRAND lady, mother of every mortal thing :
Nurse of the world, conservative of kind :
Cause of increase, of life and soul the spring ;
At whose instinct the noble heaven doth wind,
To whose award all creatures are assigned,
I come in place to treat with this my son,
For his avail how he the path may find,
Whereby his race in honour he may run :
Come, tender child, unripe and green for age,
In whom the parent sets her chief delight,
Wit is thy name, but far from wisdom sage,
Till tract of time shall work and frame aright,
This peerless brain, not yet in perfect plight :
But when it shall be wrought, methinks I see,
As in a glass beforehand with my sight,
A certain perfect piece of work in thee,
And now so far as I [can] guess by signs,
Some great attempt is fixed in thy breast :
Speak on, my son, whereto thy heart inclines,
And let me deal to set thy heart at rest.
He salves the sore, that knows the patient best :
As I do thee, my son, my chiefest care,
In whom my special praise and joy doth rest ;
To me therefore these thoughts of thine declare.

WIT.

Nature, my sovereign queen and parent passing dear,
Whose force I am enforced to know and 'knowledge
     everywhere,
This care of mine, though it be bred within my
     breast,
Yet it is not so ripe as yet to breed me great
     unrest,
So run I to and fro with hap luck as I find,
Now fast, now loose: now hot, now cold: inconstant
     as the wind,
I feel myself in love, yet not inflamed so,
But causes move me now and then to let such
     fancies go,
Which causes prevailing sets each thing else in doubt
Much like the nail, that last came in, and drives
     the former out.
Wherefore my suit is this: that it would please
     your grace
To settle this unsettled head in some assured place:
To lead me through the thick, to guide me all the way,
To point me where I may achieve my most desired
     pray,
For now again of late I kindle in desire,
And pleasure pricketh forth my youth to feel a
     greater fire,
What though I be too young to show her sport in
     bed,
Yet are there many in this land that at my years
     do wed,
And though I wed not yet, yet am I old enou'
To serve my lady to my power, and to begin to
     woo.

NATURE.

What is that lady, son, which thus thy heart doth
     move?

WIT.

A lady, whom it might beseem high Jove himself
    to love.

NATURE.

Who taught thee her to love, or hast thou seen her
    face ?

WIT.

Nor this nor that, but I heard men talk of her
    apace.

NATURE.

What is her name ?

WIT.

Reason is her sire, Experience her dame,
The lady now is in her flower, and Science is her
    name.
Lo, where she dwells; lo, where my heart is all
    possest;
Lo, where my body would abide; lo, where my
    soul doth rest.
Her have I borne good-will these many years tofore,
But now she lodgeth in my thought a hundred
    parts the more,
And since I do persuade myself that this is she,
Which ought above all earthly wights to be most
    dear to me;
And since I wot not how to compass my desire,
And since for shame I cannot now nor mind not to
    retire,
Help on, I you beseech, and bring this thing about
Without your hurt to my great ease, and set all
    out of doubt.

NATURE.

Thou askest more than is in me to give,
More than thy cause, more than thy state, will bear,
They are two things to able thee to live,
And to live so, that none should be thy peer,
The first from me proceedeth everywhere ;
But this by toil and practice of the mind,
Is set full far, God wot, and bought full dear,
By those that seek the fruit thereof to find,
To match thee then with Science in degree,
To knit that knot that few may reach unto,
I tell thee plain, it lieth not in me.
Why should I challenge that I cannot do ?
But thou must take another way to woo,
And beat thy brain, and bend thy curious head.
Both ride and run, and travel to and fro,
If thou intend that famous dame to wed.

WIT.

You name yourself the lady of this world.

NATURE.

It is true.

WIT.

And can there be within this world a thing too
    hard for you ?

NATURE.

My power it is not absolute in jurisdiction,
For I cognise another lord above,
That hath received unto his disposition
The soul of man, which he of special love
To gifts of grace and learning eke doth move.

A work so far beyond my reach and call,
That into part of praise with him myself to show
Might soon procure my well-deserved fall :
He makes the frame, and [I] receive it so,
No jot therein altered for my head ;
And as I it receive, I let it go,
Causing therein such sparkles to be bred,
As he commits to me, by whom I must be led :
Who guides me first, and in me guides the rest,
All which in their due course and kind are spread
Of gifts from me such as may serve them best,
To thee, son Wit, he will'd me to inspire,
The love of knowledge and certain seeds divine,
Which ground might be a mean to bring thee here,
If thereunto thyself thou wilt incline :
The massy gold the cunning hand makes fine :
Good grounds are till'd, as well as are the worst,
The rankest flower will ask a springing time ;
So is man's wit unperfit at the first.

WIT.

If cunning be the key and well of wordly [1] bliss
Me-thinketh God might at the first as well endue
    all with this.

NATURE.

As cunning is the key of bliss, so it is worthy praise :
The worthiest things are won with pain in tract of
    time always.

WIT.

And yet right worthy things there are, you will
    confess, I trow,

---

[1] Worldly.

Which notwithstanding at our birth God doth on
    us bestow.

NATURE.

There are ; but such as unto you, that have the great
    to name,
I rather that bestow, than win thereby immortal
    fame.

WIT.

Fain would I learn what harm or detriment ensued,
If any man were at his birth with these good gifts
    endued.

NATURE.

There should be nothing left, wherein men might
    excel,
No blame for sin, no praise to them that had
    designed well :
Virtue should lose her price, and learning would
    abound ;
And as man would admire the thing, that each-
    where might be found.
The great [e]state, that have of me and fortune
    what they will,
Should have no need to look to those, whose heads
    are fraught with skill.
The meaner sort, that now excels in virtues of the
    mind,
Should not be once accepted there, where now they
    succour find.
For great men should be sped of all, and would
    have need of none,
And he that were not born to land should lack to
    live upon.
These and five thousand causes mo, which I forbear
    to tell,

The noble virtue of the mind have caused there to
    dwell,
Where none may have access, but such as can get in
Through many double doors: through heat, through
    cold, through thick and thin.

WIT.

Suppose I would address myself to seek her out,
And to refuse no pain that lieth thereabout;
Should I be sure to speed?

NATURE.

       Trust me, and have no doubt,
Thou canst not choose but speed with travail and
    with time:
These two are they that must direct thee how to
    climb.

WIT.

With travail and with time? must they needs join
    in one?

NATURE.

Nor that nor this can do thee good, if they be took
    alone.

WIT.

Time worketh all with ease, and gives the greatest
    dint:
In him soft water drops can hollow hardest flint.
Again with labour by itself great matters com-
    pass'd be,
Even at a gird, in very little time or none we see.
Wherefore in my conceit good reason it is,
Either this without that to look, or that without
    this.

NATURE.

Set case thou didst attempt to climb Parnassus
    hill :
Take time five hundred thousand years and longer,
    if thou will,
Trowest thou to touch the top thereof by standing
    still ?
Again work out thy heart, and spend thyself with
    toil :
Take time withal, or else I dare assure thee of the
    foil.

WIT.

Madam, I trust I have your licence and your leave,
With your good-will and so much help as you to
    me can give ;
With further aid also, when you shall spy your
    time,
To make a proof to give attempt this famous hill
    to climb ;
And now I here request your blessing and your
    prayer ;
For sure, before I sleep, I will to yonder fort
    repair.

NATURE.

I bless thee here with all such gifts as nature can
    bestow,
And for thy sake I would they were as many
    hundred mo.
Take there withal this child, to wait upon thee still :
A bird of mine, some kin to thee : his name is Will.

WIT.

Welcome to me, my Will, what service canst thou
    do ?

WILL.

All things forsooth, sir, when me list, and more
    too.

WIT.

But whether[1] wilt thou list, when I shall list, I
    trow?

WILL.

Trust not to that; peradventure yea, peradventure
    no.

WIT.

When I have need of thee, thou wilt not serve me
    so.

WILL.

If ye bid me run, perhaps I will go.

WIT.

Cock's soul, this is a boy for the nonce amongst
    twenty mo!

WILL.

I am plain, I tell you, at a word and a blow.

WIT.

Then must I prick you, child, if you be drown'd in
    sloth.

NATURE.

Agree, you twain, for I must leave you both;
Farewell, my son: farewell, mine own good Will,
Be ruled by Wit, and be obedient still;

---

[1] Old copy, *when.*

Force thee I cannot, but as far as lies in me,
I will help thy master to make a good servant of
    thee.
Farewell—   *[Exit.*

WIT.

Adieu, lady mother, with thanks for all your pain ;
And now let me bethink myself again and eke again,
To match with Science is the thing that I have took
    in hand:
A matter of more weight, I see, than I did under-
    stand.
Will must be won to this, or else it will be hard ;
Will must go break the matter first, or else my
    game [1] is marr'd,
Sir boy, are you content to take such part for me,
As God shall send, and help it forth as much as
    lies in thee ?

WILL.

Yea, master, by his wounds, or else cut off his head.

WIT.

Come then, and let us two devise what trace were
    best to tread ;
Nature is on my side, and Will my boy is fast.
There is no doubt I shall obtain my joys at last.
                                    [Exeunt.

ACT II, SCÆNA 1.

WIT *and* WILL.

WIT.

What, Will, I say, Will boy, come again, foolish elf !

---

[1] Old copy, *gain.*

WILL.

I cry you mercy, sir, you are a tall man yourself.

WIT.

Such a crackbrain as thou art, I never saw the like
to it.

WILL.

Truth, in respect of you, that are nothing else but
Wit!

WIT.

Canst thou tell me thy errand, because thou art
gone so soon?

WILL.

I can remember a long tale of a man in the moon,
With such a circumstance and such flim-flam?
I will tell, at a word, whose servant I am:
Wherefore I come, and what I have to say,
And call for her answer, before I come away.
What, should I make a broad tree of every little
shrub,
And keep her a great while with a tale of a tub?

WIT.

Yet thou must commend me to be rich, lusty,
pleasant, and wise.

WILL.

I cannot commend you, but I must make twenty
lies.
Rich, quoth you? that appeareth by the port that
you keep:
Even as rich as a new-shorn sheep!

Of pleasant conceits, ten bushels to the peck,
Lusty like a herring, with a bell about his neck,
Wise as a woodcock : as brag as a bodylouse,
A man of your hands, to match with a mouse !
How say you, are not these proper qualities to
　　praise you with ?

WIT.

Leave these mad toys of thine, and come to the pith :
One part of the errand should have been
To give her this picture of mine to be seen,
And to request her the same to accept,
Safely until my coming to be kept,
Which I suspend till thy return, and then,
If it like her ladyship to appoint me where and
　　when,
I will wait upon her gladly out of hand.

WILL.

Sir, let me alone : your mind I understand.
I will handle the matter, so that you shall owe me
　　thanks,
But what, if she find fault with these spindle-shanks,
Or else with these black spots on your nose ?

WIT.

In faith, sir boy, this talk deserveth blows.

WILL.

You will not misuse your best servant, I suppose ?
For, by his nails and by his fingers too,
I will mar your marriage, if you do so.[1]

---

[1] Old copy, *clitter* (for *clatter*), which the compositor's eye
must have caught from the next line. So is agreeable to
the metre and the sense.

WIT.

I pray thee go thy ways, and leave this clatter.

WILL.

First shall I be so bold to break to you a matter.

WIT.

Tush, thou art disposed to spend words in waste,
And yet thou knowest this business asketh haste.

WILL.

But even two words, and then I am gone.

WIT.

If it be worth the hearing, say on.

WILL.

I would not have you think that I, for my part,
From my promise or from your service will depart,
But yet now and then it goeth to my heart,
When I think how this marriage may be to my
    smart.

WIT.

Why so?

WILL.

I would tell you the cause, if I durst for shame.

WIT.

Speak hardily what thou wilt without any blame.

WILL.

I am not disposed as yet to be tame,
And therefore I am loth to be under a dame,
Now you are a bachelor, a man may soon win you,
Me-thinks there is some good fellowship in you ;
We may laugh and be merry at board and at bed,
You are not so testy as those that be wed.
Mild in behaviour and loth to fall out,
You may run, you may ride and rove round about,
With wealth at your will and all thing at ease,
Free, frank and lusty : easy to please.
But when you be clogged and tied by the toe,
So fast that you shall not have pow'r to let go,
You will tell me another lesson soon after,
And cry *peccavi* too, except your luck be the better.
Then farewell good fellowship ! then come at a call !
Then wait at an inch, you idle knaves all :
Then sparing and pinching, and nothing of gift :
No talk with our master, but all for his thrift !
Solemn and sour, and angry as a wasp,
All things must be kept under lock and hasp ;
All [1] that which will make me to fare full ill.
All your care shall be to hamper poor Will.

WIT.

I warrant thee, for that take thou no thought,
Thou shalt be made of, whosoever be set at nought :
As dear to me, as mine own dear brother,
Whosoever be one, thou shalt be another.

WILL.

Yea, but your wife will play the shrew ; perdè, it
　　is she that I fear.

---

[1] Old copy, *at that.*

WIT.

The message will cause her some favour to bear,
For my sake and thy sake, and for her own likewise,
If thou use thyself discreetly in this enterprise.

WILL.

She hath a father, a testy, sour old man :
I doubt lest he and I shall fall out now and then.

WIT.

Give him fair words, forbear him for his age ;
Thou must consider him to be ancient and sage.
Shew thyself officious and serviceable still,
And then shall Reason make very much of Will.

WILL.

If your wife be ever complaining, how then ?

WIT.

My wife will have nothing to do with my men.

WILL.

If she do, believe her not in any wise.
And when you once perceive her stomach to arise,
Then cut her short at the first, and you shall see
A marvellous virtue in that medicine to be.
Give her not the bridle for a year or twain,
And you shall see her bridle it without a rein,
Break her betimes, and bring her under by force,
Or else the grey mare will be the better horse.

WIT.

If thou have done, begone, and spend no time in
    vain.

WILL.

Where shall I find you, when I come again ?

WIT.

At home.

WILL.

Good, enough, take your ease : let me alone with
    this.   [*Exit Wit.*
Surely a treasure of all treasures it is
To serve such a master, as I hope him to be,
And to have such a servant as he hath of me ;
For I am quick, nimble, proper and nice ;
He *is* full good, gentle, sober and wise.
He *is* full loth to chide or to check,
And I am as willing to serve at a beck,
He orders me well, and speaks me so fair,
That for his sake no travail I must spare.
But now am I come to the gate of this lady,
I will pause a while to frame mine errant finely
And lo, where she cometh ; yet will I not come
    nigh her ;
But among these fellows will I stand to eye her.

ACT II., SCÆNA 2.

REASON, EXPERIENCE, SCIENCE, *and* WILL.

SCIENCE.

My parents, ye know, how many fall and lapse,[1]
That do ascribe to me the cause of their mishaps ?
How many seek, that come too short of their
    desire :
How many do attempt, that daily do retire.

---

[1] Old copy, *in laps.*

How many rove about the mark on every side :
How many think to hit, when they are much too
      wide :
How many run too far, how many light too low :
How few to good effect their travail do bestow !
And how all these impute their losses unto me :
Should I have joy to think of marriage now, trow
      ye ?
What saith[1] the world ? my love alone, say they,
Is bought so dear, that life and goods for it must
      pay
Strong youth must spend itself, and yet, when all
      is done,
We hear of few or none, that have this lady won.
On me they make outcries, and charge me with the
      blood
Of those, that for my sake adventure life and
      good.
This grief doth wound my heart so, that suitors
      more as yet
I see no cause nor reason why I should admit.

REASON.

Ah, daughter, say not so ; there is great cause and
      skill,
For which you should mislike to live unmarried
      thus alone,
What comfort can you have remaining thus un-
      known ?
How shall the commonwealth by you advanced be,
If you abide inclosed here, where no man may you
      see ?
It is not for your state yourself to take the pain :
All strangers shall resort to you to entertain.

---

[1] Old copy, *doth.*

To suffer free access of all that come and go :
To be at each man's call : to travel to and fro.
What then, since God hath plac'd such treasure in
      your breast,
Wherewith so many thousand think by you to be
      refresh'd,
Needs must you have some one of high and secret
      trust,
By whom these things may be well-order'd and
      discuss'd.
To him you must disclose the depth of all your
      thought ;
By him, as time shall serve, all matters must be
      wrought :
To him alone you must content yourself to be at
      call ;
Ye must be his, he must be yours, he must be all
      in all.

EXPERIENCE.

My lord, your father tells you truth, perdè,
And that in time yourself shall find and try.

SCIENCE.

I could allege more than as yet I have said,
But I must yield, and you must be obey'd.
Fall out, as it will : there is no help, I see ;
Some one or other in time must marry me.

WILL.

In time ? nay, out of hand, madam, if it please you ;
In faith, I know a younker that will ease you,
A lively young gentleman, as fresh as any flower,
That will not stick to marry you within this hour.

SCIENCE.

Such haste might haply turn to waste to some;
But I pray thee, my pretty boy, whence art thou
    come ?

WILL.

If it please your good ladyship to accept me so,
I have a solemn message to tell, ere I go;
Not anything in secret your honour to stain,
But in the presence and hearing of you twain.

REASON.

Speak.

WILL.

The lady of this world, which lady Nature hight,
Hath one a peerless son, in whom she taketh
    delight,
On him she chargeth men to be attendant still,
Both kin[1] to her: his name is Wit, my name is
    Will.
The noble child doth feel the force of Cupid's flame,
And seeketh[2] now for ease, by counsel of his dame.
His mother taught him first to love, while he was
    young :
Which love with age increaseth sore, and waxeth
    wondrous strong;
For very fame displays your bounty more and
    more,
And at this pinch he burneth so as never hereto-
    fore.
Not fantasies forsooth,[3] not vain and idle toys of
    love ;

---

[1] Old copy, *kind.*   [2] Old copy, *sendeth.*
[3] Old copy, *force.*

Not hope of that which commonly doth other
    suitors move;
But fixed fast good-will that never shall relent,
And virtue's force, that shines in you, bad him give
    this attempt.
He hath no need of wealth, he wooes not for your
    good;
His kindred is such he need not to seek to match
    with noble blood,
Such store of friends that, where he list, he may
    command,
And none so hardy to presume his pleasure to
    withstand.
Yourself it is, [madam,] your virtue and your grace,
Your noble gifts, your endless praise in every place:
You alone, I say, the mark that he would hit,
The hoped joy, the dearest prey, that can befal to
    Wit.

EXPERIENCE.

I have not heard a message more trimly done.

SCIENCE.

Nor I; what age art thou of, my good son?

WILL.

Between eleven and twelve, madam, more or less.

REASON.

He hath been instructed this errand, as I guess.

SCIENCE.

How old is the gentleman thy master, canst thou
    tell?

WILL.

Seventeen or thereabout, I wot not very well.

SCIENCE.

What stature, of what making, what kind of port
    bears he ?

WILL.

Such as your ladyship cannot mislike, trust me.
Well-grown, well-made, a stripling clean and tall:
Well-favoured, somewhat black, and manly there-
    withal;
And that you may conceive his personage the
    better,
Lo, here of him the very shape and lively picture !
This hath he sent to you to view and to behold:
I dare advouch no joint therein, no jot, to be con-
    troll'd.

SCIENCE.

In good faith, I thank thy master with my heart;
I perceive that nature in him hath done her part.

WILL.

Farther, if it please your honour to know :
My master would be glad to run, ride, or go,
At your commandment to any place far or near,
To have but a sight of your ladyship there.
I beseech you appoint him the place and the hour,
You shall see, how readily to you he will scour.

REASON.

Do so.

EXPERIENCE.

Yea, in any wise, daughter; for, hear you me,

He seemeth a right worthy and trim young man
    to be.

SCIENCE.

Commend me then to Wit, and let him understand,
That I accept with all my heart this present at his
    hand,
And that I would be glad, when he doth see his
    time,
To hear and see him face to face within this house
    of mine.
Then may he break his mind, and talk with me his
    fill ;
Till then, adieu, both he and thou, mine own sweet
    little Will.

        [Exeunt Science, Reason, Experience.

ACT II., SCÆNA 3.

WILL.

Ah flattering quean, how neatly she can talk,
How minionly she trips, how sadly she can walk !
Well, wanton, yet beware that ye be sound and
    sure,
Fair words are wont ofttimes fair women to allure,
Now must I get me home, and make report of
    this
To him, that thinks it long till my return, i-wis.

        [Exit.

ACT III., SCÆNA 1.

WIT *and* WILL.

WIT.

Say'st thou me so, boy ? will she have me indeed ?

WILL.

Be of good cheer, sir; I warrant you to speed.

WIT.

Did both her parents speak well to her of me?

WILL.

As heart can think; go on, and you shall see.

WIT.

How took she the picture? How liketh she my
    person?

WILL.

She never had done toting[1] and looking thereon.

WIT.

And when must I come to talk with her my fill?

WILL.

Whensoever you please, and as oft as you will.

WIT.

O my sweet boy, how shall I recompense
Thy faithful heart and painful diligence?
My hope, my stay, my wealth, the key of all my
    joy!

WILL.

I pray you, sir, call me your man, and not your
    boy.

---

[1] Peeping.

WIT.

Thou shalt be what thou wilt, all in all.

WILL.

Promise me faithfully that, if your wife brawl,
Or set her father to check me out of measure,
You will not see me abused to their pleasure.

WIT.

Give me thy hand, take here my faith and troth,
I will maintain thee, howsoever the world goeth.

ACT III., SCÆNA 2.

The house of SCIENCE. WILL, WIT ; *also* REASON
and SCIENCE *behind.*

WIT.

What shall we do ? Shall we stand lingering
here ?

WILL.

If you be a man, press in and go near.

WIT.

What, if there be some other suitor there ?

WILL.

And if there be, yet need you not to fear ;
Until I bring his head to you upon a spear.
I will not look you in the face, nor in your sight
appear.

REASON.

Nay, Wit, advise yourself, and pause a while,
Or else this haste of yours will you beguile.

SCIENCE.

No haste but good, take time and learn to fight,
Learn to assault, learn to defend a right :
Your match [1] is monstrous to behold and full of
    might,
Whom you must vanquish, not by force, but by
    sleight.

WIT.

Madam, stand to your promise; if I win, I am
    sped,
Am I not?

SCIENCE.

Yea, truly.

WILL.

Good enough, if we fight not, I would we were
    dead,
No man shall stay us, that bears a head.

EXPERIENCE.

Young man, a word or twain, and then adieu :
Your years are few, your practice green and new ;
Mark what I say, and ye shall find it true :
You are the first that shall this rashness rue.
Be ruled here : our counsel do thereafter.
Lay good ground, your work shall be the faster.
This headlong haste may sooner miss than hit ;
Take heed both of witless [2] Will and wilful Wit.

---

[1] Rival.
[2] Old copy, *wit's.*

We have within a gentleman, our retainer and our
    friend,
With servants twain, that do on him attend—
Instruction, Study, Diligence : these three
At your commandment in this attempt shall be.
Hear them instead of us, and as they shall devise,
So hardily cast your[1] cards in this enterprise.
I will send them to you, and leave you for now.

WIT.

The more company the merrier ; boy, what say'st
    thou ?

WILL.

It is a good fault to have more than enou' :
I care not, so as we may put the knaves down,
I would we were at it, I pass not how soon.

WIT.

If it shall please you to send those three hither,
We will follow your counsel, and go together.

WILL.

I warrant her a shrew, whosoever be another,
God make the daughter good, I like not the
    mother.   [*Aside.*

WIT.[2]

Yet would not I for no good to have forgone her.
                              [*Aside.*

WILL.

Marry, sir, indeed she talks and takes on her,
Like a dame, nay, like a duchess or a queen,
With such a solemnity as I have not seen.

---

    [1] Old copy, *our.*   [2] Old copy, *Reason.*

REASON.

She is a queen, I tell thee, in her degree.

WILL.

Let her be what she list, with a vengeance, for me !
I will keep me out of her reach, if I can.   [*Aside.*

REASON.

If this marriage go forward, thou must be her man.

WILL.

Marriage or marriage not, beshrew me then,
I have but one master, and I will serve no mo,
And if he anger me, I will forsake him too.

REASON.

She shall not hurt thee, unless her cause be juster.

WILL.

By the faith of my body, sir, I intend not to trust
    her.

REASON.

Why ?

WILL.

Take [1] me this woman, that talks so roundly,
That be so wise, that reason so soundly :
That look so narrow, that speak so shrill :
Their words are not so cursed, but their deeds are
    ill.

REASON.

It is but thy fancy, I see no such thing in her.

---

[1] *i.e.*, Take away from me.

WILL.

Perhaps you had never occasion to try her?

REASON.

That were great marvel in so many years.

WILL.

She hath won the mastery of you, it appears.

WIT.

Well, quiet yourself; thou shalt take no wrong,
Methink our three companions tarry very long.

ACT III., SCÆNA 3.

INSTRUCTION, STUDY, DILIGENCE, REASON, WIT,
WILL.

INSTRUCTION.

Sir, we are come to know your pleasure.

REASON.

You are come in good time, Instruction, our trea-
    sure;
This gentleman craveth your acquaintance and aid.
What you may do for him, let him not be denay'd.

WIT.

Welcome, good fellows, will ye dwell with me?

DILIGENCE.

If all parties be pleased, content are we.

WIT.

Welcome, Instruction, with all my heart.

WILL.

What, three new servants! then, farewell, my part.
[Aside.

INSTRUCTION.

I heartily thank you, and look what I can do;
I[1] shall be always ready to pleasure you.

REASON.

Consider and talk together with these,
And you shall find in your travail great ease.
Take here of me, before I take my leave,
This glass of crystal clear, which I you give,
Accept it, and reserve it for my sake most sure,
Much good to you in time it may procure.
Behold yourself therein, and view and pry:
Mark what defects it will discover and descry;
And so with judgment ripe and curious eye,
What is amiss endeavour to supply,
Farewell—

WIT.

Farewell to you, right honourable sir:
And commend me to my love, my heart's desire,
Let her think on me, when she sees me not, and
    wish me well.

WILL.

Farewell, master Reason, think upon us, when you
    see us not,
And in any wise let not Will be forgot.

---

[1] Old copy, It.

WIT.

Since I must take advice and counsel of you three,
I must intreat you all to dwell in house with me,
And look what order you shall prescribe as needful,
To keep the same you shall find me as heedful:
Come.

INSTRUCTION.

[I] come.

WIT.

[I] go. *[Exeunt.*

ACT IV., SCÆNA 1.

WIT, WILL, INSTRUCTION, STUDY, DILIGENCE.

WILL.

Tush, tush, Instruction, your talk is of no force:
You tell us a tale of a roasted horse,
Which, by his wounds, except we set to it,
As fast as we make, these [1] fellows will undo it,
Their talk is nothing but soft, and fair, and tarry;
If you follow their counsel, you shall never marry.

INSTRUCTION.

To follow our counsel your charge and promise
was.

WIT.

I would I had never known you, by the mass.
Must I look so long, and spend my life with toil?
Nay, sure, I will either win it, or take the foil.

---

[1] Old copy, *this.*

STUDY.

The surer is your ground, the better you shall
    bear it.

WILL.

Ground us no ground; let him win it, and wear it.

INSTRUCTION.

Good sir, be ruled, and leave this peevish elf.

WIT.

I had even as lief ye bad me hang myself;
Leave him? no, no, I would you all knew,
You be but loiterers to him, my Will tells me true.
I could be content with a week, yea a month or
    twain,
But three or four years! marry, that were a pain.
So long to keep me, and lie like a hog.

WILL.

A life, with all my heart, I would not wish a dog.

WIT.

Will a week serve?

STUDY.

No.

WIT.

A month?

STUDY.

Neither.

WIT.

No?

STUDY.

Not so.

INSTRUCTION.

No, nor so many mo.

WIT.

Then, farewell all, for, as I hope to thrive,
I will prove him, ere I sleep, if I be alive,
And if ye be mine, and good fellows all three,
Go thither out of hand, and take your chance with
  me.

INSTRUCTION.

For my part, I know I can do you no good.

WILL.

You are a proper man of your hands, by the rood !
Yet well fare him, that never his master forsaketh.

WIT.

What say'st thou, Study ?

STUDY.

    My head acheth.

WIT.

Out upon thee, coward ! speak, Diligence.

DILIGENCE.

Against Instruction's mind, I am loth to go hence,
Yet I will make one, rather than you should lack.

WIT.

Perhaps we may find them at this time in bed.

WILL.

So much the rather look you to be sped,
Care for no more, but once to come within her,
And when you have done, then let another win her.

WIT.

To come within her, child? what meanest thou by
    that ?

WILL.

One mass for a penny, you know what is what !

WIT.

Heard you ever such a counsel of such a Jack sprat ?

WILL.

Why, sir, do ye think to do any good,
If ye stand in a corner like Robin Hood ?
Nay, you must stout it, and face it out with the
    best :
Set on a good countenance, make the most of the
    least,
Whosoever skip in, look to your part,
And while you live, beware of a false heart.

WIT.

Both blame and shame rash boldness doth breed.

WILL.

You must adventure both : spare to speak, spare
    to speed.

What tell you me of shame? it is shame to steal a
    horse.

WIT.

More haste than good speed makes many fare the
    worse.

WILL.

But he that takes not such time, while he may,
Shall leap at a whiting, when time is away.

WIT.

But he that leaps, before he look, good son,
May leap in the mire, and miss when he hath done.
        [Enter Science, Reason, and Experience.

SCIENCE.

Methink I hear the voice of Will, Wit's boy.

WIT.

I see her come, her sorrow and my joy,
My salve and yet my sore, my comfort and my
    care,
The causer of my wound, and yet the well of my
    welfare ;
O happy wight, that have the saint of your request,
O hopeless hope, that holdeth me from that which
    likes me best !
Twixt hope and fear I stand, to mar or else to
    make,
This day to be relieved quite, or else my death-
    wound to take.

REASON.

Here let us rest awhile, and pause all three :

EXPERIENCE.

Daughter, sit down, belike this same is he.

WILL.

Be of good cheer, sir; be ruled by me.
Women are best pleased, till they be used homely,
Look her in the face, and tell your tale stoutly.

WIT.

O pearl of passing price, sent down from God on
    high,
The sweetest beauty to entice, that hath been seen
    with eye :
The well of wealth to all, that no man doth annoy:
The key of kingdoms and the seal of everlasting
    joy.
The treasure and the store, whom all good things
    began,
The nurse of lady Wisdom's love, the link of man
    and man.
What words shall me suffice to utter my desire ?
What heat of talk shall I devise, for to express my
    fire ?
I burn and yet I freeze, I flame and cool as fast,
In hope to win and for to lese, my pensiveness
    doth last ;
Why should my dull spirit appal my courage so ?
O, salve my sore, or sle me quite, by saying yea or
    no !
You are the mark at whom I shoot to hit or miss,
My life it stays on you alone, to you my suit it is,
A suit [1] not much unmeet with you some grace [2] to
    find,

---

[1] Old copy, *Amity.*   [2] Old copy, *grief.*

Dame Nature's son, my name is Wit, that fancieth
    you by kind,
And here I come this day to wait and to attend,
In hope to have my hoped prey,[1] or else my life to
    end.

SCIENCE.

Good cause there is, wherefore I should embrace,
This loving heart which you have borne to me,
And glad I am, that we be both in place,
Each one of us each other's looks to see.
Your picture and your person doth agree,
Your prince-like port and eke your noble face ;
Wherein so many signs of virtue be :
That I must needs be moved in your case.

REASON.

Friend Wit, are you the man indeed, which you
    intend?[2]
Can you be well content, until your life doth end,
To join and knit most sure with this my daughter
    here,
And unto her alone your fixed faith to bear ?

WIT.

As I am bent to this, so let my suit be sped,
If I do fail, ten thousand plagues and more light
    on my head !

EXPERIENCE.

There are, that promise fair, and mean as well,
As any heart[3] can think, or tongue can tell :
Which at the first are hot, and kindle in desire,

---

[1] Prize.   [2] Pretend.   [3] Old copy, *heare.*

But in one month or **twain** quite quenched is the
    fire.
Such is the train[1] of youth, whom fancy's force
    doth lead,
Whose love is only at the plunge, and cannot long
    proceed.

WIT.

Credit my words, and ye shall find me true.

EXPERIENCE.

Suppose you keep not touch, who should this bar-
    gain rue ?

WIT.

I will be sworn here solemnly before you both.

EXPERIENCE.

Who breaketh promise, will not stick likewise to
    break his oath.

WIT.

I will be bound in all that ever I can make.

EXPERIENCE.

What good were that to us, if we th' advantage
    take ?

WIT.

Will neither promise serve, nor oath, nor bands ?[2]
What other assurance will ye ask at my hands ?

---

[1] Old copy, *trade.*   [2] Bonds.

WILL.

My master is a gentleman, I tell you, and his
    word,
I would you knew it, shall with his deeds accord.

REASON.

We know not whom to trust, the world is so ill.

WILL.

Indeed, sir, as you say, you may mend, when ye
    will ;
But in good earnest, madam, speak—off or on ?
Shall we speed at your hand, or shall we be gone ?
I love not these delays ; say so, if we shall have you,
If not, say no ; and let another crave you.

WIT.

Soft and fair, sir boy, you talk, you wot not what.
[Aside.

WILL.

Can you abide to be driven off with this and that,
Can they ask any more than good assurance at
    your hands ?   [Aside.

EXPERIENCE.

All is now too little, son, as the matter stands.

WILL.

If all be too little, both goods and lands,
I know not what will please you, except Darby's
    bands.[1]

---

[1] A proverbial expression not found in the collections. It
may signify the hangman's cord.

SCIENCE.

I have an enemy, my friend Wit, a mortal foe to
    me ;
And therewithal the greatest plague that can befal
    to thee.

WIT.

Must I fight with him ?

REASON.

Can you fight, if need be ?

WILL.

If any such thing fall, count the charge to me,
Trouble not yourself.

WIT.

Hold thy peace, elf.

SCIENCE,

Hear out my tale ; I have a mortal foe,
That lurketh in the wood hereby, as you come and
    go ;
This monstrous giant bears a grudge to me and
    mine,
And will attempt to keep thee back from this
    desire of thine.
The bane of youth, the root of ruin and distress :[1]
Devouring those that sue to me, his name is
    Tediousness.
No sooner he espies the noble Wit begin :

---

[1] Old copy, *desire.*

To stir and pain itself the love of me to win.
But forth he steps, and with strong hands by
    might and main
He beats and buffets down the force and liveliness
    of brain.
That done, in deep despair he drowns him villain-
    ously :
Ten thousand suitors in a year are cast away
    thereby.
Now, if your mind be surely fixed so,
That for no toil nor cost my love you will forego,
Bethink you well, and of this monster take good
    heed,
Then may you have with me the greater hope to
    speed.
Herein use good advice, to make you strong and
    stout,
To feud and keep him off a while, until his rage be
    out.
Then when you feel yourself well able to prevail,
Bid you the battle, and that so courageously assail.
If you can win the field, present me with his head,
I ask no more, and I forthwith shall be your own
    to bed.

WIT.

Ill might I thrive, and lack that likes me best,
If I be not a scourge to him, that breedeth [1] your
    unrest,
Madam, assure yourself, he lives not in the land,
With whom I would not in your cause encounter
    hand to hand,
And as for Tediousness that wretch, your common
    foe,

---

[1] Old copy, *breeds.*

Let me alone, we twain shall cope, before I sleep,
    I trow.

WILL.

Lustily spoken, let me claw thee by the back :
How say you now, sir, here are three against
    twain !

STUDY.

Go, that go list, I will at home remain,
I have more need to take a nap in my bed.

WILL.

Do so, and, hear you, couch a cod's-head ! [*Aside.*

INSTRUCTION.

Well, since it will none otherwise frame,
Let us twain, Study, return[1] from whence we
    came.

STUDY.

Agreed.   [*Exit.*

WIT.

And let us three bestir ourselves like men ;
Unlikely things are brought to pass by courage
    now and then.
My Will, be always prest, and ready at an inch,
To save thyself, to succour me, to help at every
    pinch.
Both twain on either side assault him, if ye can,
And you shall see me in the middes, how I will
    play the man ;

---

[1] Old copy, *and return.*

This is the deadly den, as far as I perceive,
Approach we near, and valiantly let us the onset
    give.
Come forth, thou monster fell, in drowsy darkness
    hid,
For here is Wit, Dame Nature's son, that doth
    thee battle bid.

ACT IV., SCÆNA 2.

TEDIOUSNESS, WIT, WILL, DILIGENCE.

TEDIOUSNESS.

What princox have we here, that dares me to
    assail?
Alas, poor boy, and weenest thou against me to
    prevail?
Full small was he thy friend, whoever sent thee
    hither,
For I must drive thee back with shame, or slay
    thee altogether.

WIT.

Great boast, small roast: I warrant thee, do thy
    best,
Thy head must serve my turn this day to set my
    heart at rest.

WILL.

And I must have a leg of thee, if I can catch it.

TEDIOUSNESS.

First I must quite this brain of thine, if I can reach
    it.   [*Fight, strike at Will.*

WIT.

Well shifted, Will; now have at thee, sir knave.

TEDIOUSNESS.

These friscols shall not serve your turn for all your
vaunts so brave;
Ho, ho! did I not tell thee thou cam'st to thy
pain!

DILIGENCE.

Help, help, help, our master is slain.

WILL.

Help, help, help, &c.

TEDIOUSNESS.

Where are these lusty bloods, that make their
match with me?
Here lies a pattern for them all, to look at and to see.
To teach them to conspire against my force and
might;
To promise, for their woman's love, to vanquish
me in fight:
Now let them go and crake, how wisely they have
sped,
Such is the end of those, that seek this curious
dame to wed.   [*Exit* TED.

ACT IV., SCÆNA 3.

WILL, RECREATION, WIT.

WILL.

Rub and chafe him:
For God's love, haste; see, lo, where he doth lie.

RECREATION.

He is not cold, I warrant him, I.

SING.

Give a leg, give an arm; arise, arise.
Hold up [1] thy head, lift us thy eyes,
1 A leg to stand upright:
2 An arm to fight amain,
1 The head to hold thy brains in plight,
2 The eyes to look again.
Awake, ye drowned powers.
Ye sprites, for-dull with toil:
Resign to me this care of yours,
And from dead sleep recoil.
Think not upon your loathsome luck,
But arise, and dance with us a-pluck.
      [Both sing, Give a leg, as is before.
2 What, though thou hast not hit
The top of thy desire,
Time is not so far spent as yet
To cause thee to retire.
Arise, and ease thyself of pain,
And make thee strong to fight again.

SING BOTH.

Let not thy foes rejoice;
Let not thy friends lament;
Let not thy lady's rueful voice
In sobs and sighs be spent;
Thy faith is plight, forget it not,
Twixt her and thee to knit the knot.

SING.

Give a leg, &c.
This is no deadly wound:
It may be cured well.

---

[1] Old copy, *by.*

See here what physic we have found
Thy sorrows to expel.
　　　　[*Wit lifting himself up, sitting on the ground.*
The way is plain, the mark is fair,
Lodge not thyself in deep despair.

WIT.[1]

What noise is this, that ringeth in my ears,
Her noise that grieveth my mishap with tears?
Ah, my mishap, my desperate mishap,
On[2] whom ill-fortune poureth down all mishap at
　　a clap,
What shall become of me, where shall I hide my
　　head?
O, what a death is it to live for him that would be
　　dead?
But since it chanceth so, whatever wight thou be,
That findeth me here in heavy plight, go, tell her
　　this from me.
Causeless I perish here, and cause to curse I have.
The time that erst I lived to love, and now must
　　die her slave,
The match was over-much for me, she understood,
Alas, why hath she this delight to lap in guiltless
　　blood?
How did I give her cause to show me this despite,
To match me where she wist full well I should be
　　slain in fight?
But go, and tell her plain, although too late for me,
Accursed be the time and hour, which first I did
　　her see.
Accursed be the wight, that will'd me first thereto,
And cursed be they all at once, that had therewith
　　to do.

---

[1] Old copy, *Will.*　　　　　　　[2] Old copy, *In.*

Now get thee hence in haste, and suffer me to die.
Whom scornful chance and lawless love have slain
  most traitorously.

RECREATION.

O noble Wit, the miracle of God and eke of Nature :
Why cursest thou thyself and every other creature ?
What causeth thee thine innocent dear lady to
  accuse ?
Who would lament it more than she to hear this
  woful news ?
Why wilt thou die, whereas thou may'st be sure of
  health ?
Whereas thou seest a plain pathway to worship
  and to wealth.
Not every foil doth make a fall, nor every soil doth
  slay ;
Comfort thyself : be sure thy luck will mend from
  day to day.

WILL.

These gentlewomen of good skill are [1] come to make
  you sound,
They know which way to salve your sore, and how
  to cure your wound.
Good sir, be ruled by her then, and pluck your
  spirit to you :
There is no doubt, but you shall find your loving
  lady true.

WIT.

Ah, Will, art thou alive that doth my heart some
  ease,

----

[1] Old copy, *This gentle news of good Will are.* The gentlewomen referred to are *Recreation* and *Idleness.*

The sight of thee, sweet boy, my sorrows doth
    appease :
How hast thou 'scap'd ? what fortune thee befel ?

WILL.

It was no trusting to my hands, my heels did serve
    me well,
I ran with open mouth to cry for help amain,
And, as good fortune would, I hit upon these twain.

WIT.

I thank both thee and them ; what will ye have
    me do ?

RECREATION.

To rise and dance a little space with us two.

WIT.

What then ?

RECREATION.

That done, repair again to Study and Instruction ;
Take better hold by their advice, your foe to set
    upon.

WIT.

Can any recompense recover this my fall ?

RECREATION.

My life to yours, it may be mended all.

WIT.

Speak, Will.

WILL.

I have no doubt, sir, it shall be, as you would wish.

WIT.

But yet this repulse of mine they will lay in my
  dish.

RECREATION.

No man shall let them know thereof, unless yourself do it.

WIT.

On that condition, a God's name, fall we to it.

WILL.

Nay, stand we to it, and let us fall no more.

WIT.

Will dancing serve, and I will dance, until my
  bones be sore,
Pipe us up a galliard, minstrel, to begin.
  [*Let Will call for dances, one after another.*

WILL.

Come, damsel, in good faith, and let me have
  you in,
Let him practise in dancing all things to make
  himself breathless.[1]

RECREATION.

Enough at once, now leave, and let us part.

WIT.

This exercise hath done me good, even to the very
  heart.
Let us be bold with you more acquaintance to take,

---

[1] A line seems to have dropped out here.

And dance a round yet once more for my sake,
Enough is enough; farewell, and at your need
Use my acquaintance, if it may stand you in stead.
Right worthy damsels both, I know you seek no
    gains
In recompense of this desert your undeserved
    pains.
But look what other thing my service may devise,
To show my thankful heart in any enterprise.
Be ye as bold therewith, as I am bold on you,
And thus with hearty thanks I take my leave as
    now.

RECREATION.

Farewell, friend Wit, and since you are relieved,
Think not upon your foil, whereat you were so
    griev'd,
But take your heart to you, and give attempt once
    more :
I warrant you to speed much better than before.
[Exeunt.

ACT IV., SCÆNA 4.

WIT, WILL, IDLENESS, IGNORANCE.

WIT.

One dance for thee and me ; my boy, come on.

WILL.

Dance you, sir, if you please, and I will look upon.

WIT.

This gear doth make me sweat, and breathe apace.

IDLENESS.

Sir, ease yourself awhile ; here is a resting-place.

WIT.

Home, Will, and make my bed, for I will take a
    nap.

IGNORANCE.

Sure, and it please your mastership, here in my
    dame's lap.

IDLENESS *singeth.*

Come, come, lie down, and thou shalt see,
None like to me to entertain
Thy bones and thee oppressed with pain.
Come, come, and ease thee in my lap,
And if it please thee, take a nap;
A nap, that shall delight thee so,
That fancies all will thee forego.
By musing still, what canst thou find,
But wants of will and restless mind?
A mind that mars and mangles all,
And breedeth jars to work thy fall!
Come, gentle Wit, I thee require,
And thou shalt hit thy chief desire:
Thy chief desire, thy hoped prey;
First ease thee here, and then away.

WIT.

                    [*Falls down into her lap.*
My bones are stiff, and I am wearied sore,
And still me-think I faint and feeble more and
    more ;
Wake me again in time, for I have things to do,

And as you will me for mine ease, I do assent
    thereto.

              IDLENESS.   [*Lulls him.*

Welcome, with all my heart: sir boy, hold here
    this fan,
And softly cool his face ; sleep soundly, gentleman.
This char is char'd [1] well now, Ignorance, my son,
Thou seest all this, how featly [2] it is done ;
But wot'st thou why ?

              IGNORANCE.

Nay, bumfay,[3] mother, not I.
Well, I wot 'tis a gay worched trick and trim :
Chould rejouce my heart to chance coots [4] with
    him.

              IDLENESS.

Dost thou remember how many I have served in
    the like sort ?

              IGNORANCE.

It doth my heart good to think on this sport.

              IDLENESS.

Wilt thou see this proper fellow served so ?

---

[1] *i.e.,* That business is despatched. See Hazlitt's " Proverbs," 1869, p. 352.

[2] Old copy, *fitly.*

[3] By my faith.

[4] *i.e.,* "It would rejoice my heart to change coats with
him."

IGNORANCE.

Chould give tway pence to see it and tway pence
    mo.

IDLENESS.

Come off, then, let me see thee in his doublet and
    his [1] hose.

IGNORANCE.

You shall see a tall fellow, mother, I suppose.

IDLENESS.

Help off with this sleeve softly for fear of waking,
We shall leave the gentleman in a pretty taking.
Give me thy coat, hold this in thy hand :
This fellow would be married to Science, I under-
    stand.
But, ere we leave him, tell me another tale !
Now let us make him look somewhat stale.
There lie, and there be : the proverb is verified,
I am neither idle, nor yet well-occupied.

IGNORANCE.

Mother, must I have his coat? now, mother, I
    must.
Chalt be a lively lad with hey tisty-tust.

IDLENESS.

Sleep sound, and have no care to occupy thy head,
As near unto thy body now, as if thou had'st been
    dead.
For Idleness hath won, and wholly thee possess'd,
And utterly disabled thee from having thy request.

---

[1] Old copy, *thy—thy ;* but Ignorance is to change clothes
with Wit, while the latter sleeps in the lap of Idleness.

Come on with me, my son, let us go couch again,
And let this lusty ruffling Wit here like a fool remain.   [*Exeunt.*

ACT V., SCÆNA 1.

WIT, SCIENCE, REASON.

WIT.

Up and to go, why sleep I here so sound ?
How falls it out that I am left upon the naked
    ground ?
God grant that all be well, whilst I lay dreaming
    here :
Me-thinks all is not as it was, nor as I would it
    were.
And yet I wot not why, but so my fancies gives me,
That some one thing or other in my tire [1] that
    grieves me,
They are but fancies, let them go : to Science now
    will I ;
My suit and business yet once again to labour and
    apply.
                [*Enter Science and Reason.*

SCIENCE.

What is become, trow ye, of Wit, our spouse that
    would be ?

REASON.

Daughter, I fear all is not as it should be.

---

[1] Old copy, *is my tryer.*   He has indistinct misgivings
that his clothes are not all right.

WIT.

Yes, yes, have ye no doubt, all is and shall be
    well.

REASON.

What one art thou? thereof how canst thou tell?

WIT.

Reason, most noble sir, and you, my lady dear :
How have you done in all this time, since first I
    saw you here?

SCIENCE.

The fool is mad, I ween ; stand back, and touch
    me not.

WIT.

You speak not as you think, or have you me forgot?

SCIENCE.

I never saw thee in my life until this time, I wot ;
Thou art some mad-brain or some fool, or some
    disguised sot.[1]

WIT.

God's fish-hooks ?[2] and know you not me ?

SCIENCE.

I had been well at ease indeed to be acquainted
    with thee !

---

[1] Old copy, *scot*.   [2] Old copy, *fish-hosts*.

WIT.

Hop haliday![1] marry, this is pretty cheer,
I have lost myself, I cannot tell where !
An old-said saw it is, and too true, I find,
Soon hot, soon cold : out of sight, out of mind.
What, madam, what meaneth this sudden change ?
What means this scornful look, this countenance so
      strange ?
Is it[2] your fashion so to use your lovers at the
      first :
Or have all women this delight to scold and to be
      curs'd ?

REASON.

Good fellow, whence art thou ? what is thy name ?

WIT.

I ween ye are disposed to make at me some game.
I am the son of lady Nature ; my name is Wit.

REASON.

Thou shalt say so long enough, ere we believe it.

SCIENCE.

Thou Wit ? nay, thou art some mad-brain out of
      thy wit.

WIT.

Unto yourselves this trial I remit.
Look on me better, and mark my person well

---

[1] A colloquialism, of which the exact import must be
matter of guess. Old copy, *Hope haliday.* Perhaps a corruption of *upon my haliday.*
[2] Old copy, *It is.*

SCIENCE.

Thy look is like to one, that came out of hell.

REASON.

If thou be Wit, let see, what tokens thou canst
    tell.
How cam'st thou first acquainted here? what said
    we?
How did we like thy suit, what entertainment
    made we?

WIT.

What tokens?

SCIENCE.

Yea, what tokens? speak, and let us know.

WIT.

Tokens good store I can rehearse a-row:
First, as I was advised by my mother Nature,
My lackey Will presented you with my picture.

SCIENCE.

Stay there, now look, how these two faces agree!

WIT.

This is the very same that you received from me.

SCIENCE.

From thee? why look, they are no more like,
Than chalk to cheese, than black to white.

REASON.

To put thee out of doubt, if thou think we say not
    true,
It were good for thee in a glass thy face to view.

WIT.

Well-remembered, and a glass I have indeed,
Which glass you gave me to use at need.

REASON.

Hast thou the glass, which I to Wit did give?

WIT.

I have it in my purse, and will keep it, while I live.

REASON.

This makes[1] me muse how should he come
    thereby?

WIT.

Sir, muse no more, for it is even I,
To whom you gave the glass, and here it is.

REASON.

We are content thou try thy case by this.

WIT.

                          [Looking in the glass.
Either my glass is wonderfully spotted,
Or else my face is wonderfully blotted.
This is not my coat; why, where had I this weed?

---

[1] Old copy, *These marks.*

By the mass, I look like a very fool indeed.
O haps of haps, O rueful chance to me !
O Idleness, woe-worth the time, that I was ruled
    by thee !
Why did I lay my head within thy lap to rest ?
Why was I not advis'd by her, that wish'd and
    will'd [1] me best ?
O ten times treble [2] blessed wights, whose corps
    in grave do lie :
That are not driven to behold these wretched cares
    which I [3] !
On me you [4] furies all, on me, have poured out
    your spite,
Come now and slay me at the last, and rid my
    sorrows quite.
What coast shall me receive ? where shall I show
    my head ?
The world will say this same is he that, if he list,
    had sped.
This same is he, that took an enterprise in hand ;
This same is he that scarce one blow his enemy
    did withstand.
This same is he, that fought and fell in open field :
This same is he that in the song of Idleness did
    yield.
This same is he that was in way to win the game :
To join himself whereby he should have won im-
    mortal fame ;
And now is wrapp'd in woe, and buried in despair.
O happy case for thee, if death would rid thee quite
    of care !

---

[1] Old copy, *will*.

[2] Old copy, *troble*.

[3] Old copy, *die*. The same appears to be, " That are not
driven to behold those wretched cares, which I *am driven*,
&c."

[4] Old copy, *your*.

ACT V., SCÆNA 2.

SHAME, REASON, SCIENCE, WIT.

REASON.

Shame.

SHAME.

Who calls for Shame?

REASON.

Here is a merchant,[1] Shame, for thee to tame.

SHAME.

A shame come to you all, for I am almost lame
With trudging up and down to them that lose their
    game.

REASON.

And here is one, whom thou must rightly blame,
That hath preferr'd his folly to his fame.

SHAME.

Who? this good fellow? what call you his name?

REASON.

Wit, that on wooing to lady Science came.

---

[1] Fellow. The word is frequently used, as we now use
the word *chap*, which is in fact the same, being an abbreviation of *chapman*.

SHAME.

Come aloft, child, let me see, what friscols you can
    fet ;[1]

REASON.

[If] he hath deserved it, let him be well-bet.

WIT.

O, spare me with the whip, and sle me with thy
    knife :
Ten thousand times more dear to me were present
    death than life.

SHAME.

Nay, nay, my friend, thou shalt not die as yet.

REASON.

Remember in what case dame Nature left thee,
    Wit ;
And how thou hast abus'd the same—
Thou hast deceived all our hope, as all the world
    may see.

SHAME.

A shame

Come to it !—

REASON.

Remember, what fair words and promises thou
    diddest make,
That for my daughter's love no pains thou wouldest
    forsake.
Remember in what sort we had a care of thee :

---

[1] *Fet* (or *feat*) seems to be here employed in the sense of
play or *perform*. *Friscols* has occurred before in this play.

Thou hast deceived all our hope, as all the world
    may see.

SHAME.

A shame come to it.

REASON.

Remember, how Instruction should have been fol-
    lowed still,
And how thou wouldest be ruled by none but by
    Will.
How Idleness hath crept, and reigneth in thy breast,
How Ignorance her son hath wholly thee possess'd.

SHAME.

A shame come to it.

WIT.

O woful wretch, to whom shall I complain?
What salve may serve to salve my sore, or to
    redress my pain?

REASON.

Nay, I can tell thee more: remember, how
Thou was subdued of Tediousness right now.
Remember with what crakes thou went unto his
    den,
Against the good advice and counsel of thy men,
What Recreation did for thee in these thy rueful
    haps,
And how the second time thou fell into the lap.[1]

---

[1] So old copy; but perhaps we ought to read *this hap* in
the line preceding.

SHAME.

A shame come to thee !

WIT.

O, let me breathe a while, and hold thy heavy hand,
My grievous faults with Shame enough I understand.
Take ruth and pity on my plaint, or else I am
    forlorn ;
Let not the world continue thus in laughing me to
    scorn.
Madam, if I be he, to whom you once were bent,
With whom to spend your time sometime you were
    content :
If any hope be left, if any recompense
Be able to recover this forepassed negligence,
O, help me now poor wretch in this most heavy
    plight,
And furnish me yet once again with Tediousness
    to fight.

SCIENCE.

Father, be good to these young tender years,
See, how he doth bewail his folly past with tears !

REASON.

Hold, slave, take thou his coat for thy labour,
We are content, at her request, to take you to our
    favour.
Come in, and dwell with us, till time shall serve :
And from Instruction['s] rule look that thou never
    swerve.
Within we shall provide to set you up once more,
This scourge hath taught you, what default was in
    you heretofore.

ACT V., SCÆNA 3.

WILL.

Once in my life I have an odd half-hour to spare,
To ease myself of all my travail and my care.
I stood not still so long this twenty days, I ween,
But ever more sent forth on messages I have been.
Such trudging and such toil, by the mass, was
    never seen;
My body is worn out, and spent with labour clean.
And this it is that makes me look so lean.
That lets my growth, and makes me seem a squall;[1]
What then, although my stature be not tall,
Yet I am as proper as you, so neat and cleanly,
And have my joints at commandment full of
    activity.
What should a servant do with all this flesh and
    bones,
That makes them run with leaden heels, and stir
    themself like stones?
Give me a proper squire much after my pitch,
And mark how he from place to place will squich;[2]
Fair or foul, thick or thin, mire or dusty;
Cloud or rain, light or dark, clear or misty:
Ride or run, to or fro, bad or good:
A neat little fellow on his business will scud.
These great lubbers[3] are neither active nor wise,
That feed till they sleep, and sleep out their eyes.
So heavy, so dull, so untoward in their doing,

---

[1] See Halliwell's *Dict.* in *v.*

[2] *Squich*, a word of most uncommon occurrence and of dubious meaning. From the immediate context we should infer that it signified *skip, move lightly and quickly.*

[3] Old copy, *labores.*

That it is a good sight to see them leave working.
But all this while, while I stand prating here,
I see not my master ; I left him snorting here.

[Exit.

ACT V., SCÆNA 4.

SCIENCE, WIT, WILL ; [*to them*] INSTRUCTION,
STUDY, DILIGENCE, TEDIOUSNESS.

SCIENCE.

Mine own dear Wit, the hope of mine avail,
My care, my comfort, my treasure and my trust,
Take heart of grace our enemy to assail,
Lay up these things, which you have heard dis-
    cuss'd ;
So doing, undoubtingly you cannot fail
To win the field, to 'scape all these unhappy
    shewers ; [1]
To glad your friends, to cause your foes to wail ;
To match with us, and then the gain is yours.
Here in this closet ourself will sit and see
Your manly feats and your success in fight :
Strike home courageously for you and me ;
Learn where and how to fend, and how to smite.
In any wise, be ruled by these three ;
They shall direct both you and Will aright.
Farewell, and let our loving counsel be
At every hand before you in your fight.

WIT.

Here in my sight, good madam, sit and view :
That, when I list, I may look upon you.
This face, this noble face, this lively hue,

---

[1] Query, *examples.*

Shall harden me, shall make our enemy rue.
O faithful mates, that have this care of me,
How shall I ever recompense your pains with gold
　　or fee ?
Come now, and, as you please, enjoin me how to
　　do it,
And you shall see me prest and serviceable to it.

WILL.

Why, master, whither [a]way ? what haste ? am I
　　no body ?

INSTRUCTION.

What, Will, we may not miss thee for no money.

WIT.

Welcome, good Will, and do as thou art bid ;
This day or never must Tediousness be rid.

WILL.

God speed us well, I will make one at all assays.

INSTRUCTION.

Thou shalt watch to take him at certain bays,
Come not in the throng, but save thyself always.
You twain on either side first with your sword and
　　buckler ;
After the first conflict, fight with your sword and
　　daggers ;
You, sir, with a javelin and your target in your
　　hand,
See how ye can his deadly strokes withstand.
Keep at the foin ;[1] come not within his reach,

---

[1] *Push, i.e.,* do not close.

Until you see, what good advantage you may catch.
Then hardily leave him not, till time you strike him
    dead,
And, of all other parts, especially save your head.

WIT.

Is this all, for I would fain have done ?

WILL.

I would we were at it, I care not how soon.

INSTRUCTION.

Now, when ye please ; I have no more to tell,
But heartily to pray for you, and wish you well.

WIT.

I thank you ; go thou, and bid the battle, Will.

WILL.

Come out, thou monster fell, that hast desire to spill
The knot and linked love of Science and of Wit,
Come, try the quarrel in the field, and fight with
    us a fit.

ACT V., SCÆNA 5.

TEDIOUSNESS, WIT, WILL, INSTRUCTION, STUDY,
DILIGENCE.

TEDIOUSNESS.

A doughty dust [1] these four boys will do :
I will eat them by morsels, two and two !

---

[1] Old copy, *durte* (dirt). We still say, *to make a dust.*

Thou fightest for a wife! a rod, a rod!
Had I wist this, I would have laid on load,
And beat thy brain and this my club together,
And made thee safe enough for returning hither.

WILL.

A foul whoreson! what a sturdy thief it is!
But we will pelt thee, knave, until for woe thou
    piss.

TEDIOUSNESS.

Let me come to that elf.

WIT.

Nay, nay, thou shalt have work enough to save
    thyself.   *[Fight.*

INSTRUCTION.

Take breath, and change your weapons; play the
    men.

TEDIOUSNESS.

Somewhat it was that made thee come again.
Thou stickest somewhat better to thy tackling, I
    see,
But what, no force; ye are but Jack-Sprat to me.

WIT.

Have hold, here is a morsel for thee to eat.
                                   [Strikes.

STUDY, INSTRUCTION.

Here is a pelt to make your knave's heart fret.

DILIGENCE.

There is a blow able to fell a hog.

WIT.

And here is a foin behind for a mad dog !
> [*Let Will trip you* [1] *down.*

Hold, hold, hold, the lubber is down !

TEDIOUSNESS.

O !

WILL.

Strike off his head, while I hold him by the crown.

WIT.

Thou monstrous wretch, thou mortal foe to me and
    mine,
Which evermore at my good luck and fortune
    did'st repine,
Take here thy just desert and payment for thy hire.
Thy head this day shall me prefer unto my heart's
    desire.

INSTRUCTION.

O noble Wit, the praise, the game is thine.

STUDY.

Hove up his head upon your spear, lo, here a joy-
    ful sign !

DILIGENCE.

O valiant knight, O conquest full of praise !

WILL.

O bliss [2] of God to see these happy days !

---

[1] A direction to *Tediousness*, that he is to be tripped up
by *Will*.

[2] Old copy, *blest*.

WIT.

You, you, my faithful squires, deserve no less,
Whose tried trust, well-known to me in my distress.
And certain hope of your fix'd faith and fast good-
    will,
Made me attempt this famous fact, most needful to
    fulfil :
To you I yield great thanks, to me redounds the
    gain,
Now home apace, and ring it out, that Tediousness
    is slain.
Say all at once, *Tediousness is slain.*

ACT V., SCÆNA 6.

SCIENCE, WIT.

SCIENCE.

I hear and see the joyful news, wherein I take
    delight,
That Tediousness, our mortal foe, is overcome in
    fight :
I see the sign of victory, the sign of manliness :
The heap of happy haps : the joy that tongue can-
    not express.
Our [1] welcome fame from day to day for ever shall
    arise.

WIT.

Avaunt, ye griping cares, and lodge no more in me,
For you have lost, and I have won continual joys
    and fee.

---

[1] Old copy, *O.*

Now let me freely touch, and freely you embrace,
And let my friends with open mouth proclaim my
    blissful case.

SCIENCE.

The world shall know, doubt not, and shall blow
    out your fame,
Then true report shall send abroad your everlasting
    name.
Now let our parents dear be certified of this,
So that our marriage may forthwith proceed, as
    meet it is.
Come after me, all five, and I will lead you in.

WIT.

My pain is pass'd, my gladness to begin,
My task is done, my heart is set at rest ;
My foe subdued, my lady's love possess'd.
I thank my friends, whose help I had [1] at need,
And thus you see, how Wit and Science are agreed,
We twain henceforth one soul in bodies twain
    must dwell :
Rejoice, I pray you all with me, my friends, and
    fare ye well.

FINIS.

---

[1] Old copy, *have.*

END OF VOL. II.

PRINTED BY BALLANTYNE AND COMPANY,
EDINBURGH AND LONDON.